A Broken Spear

The Spear Series

Book Three

Douglas Owen

Science Fiction and Fantasy Publications

Science Fiction and Fantasy Publications

https://scififantasypublications.com
A division of DAOwen Publications

A Broken Spear / Douglas Owen

ISBN - 978-1-998029-25-9
EISBN - 978-1-998029-26-6

Jacket Art commissioned by MMT Productions

10 9 8 7 6 5 4 3 2 1

For the two most important women in my life

PROLOGUE

Chena pulled the hood further down over her face. The wicked rain cut through the gloom of the dark day, intensifying her foul mood. She was late, and the one whom went before her had already found the mother heavy with child. The mother who would die during childbirth. Another child, found by him, another child to secure his title of Seeker of Spears. She wanted that title.

For thirty years she had followed him, hoping to discover a child he missed; she still had yet to bring an infant back for training. This irked her to no end and was a black stain on her record as a Wooder. Chena swore under her breath and trudged away from the brothel, mud sucking at her boots. Something nagged the back of her mind, but only time would tell what it was and how she could resolve the problem. She glanced into the darkness ahead of her as a shadow made its way through the gloom. A child walked, head down and hand shielding a hooded face, but the child was too old for her needs. She dismissed the figure and strode toward the outskirts of the town.

Chena recalled how unfair life had been for her. The training to be a Spear took three fingers from her left hand at the age of seven, causing the Spears to reject her, and put her on the path to become a Wooder. Changing disciplines had been hard for her at that age. The herbs and plants did not take long to memorize - she had an innate understanding of them. But she struggled to learn the healing ways. All her past training was on how to injure or subdue, but finally, after many years, Chena became of use to the service.

Lightning flashed, illuminating the thick mud on the street and a figure of a small female child before her. Startled, Chena took in a breath through clenched teeth and pulled the white cloak tighter around her. Not wanting to talk to anyone, she shifted her direction and walked on.

A tug at her cloak annoyed Chena, and she pulled it even closer.

"We need your help," the child said, and Chena felt the tug on her cloak once again.

"I am of no help. You need to find another."

"But you're a Wooder." The child ran up beside Chena. "You heal the sick and help those in need."

"No, I'm not."

"But your cloak, it's like the others. Like his."

Chena glanced at her cloak. The dirt used to disguise who she was had washed away in the rain. "What do you want from me?"

The child's face was full of anguish. "My mother is giving birth, and something is wrong."

Chena took a breath, understanding now what had caused her to pause in the miserable town of Fisheries. Not just one child being born with the mother in trouble. No, there was another. Was there one who could take care of the child if the mother died? Her mind swam with thoughts of what she should do.

Disdain filled her. "Lead the way, child."

The girl spun and ran toward a small hut several yards away. Chena glanced about, but no one watched the streets. The cold probably kept them inside next to their fires. No witnesses to the conspiracy forming in her mind.

She followed her. *Are you sure about this, Chena? If you are caught...* She shook off the thought and concentrated on what her course of action should be to secure the child coming into the world.

"In here." The girl held open a door, a jumble of cut wood held together with hemp that had seen better days. "Mother is just inside."

As if to validate her statement, a cry of pain tore through the air from inside the hut. The child ran in, and Chena stepped inside to watch her kneel beside a bed with a woman whose belly was swollen. She gaged the girl to be maybe seven, and the woman in her twenties. Without hesitation, the child took the woman's hand and winced. A convulsion shook the woman, and the girl gritted her teeth against a crushing white knuckled grip.

Chena hurried beside the child and pulled her hand free. "Never take the hand of a woman birthing. She could easily break your fingers, little one."

The girl nodded as she shook her hand. "Can you help her?"

Chena glanced about the hut and shuddered. "I can help." An evil thought entered her mind. *I can help myself to the child. Must be careful, the little one will tell if something happens.*

Chena reached into her pouch, pulling out a small purse. "Hot water, now!"

The girl hurried off to the small fire pit. She wrapped cloth around her hands, grabbed the pot, and pulled it from the fire. With great effort, she sat the pot beside Chena.

"I need a cup."

Once again, the child brought what was demanded.

"You will step outside now," Chena said.

"I wish to be here. For Mother."

Chena glared at the girl. *How am I to do this with an imp beside me?* But she kept working. The contents of the purse went into the pot. "You will see things happening that may sicken you. Your mother may not survive, but the child... Yes, the child may." She tested the water. The bitterness gripped her tongue but mellowed her headache. "A little too hot. Bring some cold rain water from outside."

The child grabbed a bowl, then darted outside.

When the convulsion stopped, the woman lifted her sweat-soaked head. "Who are you?"

"Chena."

"You're a Wooder?"

"Yes. Now lay back down before you smother the baby." Chena stirred the water. *Where is that blasted child?*

Several moments later, the girl came back. "Here is the water. But it is cold."

"That is why I sent you out. This water from the fire is too hot for your mother. It would scald her throat if she needs to drink it."

"Cinder," the woman said. "Come here, my child."

Chena took the bowl of water as Cinder stepped beside the bed. She reached out to take her mother's hand but hesitated, looking toward Chena.

"Unless you want your fingers broken ..." Chena smiled. *Maybe I should let her.*

"Wooder," the woman said. "If anything happens to me, can you take Cinder and the child to be trained?"

Chena glanced over at Cinder. "The girl is too old."

"What about my baby?" the woman asked.

The law went through Chena's mind. A child with no one to claim it is the only child who can be a Spear. She glanced at Cinder. "The law would not allow it. Your daughter can claim the child."

"I will protect him, Mother." Cinder smiled, wiped away a tear. "He will want for nothing."

"Oh, my sweet daughter. We must let this child go. Even if I survive, this birthing has taken much from me. We will not be able to support another. It is all we can do to survive without another. If your father was still alive, it would be diff–" She gritted her teeth as a contraction raged through her body.

Chena pushed the woman's legs apart. The body was not yet ready to let the child be free, so she took the cold water and mixed it with the hot. Once the temperature was correct, she pulled a cloth from her cloak, then soaked it.

Chena thrust the cloth at the girl. "Wipe your mother's brow." As the girl took the cloth, her thoughts went to what transpired. *I can cause her to pass. And with what she has said, the girl should not claim the child. I will have found one.*

The woman settled down as the contraction passed. Chena examined the woman once again and noted her body was almost ready to bring forth the child. She took another cloth and soaked it, applying the potion against the swelling of the mother.

"That's soothing." The woman frowned. "Will I live?"

Chena pulled back the cloth and saw the blood. "Your body is giving up itself to bring this child forth. You may not survive the birthing. I will try to save you." She reached into her cloak, then brought forth a small leaf with thin hair like prickles on one side. "This may hurt." Deliberately she ripped the leaf, then applied its juice against the woman's bleeding flesh.

"It burns!" the woman gasped.

"Only for a short time. Soon you will be numb there and not feel anything. This will help bring forth the child." Chena wiped the leaf's juice between the woman's legs.

The child's head started to show. Water from the birthing spilled out mixed with blood. As the child's head emerged, Chena could see the umbilical cord wrapped around its neck. "I must pull the child free. The life cord is strangling it."

The woman nodded with clenched teeth. She bore down and pushed as another contraction took hold of her.

Chena pulled out a small knife and dipped it in the potion. With a steady hand, she reached between the woman's legs once again and cut the umbilical cord from around the child's neck. *Now would be the time to act.* She reached up once again, made sure the frock hid her actions and slid the blade between the woman's legs. The leaf, having numbed the area, allowed for the murder to go unnoticed. A twist and blood spurted out.

Cinder's eyes went wide as the blood soaked the bed sheets. "Mother!"

"Let the Wooder take the child. Stay with her, and make sure nothing happens." The woman clasped the girl's hand.

With a strange feeling of tenderness, Chena held out the child and stared at the woman. "What name shall we give him?"

"He is a boy?"

"Yes, a boy," Chena said.

"His hair. What colour is his hair?" The woman's flesh grew ashen.

"His hair is fair of colour. Like the fully grown grain of the field." Chena cleaned the blood off the child. "He looks strong, and may be a good addition to the Spears if no one claims him..." She stared at Cinder.

The woman, weak from blood loss, turned her head toward her daughter. "No one claims him, right, Cinder?"

"No one claims the child," Cinder echoed, tears as her lower lip trembled.

"Then I shall name him Jon, after my father. His hair was also fair as the grain of the field."

Chena nodded and turned to the girl. "Do you have a goat?"

"Yes, several out back." Cinder did not look up, but stared at her mother as the life emptied from the woman who had brought her into the world.

"Then take this skin and fill it with milk. It will be needed for the trip to Capital. Take care to pack..."

Cinder stood, letting go of her mother's hand. It fell to the bed, lifeless. Tears fell from her eyes.

"I will fill the skin," she said, taking the empty skin from Chena. "I have very little. Nothing besides Jon now."

"You heard your mother. You are not to claim him. You do not have a brother. There is nothing to claim. I'll take you with me to Capital, and maybe the Spears will take you in as a cook or maid."

"Yes, Wooder." She bit her lower lip, more tears welled from her eyes.

Cinder strode to the back of the hut and opened the door, letting in the driving wind. The light from the fire pit flickered wildly, throwing evil shadows against the wall.

"You are mine, Jon. I will take you to Capital and they will teach you to be a great Spear. A better fighter than all those you'll come up against."

ONE

Jon sat on the ground in front of the small fire, staring into the dying flames. The crisp night air and full moon illuminated the forest's edge, casting macabre shadows between the trees. Stars shone in the cloudless sky, a beautiful panorama for anyone looking up. The sky was the reason he kept the fire small.

His fifteen-year-old legs hurt from the three days of switching between running and walking with Fletch and he worried about Bethany and Thomasyn. Even in training, they never ran so hard without a break. He neared exhaustion and needed to sleep for at least six hours to recover, but the plan as laid out only allowed for four.

"I'll take first watch." Fletch slid up beside the Spear without a sound. His robes showed a discolouration from the excursion of the last few days. "You need to rest. How are your legs?"

"Sore." Jon stretched and kneaded the muscles through tight leggings. His white cloak hung loosely about his shoulders. A headache hammered at him and he needed to eat something before sleeping, or the pain in his stomach would erupt. "Do you have any food?"

"Some dried meat." Fletch held out a small bundle of cloth. "It's not as nice as the meat the dwarves gave you, but it will do."

"Thank you." Jon unwrapped the bundle and chewed on the piece of meat. "I would not have been able to sleep without eating."

"I know." Fletch popped some meat into his own mouth. "It's a condition. You are more Elven than anything else. Maybe your mother was one of us, or even your father. When we're young, our appetites are ravenous. It has something to do with our bodies needing more energy. Probably because we live much longer than any other races."

"You think I'm part elf?" Jon could not believe what Fletch was saying. He was not an elf. He was human. Most elves were ugly with angular faces, like Fletch, and had high cheekbones with gaunt features. He explored his own cheek bones with dirty fingers.

You are not an elf. You are human, said the voice.

"I know that," Jon said.

"Are you hearing voices?" Fletch asked.

"Voices?" Jon had never told Fletch about the voice. It was private. He thought fast. "Have you?"

Fletch chuckled. "Some of us hear the voice of The One God all the time. He speaks to us when we need his guidance."

I am a god! There is more than one. The elf lies.

Jon shook his head. "No, no voices. I just have a headache."

"It's okay if you do hear voices. It would mean you're god blessed. Very few have the ability to say such." Fletch tossed a few twigs on the fire.

"I am not god blessed," Jon said as he popped the last of the meat into his mouth. "Wake me in four hours, and I'll wake you once the sun lightens the day."

"Fair well," Fletch said.

Jon stood. "What do you mean by fair well?"

"It is a saying among us. Fair well, it means when you sleep, have good dreams and a restful sleep."

"We use it to say goodbye to a friend."

Fletch chuckled. "It would take the humans to change the meaning of our words. No, it is just a wish to have a good night's sleep. Fair well, Jon. I will wake you in four hours."

With a nod, Jon turned and strode a few paces into the forest.

Suspended ropes hung between the tree trunks formed cradles, and Jon climbed into them.

It is time.

"What do you mean, it is time?"

It is time.

"Time for what?" Jon grew annoyed with the voice. "You will shut up so I can sleep."

Jon rolled to his side, but sleep would not come. He worried about what his friends, Thomasyn and Bethany, thought about him leaving. Yes, they discovered his secret, or at least he believed they did. Bethany stayed behind and uncovered the rat at the Teeth of the World several weeks ago. He could tell by the way she'd looked at him, even though he covered the carcass.

But there was more. She stared sometimes, as if she could see through him, and crying in front of her last week had not helped. A sharp pain raced up his arm. Looking down, he noticed his fingers dug into his forearm. He relaxed and pulled his cloak tighter. The voice did not return, but sleep still eluded him.

Jon tossed about to his left and then right in the rope hammock. He counted spears, but still no sleep.

This continued through the night, and before he knew what happened, Fletch shook his shoulder.

"Did you sleep?" Fletch asked.

"What do you care?"

Fletch sighed. "I care because if you don't sleep, you will not be able to run."

"And don't you need to sleep?"

"No, not as much as you. If I sleep ten hours a week, that would be sufficient. Would it help if ..."

Jon tossed his body to stare at Fletch. "What would help?"

Fletch fumbled in his cloak and then stopped. "Are you sure?"

Nodding his head, Jon raised up in the hammock. "Yes, as you said, I need to sleep."

Fletch nodded. He pulled out a water skin and unstopped it. A pinch of powder went into the container and he handed it over to Jon. "Drink this."

Jon took the skin and sniffed. It smelt of a swamp, like water left to sit too long, but still palatable. "What is it?"

"Sleep Imp. A mixture of powders, spices and herbs to help anyone sleep. Elves usually take a large amount, but for you, maybe half elf, a pinch is all that is needed."

Holding his nose, Jon tipped the skin to his mouth and swallowed.

"Slow down, little one. It is not good for the stomach to have too much of this in it at any time."

Jon slowed. His eyes wandered. Drowsiness took him, and he fell asleep.

Jon opened his eyes. Somehow, he was fully dressed and walking with Fletch. The sun sparkled in the mid-morning sky and his stomach was not complaining for the first time in days.

"How did I..." Jon started.

"We have been walking for hours, little one. You have a very interesting outlook on life."

"I walk in my sleep?" Jon examined Fletch. The elf looked no worse for not sleeping all night. His feet touched the ground lightly, without leaving imprints on the grassland. Jon glanced behind, and the forest was well out of sight. He turned back to Fletch, expecting an answer from the elf.

Fletch just kept walking, scanning his head slightly from left to right, as if expecting an ambush to come any time. "I guess you do. As well as eat and hunt. I only have to ask one thing."

"What's that?"

"Who is Danton?"

Jon stopped. How could he answer that question? How did Fletch discover that name? Danton was dead for over a year now. He died during the Hobs uprising, and Jon was the one who killed him. Master Chail had been so upset with him after the fight. It was the battle that showed he was a master fighter, even better than Thomasyn.

"Danton. That is a name I have not heard in a year. How much do you want to know?"

"Start from the beginning and finish at the end."

He glanced at the elf, and back to the grassland. How much should he tell the elf? Should he tell him as much as he knew or less? He knotted his brow, and he really wanted the voice to come and tell him what to do. Master Chail always preached to them, tell the truth and all of it when they could. He decided to open up to the elf and tell him everything.

"You do not know the story of Danton? The Spear who left the order of protectors?"

"No. I have never heard of your legends or myths."

Jon took a deep breath. "It is not a myth," Jon said. "He was a great Spear. A leader among men."

"I didn't say–"

"Yes, you didn't say it. You did worse, you made me think it." Jon halted.

Fletch stopped and glanced back at the Spear. "It was not my intention to belittle the man. I didn't even mean to diminish his ability or yours. Please, continue and tell me the story."

"Okay." Jon thought for a second, organizing his thoughts and remembering the story as it was told to him so many years ago. He took a deep breath. "It started with concern from the common folk. They suffer because they live in huts or small homes near the wild. The dangers abound, and the Hobs have always taken advantage of it."

"I hear they hunt and eat children whenever they can," Fletch said.

Jon glared at the elf. Shaking his head, he started to walk away from Fletch in disgust.

"Where are you going, Spear?"

Jon slowed, turned and walked backward away from Fletch. "You wanted to know, but you interject. The telling of a story is a sacred thing to us. When a story is told, the listeners listen. They do not ask questions during the telling."

Fletch nodded and looked to the ground. "I will honour your telling. Please, continue."

"If you promise to allow the telling, I will tell."

"I promise," Fletch said, holding his hand over his heart.

Jon took another deep breath. "One night, the Hobs attempted to steal as many children as they could. It was a daring attack by Kindra, Queen of the Hobs. She was a piece of work if there ever was one.

"Her chin," Jon said, rubbing his chin, "was pointier than all the others, and her nose hooked down to almost touch it." Jon pulled at his nose. "Ugly brown blotches spattered about her green skin and whiskers on the sides of her chin hid all but the largest boils on her face. She walked up and down her castle cave, day and night, craving the flesh of the children of man."

Fletch came up beside Jon, and they started to walk once again.

"There was something about the sweetness of the skin," Jon continued. "Silkiness of the liver and tartness of the kidneys. Yes, she lived in a castle built in a cave for the lore of shaping stone is what they know, how to dig out a cavern from the very rock. They are so good at tunnelling, they rival the dwarves in their ability. They do not crave gold or gems. Flesh and bone of children are what they lust after. The Hobs use every bit of their victims, from tanning the skin for clothes to using the guts for bow strings.

"But she declared she needed to feast in order to draw a mate from the clans far and wide so she could bring forth babies into the world, and they could overthrow the world of man. But that was not going to be, for they forgot the prying eyes of the seers of the Realm."

Jon pulled out a water skin and took a swig. He offered it to Fletch who shook his head.

"The seers of old could hear the minds of those who meant ill to the Realm, and they heard Kindra's ravenous musing loudly for months, but could not tell where the target of their attack would be.

"The seers brought their discovery to King Basson, who ordered the Spear Danton to action once they discovered the target of the attack. A main force of over five hundred of the Spears marched out of the city and started their run. They ran and ran, day and night, to get to the village the seers said would be the target of the Hobs.

"But they arrived too late, for the Hobs had taken the children, and left no one else alive. Horror fell upon them, seeing that they had failed, for they were Spears, trained and bred to protect.

"Their commander, Danton, spun into a blood rage, vowing to find and destroy the Hobs and teach them what the true meaning of killing was.

"So he drew up his Spears and followed the Hobs into the forest. For days they tracked their movements until they came upon the Hobs' caves. He left one hundred Spears to guard the exits. Danton took the remaining force deep into the heart of the Hobs city, and killed all, male and female, young and old. Whether they fought, cowered, or slept, Danton killed as his rage empowered him. He embraced it fully in his heart."

Jon felt a fever rise in him. A feeling of uneasiness as he told the story washed over him from his toes up to his ears. Something was trying to come out, but what it was, he did not know.

"They say rage is the one thing that can kill a Spear, and vengeance overwhelmed Danton, fuelling that rage. For though he had killed many, he turned and counted only two dozen of his own Spears left. He no longer commanded a force of hundreds. Victory, the bittersweet spoils of revenge, cost the souls of those he controlled. He wept for them and swore vengeance by licking the blood of the enemy from his blade."

Fletch started to say something, but he seemed to think better of it and kept silent. He motioned with his hand for Jon to keep telling the tale.

"And when Danton found the castle of the Queen, he called her forth, and what he saw shocked him.

"For Danton did not see the face of legends and nightmares, instead he saw a beauty with long hair and enormous green eyes. He fell in love with her face, her clear skin. His followers could not understand, for they saw what she was, and when they looked upon Danton, they no longer saw their beloved leader, but the ever crafty face of a Hobs. The blood of the Hobs had taken his mind. He fell to his knees and forsook his vows. He renounced the Spears and swore to be with her."

Jon took another drink, and Fletch waited for the Spear to continue. While the silence stretched, Fletch grew uneasy. Jon smiled to himself, wondering how long it would take the elf to break the calm and ask a question. He had finished the story of the origin of Danton. It didn't take much longer for the elf to speak.

Fletch chuckled. "There's a little bit of miss-information about the Hobs in that story."

"What is that?" Jon asked.

"Well, for one, the Hobs are almost all males. There are very few females. And the females all run the clan as queens." Fletch reached out and ruffled Jon's hair. "Come, tell me more of the story you're keeping to yourself."

At first, Jon did not know what Fletch meant. That was the story of Danton. There was nothing else to tell the elf. But something in the back of his mind said there was more. He took another swig of the water and put the skin away as it hit him. Fletch wanted to know about the ending of Danton. He wanted to know the story of the killing. How Danton died.

"You want to know about his death, right?"

Fletch smiled. "Yes, his death. Tell me about how he died and what caused him to fall."

"We found him."

"Who found him?"

Jon glared at Fletch for a second. "I found him."

"So tell me, what happened?"

"Five of us travelled to the Teeth of the World, the mountain range that separates the Puddle Islands from the Realm. We arrived at the Town of Lands to find the Spear post there empty. We listened to the townfolk, and they told us about a man coming in from an outpost. He told of an invasion, and the Spears went to investigate."

Jon smiled at the thought of them finding the Hobs' army. "We travelled to a home well outside the town and found the family missing. When the sun settled, we saw fires in the distance. After climbing a hill, the Hobs' army camp came into view. It was a large invasion force for the Hobs, but not large enough. We sent Bethany to Capital in order to call the Spears while Thomasyn, Shail, Garion and me stalled the invasion."

"Four against an army? Sounds unbelievable," Fletch said.

"No. We did it. Ambush, run, hide, ambush again. Strong tactics when you think of it." As he recounted the adventure, Jon snickered.

The bloodshed was glorious. But then he caught himself. "We figured out the Hobs do not think when they are angered.

"I was one of the first to attack the enemy. Thomasyn rigged an arrow barrage to excite them. Once they ran toward the source, we attacked from behind."

"Jon," Fletch said. "How about telling me what happened to Danton?"

Jon thought that was a strange demand. Why would Fletch not want to hear about the whole story? Why just the end of the story? He realized that maybe all the elf wanted to know was his fighting ability. Fletch was taking a risk in bringing him home. Too many chances, so he decided what the elf wanted, the elf would get. He would tell him about the end of Danton.

"The Hobs' army was decimated. Only a handful of them were left after the Spears finished slaughtering them. Danton stayed back with a mage who kept him alive over all those hundreds of years. He challenged Master Chail to allow me to fight him, and I did. He was strong, but predictable. While fighting, he fell into a pattern. He struck left, then right, up and down. I followed it and played it against him. It was really easy.

"After a short time, I nicked him, and that is when I knew I won." Jon fingered the sword hilt at his side, the one he had taken from Danton. He noticed a small bump in the grip near the guard that he never noticed before. It was just under the leather wrap, and it was hard. "Once he was exhausted, I caused him to fumble. That is when I took advantage. I don't think he even knew what happened."

Fletch waited for a second, then blurted out the big question. "And then what happened?"

"I drove my sword through his skull."

Two

Jon studied Fletch's face for any sign of emotion. The elf's steady blue eyes blinked and his grayish hair spilled over his thin, angular face. He was disappointed to find nothing. He expected something to show through the stone face of the elf. The strongest Spear in history beaten by a newly promoted Spear in Flight. How could the elf not be impressed with the fighter before him?

"Is that it?" Fletch asked as he scanned the horizon before them with disinterest.

"What do you mean 'is that it'?" Jon asked. "I fought the best Spear the world had ever known and won. Me! The year I was released from training! I told them all I was the best. They didn't believe me. 'Thomasyn is the chosen one' is all I kept hearing. He would be the one to save us all. And I won the biggest fight any of them had seen. At the age of 14. You saw me fight. Am I not the best you have ever seen?"

Fletch rubbed his chin and stared beyond the path they walked. "You are one of the best fighters I have ever seen, but you still lack something..."

"I challenge you to tell me what I'm missing."

Fletch locked his eyes on Jon. "If I were to guess, you are lacking in patience."

Jon stared at Fletch, not believing what he said. Was he right? Did he lack patience? He could remember no real time when being patient affected the actions he took. There was something else, something that should not be in his memory. A feeling of remorse or loss. There was a remembrance of a woman with green skin and long, dark hair. He really wanted to see his children again.

No, there was something wrong with that thought. He did not have children. He could have children at fifteen years-old, but he did not. It would be different if he was not a Spear, working in a field. He would have a wife by now, if not more than one child. The workers who tend the fields outside of Capital marry by the age of fourteen. Some even as young as thirteen.

Jon balled up his fist and rubbed the knuckles against his forehead. He decided the small amount of food he ate over the last three days could have something to do with the headache pounding against the back of his eyes. The sun did not help. It was brite, and when he glanced at it, the pain in his head intensified.

"Are you lost?" Fletch asked.

The sudden question confused Jon. He glanced up at Fletch and shook his head. "Lost in thought."

"What are you thinking about?"

"Life." Jon stared ahead. "How much further until the coast?"

"Still a long ways." Fletch gazed out into the distance. "We have almost a month's worth of travel. But we have another place to stop off at first."

"Where?"

"A place. I made a promise to a friend that must be kept."

They walked on, Fletch leading Jon on an unfamiliar path.

THE NIGHTS STARTED TO WARM UP, AND JON WAS MORE comfortable than before. He eventually told Fletch about the headache that pounded in his skull. The elf seemed worried and left Jon to set up camp while he hunted for dinner.

Jon figured Fletch would be gone for a few hours hunting pheasant or rabbit. Either one would be fine with him, as long as it happened sooner rather than later.

To keep himself occupied, Jon set up their two tents and placed blankets inside them, begrudging the hard ground. Once done, he gathered stones and constructed a crude fire pit. The fire was easy to light with the dry, fallen branches he collected. He kept the flames small, to limit the smoke. He waited.

Jon poked the fire with a knobby stick and thought about what went wrong between the small group of friends he once travelled with. He missed them. But this was for the best. Something changed between them, and he did not want to be around the pitying glares they gave him. Just the idea that they would not accept what he had done to protect them concerned him. And he did not like the feeling. The voice worried him.

Still, one month's worth of travel to get to the coast was not much. He tired of long distance travel, but would survive. The trip to the Teeth of the World took three months, and they had horses. But Jon knew man could travel further over time than a horse could. He chuckled at the thought of running beside the horses as they trotted. Laughing as the beast stopped after only two hours and chided them for not being able to outdistance a small man. That would change over the next year or two. He expected to grow at least another six inches to a foot. Yes, it would not be long before his strength would rival even Master Chail's sturdy six-foot frame.

The embers in the fire pit glowed fiercely, out shining the flames. Jon poked at them. Sparks danced to the sky, and he let caution go. He piled on more branches. Flames licked skyward as they ignited.

The wet ground and low-lying land funnelled into a valley. Thirsty and low on water, he found a soft, sandy area and dug a foot. The ground became dark and wet. He dug another half foot and waited. The water table, just a few inches underground, started to fill the hole. The water would be safe to drink, the sand filtered out all the bad. A cloth from his pocket served to screen out the sand as he filled his three water skins.

He drank. The water tasted sweet, as if the sap of maples flavoured it. Jon blinked and noticed the water skins full on the ground and the sun already dipping below the horizon. The smell of cooking meat captured his attention, and he made his way back to the camp.

Fletch sat by the fire. Three pheasants cleaned and dressed over the flames. He glanced up as Jon approached, nodded, and turned his attention back to the cooking birds.

One of the birds was already missing a wing and leg. Small bones lay at Fletches side of the fire, stripped of meat.

Jon flopped near the fire and held out two of the skins to Fletch. They sat without speaking. He reached and took a leg off one bird and bit into it until his mouth was full. Most of their meals these last few days had been dried meat and only just a few bites at a time. Not enough for him to survive without ill effects.

A Wooder had once told him his body burned brighter than most, and that meant he must eat more than most people. And if he could, he should eat more often. Jon had not shared the information with anyone, not even Bethany and Thomasyn. He did not want to have special treatment due to his body's short comings. It was his pride, and it got in the way more times than often.

Jon believed that Fletch had information about his condition. But if he did, the elf did not share it all. Instead, his companion kept feeding him as much as he needed when they had it, and sometimes when they did not. At least they had no issues finding food during their journey. Both were capable hunters, and there was an unspoken competition between the two of them on who could find the most food the fastest. They were in a dead heat. The most birds caught at any one time were five by Fletch, but Jon had captured four rabbits that weighed about the same, and he had done it faster.

One thing that Jon noticed was Fletch did not leave much in the way of tracks, nor did he make much noise when moving. Even when they came across ground littered with pine needles and twigs, he could hardly hear the elf walk. Even the twigs went unbroken.

"How do you do it?" Jon asked between bites.

Fletch glanced up while eating. "Do what?"

"Walk so quietly." Jon flourished a pheasant leg to point at Fletch's feet.

Fletch continued to eat for some time. "To tell you the truth, I really don't know," Fletch said. "I guess it's just something I learned to do. Most of my kin can move about so quietly that even a deer is not disturbed, or even the birds in the trees." He let out another one of his slight chuckles and took a swig of water. "It's why I'm able to keep up with you while hunting, I think. My aim is not as good as yours when it comes to throwing rocks."

"I don't throw rocks, usually." Jon crossed his arms.

Fletch's eyebrows arched, and his eyes widened. "Then how did you catch the rabbits the other day?"

"Threw a spear, butt first." Jon held his right arm back, then swung it forward.

"That's a good way of killing the vermin without destroying the body." Fletch held out his hand. "May I see the spear?"

Jon pulled a three-foot short spear from its back holder, then handed it to the elf.

The head of the spear, a bladed point fitted over an oak rod, gleamed in the light of the fire. Fletch tested the edge and it easily cut into the skin of his thumb. He turned it and examined the butt. A slight indent at the butt of the spear allowed the bone, a small piece of wood with a hook at the end, to hold the weapon. Jon also handed that to the elf.

Standing now, Fletch held the bone and placed the spear so the indent enveloped the hook. He glanced at Jon. "Like this?"

"Yes," Jon said, trying to hold back a laugh. "But I wouldn't consider trying such a manoeuvre, less you want to pin your foot to the ground with the spear."

Fletch frowned. "What do you mean?"

Jon stood and came up beside the elf. "You have to put your other arm out and aim along it. Having it down at your side puts you off balance when you throw. It would cause the spear to arc wrong and head upward instead of outward. It would only go up a few yards and then come down, almost straight." He lifted Fletch's arm up, opened the fist and levelled it with the ground, palm down. "This is how you sight with a fighting spear and bone."

Fletch nodded, taking in the stance until Jon kicked at his front foot. "This foot needs to go forward." He kept kicking at the foot until Fletch had it out to counter balance a throw. "Now, when you throw, let your arm go back with the bone. Use it to propel the spear forward, and at your target." When Fletch did not throw the spear, Jon shook his head. "Go ahead and throw it."

"But you will lose the spear in the darkness," Fletch said with concern.

"I think not. Go ahead."

Fletch reached back his arm and drew the bone forward. Or, at least that must have been his intention. Jon laughed at the sight. Instead of using the bone to twist the most out of the arc, the elf threw his arm forward like a punch, and almost lost the spear from the cradle half way through the throw. The spear flipped in mid-air and dropped to the ground two feet in front of the elf.

Fletch handed back the bone and picked up the spear. "Okay, you show me."

Jon took the bone and spear from Fletch. He smiled, pointed at the tree just visible at the edge of the firelight over twenty yards away and, with one fluid motion, placed the spear in the bone, sighted down his arm. When something scurried along the trunk, he threw. He tried not to grunt, but in order to make a point, his full weight and strength needed to go into the throw. The spear flew through the air and hammered into the tree with a heavy thud, its end vibrating for a few seconds.

Fletch stared at the spear, then at Jon. "Well thrown. I could swear the spear hardly arced in flight!"

The two of them walked toward the tree, and Jon smiled as Fletch gasped. The spear had not only struck the tree dead centre of the trunk but also impaled a squirrel that had been climbing it.

"A very well thrown spear." Fletch pulled at the weapon, but it did not move until he threw his weight against it. He examined the hole in the tree and Jon saw the elf's finger go in to the second knuckle joint. "How did you learn such skill?"

"Practice. I've been throwing spears since I was five." Jon took the spear from Fletch and put it back into his holder. "We threw spears with and without bones each afternoon for a year to learn how to use them without killing. It is the way we are trained. And every Spear has it drilled into them how to use a spear for attack and defence. Master

Chail held contests to see who could clip the wings off a fly." Jon giggled a little. "I think that is where they get the name of a Spear in training. It probably started as 'Spear in flight' and became 'A Spear in Flight', hence the name of a Spear in training."

Fletch nodded. "A Spear in flight," he said.

They spent the rest of that night, and the next, in silent contemplation. Every few days, Fletch would question Jon on how the Realm trained the Spears.

"How many times did they make you run?" Fletch asked.

"Every day. Usually in the mornings." Jon pushed a few strands of blond hair out of his eyes.

"Every day?" Fletch shook his head. "Just for a few minutes, probably."

"No. Sometimes we ran for an hour, sometimes all day."

"You didn't run all day. They probably let you nap."

Jon shook his head. "Bethany ran three days and nights straight last year. From the Town of Lands to Capital."

"And you said you're faster than she is?"

"A little bit."

Fletch stopped. He stared at Jon and then walked away, shaking his head in disbelief.

Jon followed him. "Why did you walk away?"

Fletch scowled and waved a hand.

"What did I say?" Jon asked.

"You lie," Fletch accused.

Jon was taken aback. He prided himself on always telling the truth. *I do not lie, but how can I prove it to the elf?* Then he had an idea.

Jon jumped ahead of Fletch and stood in the Elf's path. "I don't lie."

"A human cannot run that long. We rested every night after our first three days when leaving the others."

The reminder of his friends stung, but Jon needed to prove how strong a Spear could be. Any Spear. "I'll prove it to you."

Fletch turned and faced Jon. "How?"

Jon smiled. "Tomorrow morning, you and I will do a fast run, just like the ones I used to go on when I was a child. Then you can see how a Spear can move about the Realm."

"That I would like to see. And when you stop halfway through the morning panting like a tired dog, I will laugh at you." Fletch pointed a finger at Jon.

"Then it is settled," Jon said. "In the morning, we will run. I suggest you get as much sleep as you can tonight. Do you happen to know how far away the nearest town is?"

Fletch put his hand above his eyes and motioned toward the horizon. "About three day's walk away."

"Not very far. Sure, it will do. You'll have to disguise yourself like you did before, but we'll stop just outside their sight by the afternoon." Jon headed back to the tents, smiling.

"In the afternoon! Will you be calling a flying beast to carry you to the town?"

"No," Jon called back. "But you may want to."

THE NEXT MORNING, JON WOKE WITH THE SUN AND LET Fletch sleep. While the sun climbed, he lit the fire and boiled some water. Leaves and twigs went into the shallow pot to add flavour. The night's catch of rabbit went on a flat rock beside the fire to warm up.

As the water boiled and meat cooked, Fletch poked his head out of the tent. "You are up already."

Jon smiled. "Yes, since the sun pushed back the darkness."

Fletch gawked at him. "Really? But you slept most of the mornings before. Why different this time?"

"Because we have a run to do. It is exciting. Much better than walking, don't you think?"

Fletch climbed out of the tent and stretched. "You are a strange man, Jon."

"You better eat if you want to keep up with me today." Jon popped a piece of the meat into his mouth and dipped a cup into the boiled water.

"What did you put in the water?" Fletched asked.

"Just leaves and twigs. You'll like it. Tastes like bird droppings." Jon smiled.

Fletch dipped a cup into the water and made a face as he drank. "At least the meat is warm and palatable."

"You better eat. I'll wrap what is left. Let me know when you are done." Jon stood and walked off to pack up the tents. He watched as Fletch hesitated and smiled. He could tell the elf was unbalanced and unprepared for what was to come. No, the elf was fast, and had good wind, but could he run as fast and as long as a Spear without stopping? Could he keep up? Only time would tell.

Finished packing the tents, Jon turned to Fletch. "Are you ready?"

Fletch stood, then looked about. He went to his pack. With deliberation, the elf started to place everything in it.

"You'll need this," Jon said, handing over a small package of wrapped leaves.

"What's in here?"

"Meat. You'll need it on the run."

"But you said we'll be there in the afternoon. Why do we need meat during the run? Are we going to stop?"

With a laugh, Jon popped a small piece of meat into his mouth and took a swig of water. "For this type of run, you will want to keep some meat in your mouth. It will help your mouth stay wet. Once it has fallen apart, swallow and replace it."

"Is this the trick you use to run?" Fletch asked.

"No," Jon said. "I use it to keep from getting too hungry like I did before. You must have seen me do it. But it is the best way to keep from getting overwhelmed by the pain of no food." He handed a water skin to Fletch as well. "You'll need to drink while we run as well. And if you feel the need to make water, stop and do so, but catch up. Some Spears learn how to hold it during the run, but that can cause pain. Empty yourself before the run and you should be good."

Fletch nodded and moved to the forest to empty himself.

Jon followed and emptied himself. A tingling feeling ran through him concerning the upcoming race.

THREE

Fletch slowed with a hand on his abdomen, and then with a violent heave emptied his stomach on the ground, showering the grass with chewed meat, bile, and water. Jon stopped and helped the elf by holding Fletch's hair away from the eruption coming out of his mouth. With his body still shaking, the elf took a swig of water, coughed, and sighed.

"How are you running so fast?" he asked.

Jon rubbed the elf's back. "From the time we could walk, Master Chail took us for runs around the training ground. At first, just a few minutes, and then more and more each day." He stopped and took a settling breath. It must have been the rolling hills they ran that caused Fletch to be ill. All that up one side and down the other. The forest on one side did not help matters. It helped with the illusion of being on water. He decided not to tell the elf about all the training, just a few parts he may need to know. "Master Chail told us running would be a way of life."

"I will be ready to keep going soon." Fletch sat back on his haunches.

"Then we will run some more. But I'll slow the pace for you. And don't make me look back at you all the time. If you feel sick, call out and we'll stop. It would not be good for you to empty your body all the time during the run, for you'll be very sick tomorrow and not be able to move for a few days." Jon took a swig from his own water skin.

Jon took Fletch's nod as a good sign. He stared into the distance, toward the direction they were running. Something was moving out there, ducking in and out of the tree line, but he could not see what it was. His curiosity took hold. With a glance back at Fletch, who was now sitting cross-legged and drinking heavily of the water, Jon decided to investigate.

"I'll be back. I just want to see what is out there."

"Be careful. We are in a strange area of the world. Far away from your Capital."

Jon nodded, then ran down the small hill. He dug deep into his body's reserves and pushed himself to sprint. Whatever caused the movement had vanished over a small hill. In fact, it was the first time in many months he was able to let loose and be free of someone constraining him. The wind of his running rustled through his hair, and it felt good.

The journey from the Teeth of the World felt slow compared to now, and he knew it had been on purpose. Jon loved to run and had wanted to continue in order to get back to Capital fast. Bethany had held them back. If she had her way, they would have crawled to the gates. But now he was alone, nothing to keep him from flying over the land. A smile crept across lips that had been used to frowning for months and victory bubbled inside. It was good to be free.

Jon reached the crest of the hillock, but did not see anything on the lee side. There were impressions in the short grass. He bent, his finger tracing the outline, measuring the depth of the grass. They were Hobs' prints.

A quick scan of the tree line, then John pulled his sword and listened. Simple shrubs dotted the landscape, but nothing a body could hide behind. The forest was another dark expanse of trees and underbrush. He spotted a number of places where a small troop could wait in ambush. But he still heard nothing. Not even birds chirped, and that alarmed him. Forests were never quiet.

The smell of smoke drifted to him. It was coming from inside the forest, but Jon did not see any smoke trail in the sky. *It must be a small fire. Someone is around here, and they are well hidden.*

Jon thought about his last experience with the Hobs, and how they could not take simple commands to stay still. It could not be a Hobs' army; they would have attacked without thinking. No, he realized, the hidden foe had to be something else. But who, or what, could it be? The idea of not figuring out who was scouting caused a finger to run up his spine. With a quick movement, he stood and ran into the forest after the smell. He followed it, dodging between trees and jumping over fallen limbs.

It did not take Jon long to find the tiny fire. He located it in a small clearing, with several branches strewn aside and leaves piled up for sleeping. Footprints heading in different directions on the ground uncovered dark dirt underneath. Small twigs, still green and lay strewn about, pointed in the direction he had come from. And he surmised the camp owner had been watching him. Could his movement toward the creature be enough to scare it off? Jon did not know, but he had suspicions.

A headache started to pound in the back of his head, and Jon sat for a few seconds, wondering if the pain would pass. To help, he took out a piece of meat and chewed. Unfortunately, the pain did not recede. Something had to give, and it would not be him.

Jon realized he needed to get moving, had to get back to Fletch, to make sure the elf was okay.

With a plan in mind, Jon ran out of the woods. Not as fast as before, but still faster than Thomasy or Bethany would have. Such quick movement through the unknown would have unnerved Bethany, but not him. As he ran, he watched about him for any food to grab. One tree bore fruit and he recognized it as a citric. He stopped and grabbed a few of the low-lying yellow fruit, put some into the catch pockets inside his cloak, and then bit into one. The tart juice refreshed his throat and filled the emptiness in his belly. The rush of natural sugar started to chase the pain in his head away, but it still lurked there in the background. Once again, he started to run.

He broke out of the woods and started to sprint up the hillock. As he rounded the top, he spied a figure darting away from where he had left Fletch. Jon gritted his teeth and quickened his pace, expending all the energy the meat and fruit had given him. The pain in his head increased in ferocity, but he ignored it and took a swallow of water from his skin.

Fletch was more in view now, and he could see the elf lying on his back. The worst thought came to Jon as he approached the spot. Fletch, not moving. Jon feared the worse that whoever followed them had killed the elf. They must not have followed them directly, but shadowed them from the side. Keeping out of sight, making sure they were not seen.

Jon reached Fletch, and to his relief, the elf was still alive.

Fletch roused as Jon approached. The elf's face was waxen, and he appeared to still be suffering from running sickness. Jon handed one of the fruits to him and scanned the distance for the figure. Fletch ate slowly, removing the rind and placing each slice of the fruit into his mouth.

"Thank you."

"You needed it." Jon tossed him the second fruit.

"Most people would have just left me. I now know that I'm slowing you down. I... I did not realize how much." Fletch stood, wavered on wobbly legs, then steadied. "I can travel now."

Jon shook his head. "No, not now. We'll walk a little to the next hillock and camp at the base of the forest until tomorrow. We don't have to be at the next village today." Jon took out some dried meat and held it out to Fletch. "Besides, you need to recoup your energy. We will make it if we walk, or jog, tomorrow."

"Still, you won."

"Won?"

"Yes. Remember we made a bet yesterday? Who could run the fastest and longest this morning?"

Jon rubbed the back of his neck, but a smile crept across his face. "I was not going to say anything about it."

"Still, you won." Fletch reached into his tunic and brought out something that glinted in the sun. He held his hand out.

"What's this?" Jon asked.

"Your prize."

Jon reached out. Fletch turned his hand around and dropped the treasure.

"What is it?" Jon asked, bringing his hand back and looking at the small ring.

"Magic," Fletch said.

"How can such a small thing have magic?"

"The Elven seers imbue metal with power. The power is formed into an object. The object there, a ring, is worn on a finger in order to make it work."

Jon lifted the ring to the sky and examined the inside of it. The sun caught something on the inside and he rubbed his finger against it. The ring vibrated, and a slight hum filled the air. He pulled back and dropped the ring.

Fletch laughed. "It won't bite you."

"It vibrated a little. And my finger started to go numb," Jon said.

"It never did that in the past. What did you do?"

"Rubbed the shiny part."

Fletch picked up the ring and examined it. "I never saw a shiny part on the ring before. How did it appear?"

Jon took the ring from Fletch. "I just took it and rubbed like this." He rubbed his finger on the inside arc. "And I just felt it rise up."

The ring started to vibrate in Jon's fingers once again. He did not understand what caused the pulsation, but it did not hurt. Drawing the ring closer to his eyes, he focused on the inside. The smooth surface did not bear any blemish. In fact, the whole surface of the ring was smoother than any calm lake water. It reflected everything clearly, with the distinct warp due to the arc of its surface.

Jon could see the elf's reflection when he held the ring between them. The surface felt warm, and the vibration stopped. His headache receded, leaving emptiness behind. There was much more than he could explain, like leaving a needed belonging somewhere, but not remembering where or when it was left. This he felt throughout his being. But more than that, he felt a sense of loss.

Fletch stared at him through the ring. "Why don't you try it on?"

"It's yours."

"No. You won it fair. Even after warning me, you still won. So it is yours. Go ahead and put it on."

Jon hesitated for a second and then started to put the ring on his middle finger.

"No, not that one. The next one. The finger beside the little finger on the left hand." Fletch pointed at Jon's left ring finger.

"Why that one?" Jon asked. That was the finger of marriage. So why was it important to put this ring there? He ignored the request and resumed putting the ring on. Fletch reached out and shook his head.

"There are reasons why it is to be put on that hand. It will not have the power if on the wrong finger. The left hand, ring finger. Beside the small finger."

"That is the marrying finger. Would it not be better to put the ring on another finger to see how it works? Then I can change it if I like what it does." Jon edged the ring to his right hand and eyed the elf. He saw the tentative way his eyes shifted; fingers twitched and tried to look unconcerned. "Okay, then it's settled. I'll put it on this one for now."

Jon slipped the ring on, and his world went black.

THE RING CLATTERED TO THE GROUND. JON OPENED HIS EYES and looked about. The blackness around him was not one of night, nor did the ground feel right to him. Something was wrong.

Above him was darkness. Not the colour of the night sky, with all the stars shining down on him, but the black of no light. The ground was not so much ground as rock. A musty odour permeated the air.

Jon fumbled about the ground, searching for the ring, which was the last thing he truly remembered. It should have been on his right hand, but nothing was there. He remembered the sound of metal hitting a rock on the ground and realized it had slipped off. But when he had put it on, the ring was snug. Why did it slip off?

His eager fingers found the round metal object, and he picked it up. It did not go on his finger, but instead, into one of the catch pockets in his cloak. Something itched in the back of his mind, near the area where his headaches usually started. He touched the sword at his side. It was his protection. What kept the evil at bay.

"There you are, little one," Fletch said, his voice echoing in the darkness.

Jon spun and pulled the sword from its scabbard in a fluid motion. He could see the outline of Fletch before him, but for some reason the sound of the elf approaching was loud, and not muffled. "Where did you come from? And where am I?"

"Don't worry, young Spear. We are in a cave. Shield your eyes and I'll summon light for us."

Lowering the sword, Jon raised his free hand to shield his eyes as instructed. He could hear Fletch fumbling around in his tunic.

"*Klasseeg Flothol Toong Ba!*"

A light sparked and grew to illuminate the area they were in. At first, Jon thought the spark floated in the air, but it was on the end of a stick that Fletch held. The elf had that strange lopsided smile he usually wore when showing his superiority in something. Jon nodded. He glanced about for the entrance and sky that should have been close by.

"You didn't tell me how we got here." He sheathed the sword in a fluid motion.

"Don't you remember? It was your idea to seek out a shelter from those who followed us. This cave, it was where you said it would be and thus we walked to it. Look, you even cooked dinner before we went to sleep." He motioned toward a small area with stones encircling a fire. Small embers struggled against the ash to stay alive, and the bones of rabbits littered the ground. "Dinner was good, and I appreciated you finding those rabbits before we came here."

"No," Jon said.

Fletch stared at him, eyebrows coming down to shelter his eyes. "No, what?"

"No. I don't remember." Jon clutched his head with both hands. His eyelids closed tight enough to shed tears and the corners of his mouth attempted to meet the jawline. "I don't remember how we got here!" He crouched low to the ground.

"Jon? Are you all right?"

"I don't understand what is happening to me!" Jon started to cry.

"I do." Fletch rubbed the young Spear's back. "Something is happening to you, and you're not sure what it is. All will become clear in time."

The pain in the back of his head erupted once again. It hammered against his eyes. Thoughts escaped in blinding flashes of light. Memories, not his own, but someone else's, flashed around. A woman, blonde with sculpted cheek bones covered in smooth pink flesh and green eyes, held a baby up to him. The softness of a warm bed before a fire. The kiss of a girl unknown to him, but familiar. The taste of some vegetable he'd never seen. A burn on his hand. Jon tried to remember his own upbringing. The fight between two huge fighters when he was ten. He remembered parts of it, but they slipped away.

Jon figured he needed to concentrate on one thing and one thing only. He thought of Bethany. Her auburn hair falling down over her shoulders. The gentle slope of her nose. Pale pink lips. Eyes so blue that the ocean grew jealous. Then, nothing. Not even the touch of her hand as she comforted him. He felt confused.

"Is it almost finished?" Fletch asked.

"Finished? What do you mean, finished? I'm losing myself. Nothing is left. No past. No tastes. Nothing! Where are my memories?"

"Put the ring on, Jon. All will become clear with the ring." Fletch smiled in the waning light.

Jon felt the cold metal being pushed into his hand. It was inviting. The ring was comfortable in some strange way. How could this one thing be so good for him? He lifted the ring up and looked at it. Nothing had changed, but it was also not familiar to him either. At first, he wanted to throw the thing as far away as possible, to push it so far from him that it no longer enticed him. But no matter how much he wanted to do it, the muscles needed would not obey his commands. Instead, his fingers tightened around the ring.

"I... I can't," he said, thrusting his hand out. But it was not the one holding the ring. That one he held close to his heart for some reason.

"Put on the ring, Jon." Fletch pried open the hand holding the ring. "It is easy. Here." He opened Jon's left hand and put the other hand before it. The ring was now supported between three of the fingers on

Jon's right hand and his left ring finger just before the circle of gold. "Put it on, now!"

As if propelled by some magical force, the hand holding the ring slipped it on the left ring finger. It stopped just before being fully past the second knuckle. Jon looked up. "What will it do?" His voice shook.

"It will free the mind inside you. Take away the vale. Open up the future. You are the right age. The source has been passed. It is ready. You are ready." Feltch rubbed Jon's shoulder.

"Will it take away the pain?" Jon asked. He looked up at Fletch, his eyes still filled with tears he could not hold back. The salty water flowed from his eyes and tumbled down his cheek.

"It will take away the pain," Fletch said.

Jon pushed the ring on the rest of the way and his mind exploded in agony. He fell to the ground and rolled, clutching at his head. It felt like hot needles were being pushed into his eyes from behind.

"You said it wouldn't hurt!"

"No, I said it would take the pain away. And it will."

Jon stared at Fletch, but he was no longer Fletch, but a Hobs grinning with an evil visage on his green fleshed face.

"Who are you? And where is Fletch?"

"Fletch is no longer with us. I took care of him on the hill." The Hobs smiled now, showing the small razor-sharp teeth.

"But who are you?"

"Soon you will know who I am. Soon the ring will work, and the spirit locked inside you will be released. And I will have my friend back."

Jon convulsed. His body shook hard and long, thrashed about. He fell to the ground, shaking and rolling from side to side. For minutes he convulsed on the ground, not able to control himself while his mind explode. Then it was over. Jon sat up slowly and ran shaking fingers through sweat soaked hair.

"Jon," the hobs said. "Are you there? What is your name?"

Jon stopped scratching his head and looked about with wide eyes. "Who is Jon?"

"What is your name?" the Hobs asked again.

"Pin, you know me. I'm Danton."

FOUR

Thomasyn stood before Bethany's tent. He could still hear her soft sobs coming from within, and he did not know what to do about it. After a week of searching for Jon, he decided they needed to get to Capital and hand the dwarves' contract to the new king. They were already behind schedule and travelling the wrong way across rolling hills of clover. They needed to travel away from the sparse forest to the North.

Thomasyn reached out a grimy hand, one that had not been cleaned for several days, to open the flap. But he hesitated, not believing it was the right thing to do. He had to do something. Bethany had not eaten in two days and pushed herself to keep up with him, even when her strength had waned. Her features were becoming gaunt, and that worried him.

No, make some breakfast first. The smell of food will bring her out, and then she will eat.

He strode to the forest with loud steps and examined the tree limbs for signs of birds taking off as he approached. Two song birds took to the air and circled around the tree. Thomasyn gripped a low branch, pulled himself up, then reached for another.

After getting past a few branches, he made his way out on a limb and approached a nest. Four eggs sat nestled among the twigs. He took two. They were loose inside; none were ready for hatching, perfect for cooking.

The underbrush rustled below him. He pulled out a knife and flung it toward the sound. It struck true, and a small hog fell to the ground, its spine severed near the head by the knife.

Thomasyn climbed down and recovered his knife. With deft movements, he sliced the small animal's neck and allowed the blood to drain free. He then gutted it to lose the excess parts. It would feed them for several days, and now he would be able to carry the carcass with ease.

He tied the front feet together, then the back, and slid a stick between the limbs. Once he hoisted the carcass on his shoulders, Thomasyn made his way back to their camp.

Bethany sat by the fire. Several more logs flamed on it than when Thomasyn had left, and the warmth coming from it was inviting when he approached. He glanced over at her and then looked to the fire. Thomasyn was sure he did not look any better than she. Neither of them had taken the time to clean after each day of searching.

The last several days of running and looking for Jon had taken a toll on both of them, but Bethany showed signs of aging beyond her fifteen years. Her sunken eyes, with great dark circles under them, stared into the fire. Her usually healthy skin was pulled tight, showing sharp cheek bones. Her hair no longer had lustre, and the ends were split.

Thomasyn dropped the pig next to the fire and held out the light pink eggs to her. He noticed how thin his fingers looked. Bethany took the eggs and placed them into a small rock pile next to the fire in order to cook them. He started to cut up the pig.

"How are you feeling?" Thomasyn asked.

"Tired." Bethany stared at the fire.

He nodded and put some of the pig meat on the flat of a rock in the fire. It sizzled as it hit the hot rock.

"Do we have water?" Bethany asked.

"Some, but not a lot. We have to fill our skins when we find a stream." He handed her a water skin.

Without Jon to help with the hunting, one had to set up the tents while the other scavenged for their evening meal, and hopefully the mornings as well. Last night there was no game to be found, and Bethany had come back to camp crestfallen. Thomasyn did not want to start the day off with an empty stomach, and now they had sufficient for several days. It would make the next week easy; not having to hunt when they stopped at the end of the day meant less time setting up camp.

With over three weeks' worth of travelling before they reached Capital, the two were at least a week away from reaching a town. Thomasyn built a fire; both erected their tents and then sat to eat the last of that morning's breakfast.

"I don't want to stop at another town." Bethany took a swig of water.

Thomasyn poked at the fire with a stick. "I understand. It would be nice to sleep in a proper bed." He glanced at his hand; dirt drew a black line under his fingernails. A quick sniff made his face screw up.

A cold wind pushed the flames of the fire sideways, causing the hair on his arm to stand. He put more wood on the fire. "We trained for this."

"For what? Losing one of our own?" Bethany's lower lip trembled. "We lost so many during training, and now we lost Jon. How did they train us for that?"

Thomasyn shivered. With dirty fingers, he stuffed the last bite of his meal into an empty mouth. The sky grew darker and another cold wind rolled over their camp.

Bethany stared at the fire. "What are we going to do?"

"We need to stop somewhere." He stood.

She opened her mouth to say something.

"No," Thomasyn said. "We do need to stop, warm ourselves, get clean, eat a decent meal. Capital's not going anywhere."

"I know, but we're not stopping until we get home."

Bethany stood, ducked into her tent, then closed the flaps.

***

Thomasyn stared at the roof of the tent, waiting for the sun to brighten the day. After travelling four days, he planned on them intersecting one of the larger towns just south of them. And if they spaced out running and walking for a few days, it was less than a week away.

"We should pack up and warm ourselves with a run," Thomasyn said, flipping the meat on the rock with the tip of his knife. "Run until noon and then cook up the rest of the meat."

Bethany stared at the fire. "I... I miss Jon." A tear escaped her eye, rolled down a smooth cheek and left a trail behind it.

Thomasyn missed their friend as well. Even Jon's brash attitude and air of superiority was something he'd grown fond of. He put another slice of pig on the heated rock.

"Are you hungry?" Thomasyn asked.

"Very. I want to be full for once."

"That's something Jon would say."

Bethany pushed aside the small rocks holding the eggs. With cloth in hand, she pulled out two eggs and handed one to Thomasyn. He took it with a cloth and rolled it on his leg, applying a little pressure to crack the shell.

"He loved eggs," Thomasyn said.

"And roasted pig."

"Yes."

They ate the rest of the meal in silence, cutting the cooked meat with their dirks. After ten minutes, the meal was complete. Thomasyn tore down the camp while Bethany smothered the fire and attempted to make the fire pit invisible. It was something Master Chail taught them years ago. Leave the land as close to what it looked like before you camped. It was the way of the Spears, honouring nature.

With the camp torn down, they started to run.

After four days, they crested a hill, and Bethany stopped. She glared at Thomasyn, and he felt a chill go through his body. An upset Bethany was something he did not want to have to deal with as tired as he was.

"I told you I didn't want to stop at a town," Bethany said.

The town of Pillers lay at the bottom of the valley. The crisp wind of fall blew across the tops of homes, scattering the smoke of fires. It was not as large as Capital, but larger than most settlements in the Realm. Thomasyn estimated the size would be well over 700 souls.

"We need a proper rest." He squared his shoulders and started to walk toward the town.

"Is it safe? There is only the two of us."

Thomasyn shook his head. "We can fend off anything in this town. It's not like there's going to be a group of hoodlums around every corner." He motioned with his arm. "Come on."

He waited for her to take a tentative step forward. "Do you think there's a Spear in town? Or maybe a Wooder?"

Thomasyn noted some buildings that would not be homes, but could be an inn or outpost. He pointed to the large building. Small plumes of smoke rose from the stone stacks. "That building, just on the outskirts. I think that could be a Spear outpost."

They walked at first and then jogged into the town. There were people moving about and venders selling food in a small market place. The Outpost building sported a spear across the main door, and that designated it as an Outpost for the Spears. They approached the door and stopped before entering.

"I hope they are nice here, not like the last town," Bethany said.

"The way the people hardly noticed us, I would be surprised if there was not a garrison waiting behind the door."

Thomasyn reached out just as the door opened. At first they stared without making a noise, and then Bethany frowned.

"Sandra?" Thomasyn asked.

The tall girl before him shook her long blonde hair and focused her piercing, ice-blue eyes on him. They grew wide and a smile spread across her face. "Thomasyn? Bethany? I thought you were in the Teeth?" She flung open her arms and hugged them.

The aroma of oranges filled his nose as she embraced them. He felt Bethany stiffen during the grasp and remembered one of the times the two girls had a confrontation years ago. Something stirred inside him, and the inappropriateness of the prior encounter struck him. They were too young for them to have any type of intimate contact, even though they had tried.

Bethany pulled away first, but Thomasyn wanted to share the warmth of Sanda's body a little longer. He felt a sharp finger stab into his side, and Bethany's frown warned him she was starting to get angry.

"We need to get to Capital," Bethany said. "We just stopped to get supplies."

"Are you sure?" Sandra asked.

Thomasyn reached out and took Bethany's hand. He gave it a squeeze. "We really need a good meal and hot bath. We've been travelling for a long time."

"Yes, you must be cold. Winter is almost on us. Come in." She stepped aside and swept her arm, motioning them inside. "We'll make up a room for you two and have a bath drawn. There are only three of us here, and the other two," she said in a hushed voice. "The other two are old and almost ready to take time at Capital."

The Outpost was warm, and Thomasyn could feel the cold releasing its hold on his body. Rubbing his hands together, he moved into the room. An eating hall with a roaring fire in the centre pit opened up to them. Two rows of tables stood empty, the last meal already cleared.

"Barion and Mitch both went to the market. They should be back in a few hours, but I'm sure they will be fine with you two staying for a couple of days."

"We don't have a couple of days," Bethany said, hands shoved under her arms.

"We can stay for two days," Thomasyn said. "Our arrival at Capital will be well within the time timeframe given to us."

"Yes, stay two days at least," Sandra said. "I would love to catch up with you both. It has been a long time since I've seen you. Bethany, you get the first bath. I'll draw it myself." She turned and started toward a doorway at the end of the hall, then stopped. "Where is Jon? I thought he went north with you."

Thomasyn frowned. When he looked over to Bethany he saw a tear forming in her eye. This was not the way he wanted to start their reunion. The explanation of what happened to their friend could collapse the tenderness of the meeting. But Sandra was not one of the people who liked Jon. She was more drawn toward Thomasyn from the early days of their training.

"Jon left." Bethany finally started to cry.

Thomasyn put his arms around her, and she leaned into him. Bethany's shoulders shook with the power of her grief. And then Sandra was taking her away from him. She looked back and nodded, mouthing the words "Jon left?" and shooing him to another door. He wondered if Bethany would put up with the close contact of a girl she had once hated. But seeing how Sandra took over comforting her, he was sure nothing untoward would happen between them.

He headed to the room Sandra motioned him to and was surprised with a large kitchen and stove giving off heat. Three large metal buckets hung from a crane. Fire licked the bottom of the buckets, making the water dance.

Thomasyn grabbed a wet towel from a chair by the fire and removed one of the heavy buckets. He emptied the water into a large bowl sitting on a table and placed it on the floor. A larder stood off to the right, and he went to it. Inside, he took down some preserves and bread.

Sandra had returned to the kitchen. "There is a hand pump outside for the well. Fill the others for me and the two outside. Put them on the crane for Bethany's bath." And she was gone.

"Figures," Thomasyn said.

He picked up the bucket and took it outside. He filled the first, glanced about and saw the two other Sandra had mentioned. He filled them as well.

With a grunt, he picked up two and went back to the kitchen. He hung them on the crane in the fireplace and went back for the third. After hanging it, he sat down at the table and sighed. He was about to get up and find something to cook when Sandra came into the kitchen.

"She's soaking. Are you hungry?"

"I was just thinking about that." Thomasyn motioned to the bread and preserves he had taken from the larder. "I can't remember the last time I had bread."

Sandra wrinkled her nose. "And a bath, it seems. I'll have to change the water before Bethany's clean." She went to the larder and returned with a small wheel of cheese and shank of dried meat. "You have to tell me what happened."

Thomasyn sighed. "It's a long story."

"I heard about the march against the Hobs. Is it true that Danton was still alive?" She put the cheese and meat on the table.

"Yes," Thomasyn said as he ripped off a piece of bread. "Jon killed him."

"Really? I thought he was a Master of Spears!"

"He was. And he was also over 400 years old as well as suffering after a blood magic spell. The Hobs had a seer with them, a very powerful seer." Thomasyn ripped off a chunk of bread and spread some crushed fruit preserves on it. "It could have been the magic that weakened him, allowing Jon to make him fall into a pattern of fighting. You know what Jon is like. Find a pattern and use it against his opponent."

"I remember." Sandra rubbed a scar on her hand. "I never fight using a pattern now." She stood and took a jar from the larder. "Here, try this." She poured an orange liquid from the jug into a cup. "Don't drink it too fast."

Thomasyn took the cup and smelled the liquid. "What is it?"

"The juice of oranges and distilled potatoes. Mitch swears it will take the cold out of a winter giant's bones." Sandra giggled and whipped hair the colour of straw back. "Every once in a while, Mitch drinks too much and stumbles about the kitchen. Once he spewed all over the place."

Even though he did not know this Mitch, he laughed. The lightness of the vision in his head only lasted a few seconds, and then he remembered. He was telling Sandra about what happened to Jon. His head dropped, and he sipped at the drink. It burned a little.

"When Jon and me fought the fast war–"

"Fast war?" Sandra asked. She took a quick sip of her drink and nodded apologetically for interrupting him.

Thomasyn nodded back. "That is what Master Shail called it. Attack quick and withdraw before they can react. Keep them from understanding what is happening to them and stop them from forming a plan of defense or attack. They were so confused that we kept them from advancing on the town for almost a week."

Sandra nodded and broke off some cheese.

"Jon argued about a lot of things, but after he acted as a decoy, it was like his mind snapped. From taking chances to following Bethany and us from a distance. Something changed in him…" He could not keep going. With his head bent, Thomasyn let out a loud sigh. There was very little that depressed him, but this was one of those things. He collected himself and raised his head. "He started killing animals for pleasure. Bethany found a rat that he dismembered while it was still alive."

He glanced up at Sandra to see her staring back at him, wide eyed. It was a shock to her, he knew, to discover a Spear tortured animals. To only take what was needed from the wild and leave the rest to continue their line. And Jon was one of the best hunters any of them had ever met. Even as a Spear, he had very few equals.

Sandra was the first to break the silence. "Is that why he's no longer with you?"

"No," Jon said. "We were going to take him to Master Chail to see if anything could be done. On our trek back from the Teeth of the World, we stumbled upon a town of elves."

"Elves? In the Realm?"

"They didn't look like elves. There was some type of spell to disguise them."

"Then how did you find them out?"

Thomasyn took some cheese and bread. He did not like the drink that much, but he didn't want to insult Sandra. So he drank, ate, and between them he talked. "The one elf came back with us, and that is when Bethany found out his secret. He didn't even try to lie about it, just dropped the act and showed us what they are like."

"And what do they look like?" Sandra asked.

"Ugly. Long faces that look like they're starved most of the time. Long hair, grey skin, very thin lips and pointed ears. He knew magic."

"Magic?"

"Yes, but he needed blood to cast the spells he used."

"Mitch told me something about that." Sandra stood and went to another room. She returned with a large book. "This is one of the books he has."

"It looks old."

"It is." Sandra put the book on the table and opened it. "There are some pictures on a few pages, but most are a lot of hard to read words." She turned the pages.

"Here's something," Thomasyn said, pointing at the middle of a page. "He looked like that."

"They really aren't easy to look at." Sandra's fingers traced the drawing.

The thin lines made up the sketch that resembled Fletch. From the long hair to the thin face. "This looks so much like Fletch. How could that be?"

"Maybe they all just look alike." Sandra ran her finger over the handwritten text. "It says blood magic is evil. All elves who do not fight use it to bring death to any who might oppose them." Sandra looked up. "Did Jon oppose the elf?"

FIVE

Bethany let the hot water pull all the knots out of her body. This was the first civilized thing she had been able to do since leaving the Teeth of the World, and she was not going to let it go to waste.

At first, she had struggled against Sandra, but she relented. All her clothes were gathered up and removed, even her cloak. And once she surrendered her clothes, fresh towels and a robe were brought.

Bethany did not start cleaning when she first immersed herself in the hot bath. She let the warm water strip away all thoughts of the long road travelled. With the water up to her neck, she leaned back in the tub. She let her mind go blank, but it did not last long. Soon Jon's face came unbidden to her mind, and she could only think that he was in trouble.

With her imagination wandering through the last few months, Bethany started to cry. The tears flowed, and she could do nothing to stop them. For the last week she pretended to be strong for Thomasyn, but the loss of Jon broke down the last of her iron will, and something told her Thomasy could see past her façade. The Spear was too smart for his own good, and her liking.

As if to relieve her, memories of the last time she really talked to Sandra came to mind. The day Thomasyn and Sandra imitated what Master Dress did to Michael, which caused the young Spear to take his life, before the Spears took their revenge on the molester. It was the time she planned to tell Thomasyn of her love for him.

That was a long time ago, and Bethany knew it was a child's love. Similar to the crush she had on Master Chail, but not as intense.

Bethany did regret one thing, and that was not coupling with Thomasyn after they saved the Town of Lands. Instead, she let them both drink too much of the strong mead and they fell asleep in the field. Why did I insult him that morning? He did not brag. All he did was show concern for me.

There was nothing Bethany could do about the past, for now she could only treat him with respect, the way he always treated her. But every time they had a chance to be a couple, she was having her time.

Bethany untied her hair and started to wash it. The grime mixed with the soil from her body muddied the water until the water became dark. She reached for the soap Sandra left for her. It smelled faintly of oranges and reminded her of Sandra's hair. But if this is what Thomasyn liked, she would do it. Maybe if she let him do more, carry her pack, do all the packing and setup all the tents, because he always seemed to want to.

Bethany wondered if Thomasyn found her attractive. She was not like Sandra. Yes, her hair was almost as long, but while Sandra's hair was like golden sunshine, hers was a dark rust colour. Both were strong, but even though Sandra was well trained, only she was a match for Thomasyn in fighting, though he was just a little bit better.

Sandra was not much of a fighter. Most of the practice showed her skill to be just passable, so why did Thomasyn want to be around the girl?

The door opened, and Sandra came in with two buckets of steaming water.

"I figured the water would need changing." She came beside the tub and examined the water. "Yes, time to change it."

"It doesn't have to be changed right now," Bethany said, and folded her arms around her chest in modesty. "The water is still warm."

Sandra reached down and pulled the stopper. Water rushed out through a grate recessed in the floor. "If we do it now, there will be clean water for you to get the rest of the dirt off."

Worry crept into Bethany's mind as the water level lowered. She hugged her chest tighter and crossed her legs. "How hot is the water in the buckets?"

"Very, but for every hot bucket, there is a cold one at the side. Did you want to get out first while I fill it?"

Bethany shook her head. Her blood flowed, and she did not want to share this with Sandra. "I'll stay in the tub."

"Of course, I just want to make sure you're comfortable. Scoot up a little; I don't want to scald you." Sandra replaced the stopper, then lifted one bucket up to the edge of the tub.

Bethany scooted up. Sandra only dumped a third of the buck in, then grabbed a cold water bucket. She alternated with the first hot bucket in order to make the filling comfortable. Once done, Sandra left to fill the empty buckets. Bethany relaxed once the girl was gone.

She grabbed the soap again and took advantage of it. At first, she was only going to rinse her hair, but after running her hand through it, she changed her mind.

Sandra returned with buckets full, filled the tub, and took the empty ones out, smiling back at Bethany. She was alone once again. Free to clear her mind once again. Her stomach rumbled, and the realization that breakfast was several hours earlier in the day hit her. She would have to eat, and soon.

Bethany grabbed a scrub brush and scrubbed the dirt off her body, then washed her hair to remove the grime. Taking the knots out of the mass was the hardest task she had to perform.

When Bethany got out of the bath, she noticed a hair brush on a small table just under the mirror. She picked it up and wondered when Sandra had dropped it off. Before brushing, she stared at her reflection for the first time in several weeks. The amount of weight lost over the year showed. Her sunken cheeks made the bones of her face protrude. Her skin, pulled tight, was pale compared to her dull auburn hair. She would need to eat a lot to gain back what was lost. Even her muscles appeared to have shrunk, but not her strength. No, she was still stronger than most, thanks to the training.

The robe engulfed her in a soft hug, and once draped over her shoulders, the fabric, though lighter than the dwarven robes, was much warmer. It fell to her mid thighs, leaving her skeletal legs naked against the cold.

She glanced at the scars on her feet from the hard run over a year ago. The ugliness of them repulsed her. She looked away.

No, Thomasyn was not the one she wanted to be with. She did not know if she wanted to be with any man. Not Jon. Last year Bethany thought she wanted to be with Master Chail, but that was not to be. He loved Tess and was too old for her.

The image of King Darrian drifted from the fog of her thoughts. She knew he was interested in her; it was made clear the last time they spoke. The king was not like his father. Darrian was kind, generous, and easy to talk with.

A rap on the door brought her back to reality. "Yes?"

Thomasyn entered the room, carrying two steaming buckets of scalding water. "Are you finished?"

"Yes," Bethany said. "Just finishing up." She put the brush down and clenched the robe tighter about the front of her chest. She left him in the room.

Sandra stood just outside the door, waiting for her to exit. She motioned for Bethany to follow her and showed her the way to the kitchen. "Would you like some tea?" Sandra asked.

"Yes."

"Do you want something to eat?"

Bethany rubbed at her stomach as it complained about how empty it was.

Sandra glanced back and smiled. "I'll take that as a yes."

The table looked inviting when she entered the kitchen. Bread and butter, preserves and cheese, meat and fruit. The aroma of gravy simmering caught her attention, and she saw a small pot on the stove.

"Sit. I'll grab the gravy and we can eat while Thomasyn becomes less gross." Sandra smiled and motioned to the table. The pot came off the stove and followed the other food to the table. A few seconds later, plates were put down.

Bethany put bread on her plate with some of the meat and cheese. Sandra pushed the pot toward her, spoon extended. Bethany took it and dolloped a bit of gravy on the plate.

"Jon told me a little about what happened." Sandra placed a cup in front of Bethany.

"Honey?"

Sandra went to the larder and returned with a jar of honey, some of the comb still in the liquid. Bethany added a dollop to her tea.

"What did he say?" Bethany asked.

"Not much, really. You know how boys are. They talk a good game around each other, but when it comes to telling us what is needed, they clam up."

Bethany let out a snort. "He can be very understating."

"Almost like you." Sandra glanced up from under a bent brow.

"What?"

"Come on, Bethany. We've known each other since we were small children, barely able to lift our heads. Grew up together, trained together, and went through a lot. Why do you hate me?"

"Michael," Bethany said.

"What? Michael? I don't know a Michael."

Bethany took a bite of bread dipped in gravy. "We did."

"No, I don't. There is no Michael– you mean the Michael Master Dress molested?" Sandra's mouth was agape.

Bethany nodded. "Yes, that Michael."

"I didn't do anything with him. It was Dress who did. At least he's not able to do anything to another child again." She put down her cup and levelled a gaze at Bethany.

"Exactly. If it wasn't for you, Michael would still be alive. Maybe not a Spear, but alive." Bethany bit into a piece of cheese. "And Thomasyn would not have killed Dress and learned how strong a fighter he really was. It's what broke him, you know. Learning how much better he was than everyone else. He doesn't even try and wins."

"Are you kidding me?" Sandra asked.

"No," Bethany said. "That was the time he became different than the rest of us. We watched him kill Dress without any effort. How could a kid do that to an adult? Dress was a fully trained Master of Spears, killed by one of his students during a duel. And what were you doing with him before Nanny Tess caught you?"

"We were... I was... It was personal. Between the two of us." Sandra blushed and lowered her head.

"Did you?" She could feel the heat from Sandra's cheeks after saying it.

"We were young. Didn't know what we were doing." She stood and went to the stove, then turned. "Kids did it all the time. They examined each other during training, even after they separated us from the boys." Sandra started to wring her hands. "We watched them bathe. Remember Bastion? His..." She made a motion toward her crotch. "... you know what, pointed up at his face all the time? He touched just about every girl he could. Never you or me, but remember Elana?"

"Yes, she lost her eye when we were six." Bethany remembered the training accident. A sliver of a wooden sword took her eye.

"Yes." Sandra returned back to the table and sat. "When we were twelve, he had her undressed and pressed against a wall, pushing himself into her. He took the maidenhood from many of the girls in our clutch."

Bethany shook her head. "But he was–"

"Ugly? I thought so also. But what girl could resist a Spear's attention? Even another Spear!" Sandra went to sip her drink, paused, then put the cup down. "If Thomasyn wanted, he could have been with every girl. But he was so pure. Even Jon. All the girls wanted to be with them both. They were the special ones." She pulled her chair closer. "I pulled Thomasyn away from the group of girls because I wanted to try. We could do nothing, being as young as we were. But I was jealous of how you three were always together. It was like you protected each other against all the possible advancements of others."

"We never protected each other, except when fighting."

"I realize that now," Sandra said. "Back then we were just children ... Who knows what we could have done, but nothing could have come of it."

Bethany finished the food on her plate and pushed it away. "What does that have to do with anything?"

Sandra let out a grunt of frustration and pushed away from the table. "Do you realize how frustrating you are?" She stood and paced between the stove and table. "You three mastered everything they threw at you. Throwing spears, crossing swords, fighting with hands. Even the trainers commented on it, and yes, I know they did, for I heard it one day. 'Those three are naturals. They pick up everything so fast'. How do you think that made us feel? We were like ants scattered around the yard while you three stomped about and made the trainers sweat."

"We sweated just as much." Bethany stared at her plate, uncomfortable with the situation.

Sandra threw her arms up in the air. "That's not the point. The rest of us sweated hard, barely made the trainers sweat, and while you did sweat, it was nothing compared to what the trainers went through just to get you at that level." She stood and walked to the oven. "I've learned a lot being at this Outpost. Seen a lot of things that people do to each other. But I'm limited here, and only one week away from Capital. You. You and Thomasyn and Jon went to the Teeth! Three months' travel away. The other side of the Realm. I feel as if every time I got a chance to shine, you three stepped in and took it away from me. And I'm not the only one who felt that way. Many of our clutch did!"

"There has to be someone who is the best." Bethany put the tea down and rubbed the back of her neck. "Having been to the Teeth, I would gladly trade it for a posting here." She glanced up at Sandra. "You don't know what it was like."

"But I would like to."

Bethany motioned Sandra to sit, and she did. Then Bethany told her about all that happened during their travel. After an hour, Sandra no longer wished to travel to the Teeth. The hardship of the journey itself was more than she could have believed, but to find out that the dwarfs welcomed you with open arms and then all but starved you for almost a week was too much. She understood it was a tradition, but still, there was a line that should never be crossed.

"I had no idea," Sandra said. "They really forced you into seclusion for almost a week?"

"Yes," Bethany said. "It was horrible at first. The only visitor was a mute woman who brought us some bread and a little meat. But we got along."

"I just remembered. I left Thomasyn in the bath." Sandra stood and straightened out her tunic.

"You still like him?" Bethany's question came out more like a statement.

Sandra blushed and looked at her feet. "Yes." She glanced up, and with more affirmation, stated, "Yes, I do."

Bethany nodded. "Take a bucket of hot water with you. He likes to take steaming hot baths and the water will have cooled down by now. Actually, if the water is dirty like mine was, it would be best to refresh it for him. Maybe spend a little time talking and finding out how he is."

"We talked while you were in the bath."

"About much?"

"Just old times," Sandra said. "Nothing much."

"How did he act?"

"He felt distant. Like there was something that he missed but could not put a finger on it. I don't know. Maybe it's not the best time to talk to him. He obviously has his head full of what you two are trying to do."

"No." Bethany stood. She wanted to just shake the girl and tell her to try something with Thomasyn, but she didn't. After being with him for so long, she knew that the best way to deal with him was to be straightforward, and not to dance around the subject as if you were testing an opponent's skill with the sword. "You should tell him how you feel and get his mind thinking about being with you."

"Are you sure?"

"Yes. And no matter how I feel about it, you are not the worse person he could be with. In fact, I think it would be good for him to be with you." Bethany started to cry inside. She did not want to give up even the remote possibility that she could be with Thomasyn, but it was for the best.

"Does that mean we're friends?" Sandra asked.

"Well, it means we're not enemies." Bethany stood and hugged the woman. She realized how much muscle was lost in the attempt to arrive home quick and understood why Thomasyn had insisted on stopping. They did need a rest, and some place to stay, in order to recuperate from the journey. She lingered in the embrace for a while longer before releasing.

"When are the others going to be back?" Bethany asked.

Sandra glanced at the two pails filled with hot water and Bethany grabbed the empty ones.

"I'm surprised they're not back now. All they needed to do was get some vegetables and a little meat. Did you see any Spears in the market on your way here?"

"None." Bethany shook her head. "Maybe they went somewhere else."

"No, Mitch is very particular about who he purchases supplies from." She took the two pails off the crane. "I'm going to get these to Thomasyn."

Bethany thought about that question for a while. "I'll be good. Maybe eat some more of this fine cheese you have here and make some tea."

"Well, if you need anything, just call out and I'll be here fast." Sandra started to leave.

"Sandra," Bethany said. The girl stopped in her tracks and looked back. "Did you... Have you... You know... Coupled?"

"With Thomasyn? No, but I would like to."

"No, have you coupled with anyone yet?"

Sandra stared at Bethany for a few seconds. "No, I never did."

"Not even Bastion?"

"Not even Bastion. He was conceited, and I didn't want my first time to be with someone like him. No, I've never lain with a boy, but if I did, I would want it to be with Thomasyn. Will that be a problem?"

Bethany thought for a while. "No, it is alright. Just be careful not to break his heart. It has been through so much over the last few weeks."

Six

Bethany turned her attention to the meal laid out in front of her. She only heard Sandra stand and make her way out of the kitchen. She hoped Sandra would wait until later to visit Thomasyn, for he was vulnerable in the heart at this time.

With her empty cup in hand, Bethany stood and walked to the stove to make more tea. The leaves still soaked in the pot, she strained them free. The tea was strong, having been allowed to steep, and the bitterness was refreshing to her. There was still something missing. People.

All that time Bethany had trained and pushed herself. She had not been alone. Now she felt it. Once again, she sat and lowered her head onto the table, and wondered what happened to Jon.

After twenty minutes, Bethany lifted her head. She grew tired of feeling sorry for herself. Sandra was prettier. Definitely her body was not built the same. The blonde just had to smile a little and boys fell over their tongues trying to get her attention.

I wonder what it would be like. In order to pacify her curiosity, Bethany took a handful of rags and placed them under her robe. She glanced down at herself and realized she looked strange. Nothing like she should. No one would recognize her and, when she moved her arms, the bundles got in the way. They kept her from the follow through swing of her sword arm.

The front door to the Outpost opened and Bethany heard the voices of two men talking. She quickly removed the rags and straightened out her robe. And for a moment, she wished her tunic was on to hide her body.

A thin and tall man with brilliant red hair walked into the kitchen carrying two large burlap sacks. He stopped upon seeing Bethany.

"Hello, little one." He placed the bags on the table. One tipped, spilling out a potato, and he grabbed it up with a quick hand. "What brings you here?"

Bethany glared at the man, then realized it was because she was not wearing her regular tunic and cloak that made him react in such a manner. "My name is Bethany, not little one."

"Oh, well, hello, Bethany. What brings you here?"

She sighed. "Sandra is one of our clutch."

"Our clutch? There are more of you?"

"Thomasyn is taking a bath." She pointed to the other room.

Another man came into the kitchen, shaking his head. He was shorter than the other, with a thick stocky body and balding head. "Mitch, you won't believe what I just saw–" He noticed Bethany and stopped. One finger came up and pointed at her.

"Her name is Bethany, a clutch mate of Sandra," Mitch said.

"You must be Barrion." Bethany sipped her tea. It was cold.

"Yes, I'm Barrion. Sandra told us about a Bethany. You the one?" He extended his hand.

Bethany took it. "I guess so."

"She probably only has a few words left in her," Mitch said. He emptied the two sacks and started to put the contents in the larder.

"Too bad. Well, I have enough words to go around." Barrion smiled. "Anyway, you know what's happening in the bathing room?"

"I don't want to know what's happening," Bethany said

"No one asked you. Okay, Barrion, what did you see?" Mitch returned to the kitchen.

Barrion grabbed a cup and poured orange liquid into it. "I saw her in the bathing room with some boy. Let's just say he has a smile on his face and leave it at that. I bet that girl could breathe through her ears if she put her mind to it."

Mitch laughed. "Kinda like that little blond thing she brought home one day? I remember being that active."

"What?" Bethany said. "Are they–"

"No," Barrion said. "She was still dressed. I just popped in and told her to hurry up." He started to laugh.

"You didn't. I bet you just closed the door as quick as you could and came over here. Did you put the package away?" Mitch tapped his finger against the long nose on his face.

Barrion nodded. "Safe and sound."

Bethany looked from one to the other, trying to understand the reference. "Look, if you two are going to share private jokes, then maybe you can let me know what it refers to."

Mitch smiled. "A little surprise for our young Spear. She's felt a little ignored as of late."

"Yeah, just a little." Barrion nodded.

"Tell me, Bethany, what brings you here?" Mitch pulled up a chair and sat beside her.

"It's a long story."

"We have time." Barrion sipped the tea and made a face. "How long has this been steeping?"

Bethany glanced over at him. "About an hour."

"No wonder it tastes like bark." Barrion threw the tea out the window. "I'll make more, but only if you tell us about what brings you here."

They were Spears, so telling them would not violate anything. But it was an assignment shrouded in some secrecy. Though who would they tell? Another Spear? No, she started to tell them about their task. The two men listened intently, asking questions only when it was appropriate. The death of Danton surprised them, and that was where they asked the majority of their questions. Most centered on how he survived all those years, but Bethany did not have an answer to that question.

When she mentioned Jon leaving, their faces went from flaccid masks to disbelief.

"How can a Spear leave?" Barrion asked.

"Yes," Mitch added. "There was only one instance of a Spear leaving the order, and that was Danton."

"I know. But who could have guessed that he would leave?" Bethany held out her cup for more tea. Barrion poured it.

"You never know why people do what they do." Barrion returned the pot to the stove. "But you and Thomasyn have not wavered."

"That is true," Mitch said. "And it seems not to be over yet." He put his hand on Bethany's shoulder. "But more can wait. You look like some sleep in a proper bed would do you good."

Bethany's voice became distant, and she looked into the distance. "A real bed."

"Yes," said Berrion. "A real bed with fresh covers and a pillow made of goose feathers. Does that sound nice?"

Bethany nodded her head. It did sound nice. Almost too nice after the last month. "I would love to sleep in a nice, warm bed."

"Then it's settled." Mitch stood and held out his hand. "Come with me, young Spear. There is a good bed just down the hall waiting for you."

SLEEP CAME EASILY FOR BETHANY. IT SEEMED TO HER THAT once she put her head down, the dreams started to come. But they were not what she wanted. The dreams pushed her thoughts toward what could be happening to Jon. She imagined Fletch taking him to a place across the sea and torturing him for the secrets of the Spears.

The training they went through would be divulged, and before anyone in the Realm knew what was happening, the elves would be marching to an invasion drum.

Just when she thought the dreams could not get worst, she would roll over and a new nightmare entered unbidden. In this one, Jon was taken to the Hobs and eaten in one of their bizarre rituals. Her clutch mate, bound to a stake, roasted slowly on a fire. His eyes boiled in their sockets and fingers burnt black.

The last dream disturbed her the most. It involved Jon surrendering to an outlandish race of reptiles and leading them into battle against the Realm. He pushed through the lines of defenders and ransacked the people she had sworn to protect. From the start, she envisioned the evil madness in the eyes of her friend. And that image burned itself into her mind.

When she awoke, it was hard to believe the sun was still in the sky, slowly sinking in the west.

She was warm and noticed an extra blanket of sheepskin laying over her. Mitch, coming in to place the blanket on her, was the foremost image in her mind. She smiled and felt completely safe for the first time in months.

There was no desire to move. Bethany only wanted to stay warm and sleep without the worrying interruption of the dreams. She pulled the covers around herself a little tighter and was about to fall asleep when the aroma of venison roasting in an oven found its way to her nose. She could even tell that the vegetables were cooking with the meat from the mingling of their odour. Grumbling just a touch, she slowly pulled off the covers and found a change of clothes laid out on a chair for her. She dressed in the white shift and skirt. It must have been Sandra's.

Bethany did not worry about it; she gathered and tucked in as much as she could. Once fully dressed, she made her way to the kitchen and saw Mitch, Barrion, Sandra and Thomasyn sitting around the table, talking. They quieted when she entered, and Thomasyn stood to get her a chair.

"I hope you're hungry," Mitch said. "Sandra went out and purchased a large shank of venison for dinner."

Sandra blushed. "It's been so long since we saw one another that I wanted to make it a special meal."

"Thank you," Bethany said.

"Yes," Thomasyn said, his voice a little slurred. "It is nice you did this thing for us."

Barrion reached out and took the cup from Thomasyn. "How much of this have you had?"

"Not so much," Thomasyn replied. He reached out for the cup, but Barrion moved it well out of his reach.

"More than you really need," Mitch said. "We better get some food in you."

Sandra was already up and fussing over the oven. Mitch got up and joined her, and soon she let out a yelp. He shooed her away. She returned to the table and sat down, sucking on the tip of her thumb.

Barrion laughed. "She does not cook very often. I think Sandra would burn her fingers off if we made her cook a fair share of the meals." He reached over and pushed her shoulder with tenderness. She rolled with the touch.

"I'm nothing but burnt thumbs around the stove."

Mitch laughed. "But she is a good judge of meat."

"But not vegetables," Barrion said. "The potatoes she buys usually have black centres, and last time she brought home horse carrots."

"If you two keep this up, I'll buy nothing but spoiled meat from now on," Sandra said, then stood up to help Mitch move the large oven doors. Once the doors were opened, they took a large pot off the crane and placed it on the table.

Bethany sniffed the air, taking in the amazing aroma of the meal. Then the lid came off and filled the kitchen with steam as well as the scent of cooked venison. Her mouth watered and she swallowed.

"Dig in," Mitch said. "We don't stand much on ceremony here."

The pot was big enough for two to reach in at once, so when Bethany stretched her fork forward, so did Barrion. He held down the roast and reached in with a knife to cut pieces of the meat. He smiled and pulled out a cut for Bethany's plate. She smiled back, thanking him for the slice.

Each took plenty to eat, and the roast was enough for all of them, leaving a good portion in the pot for later. The carrots, potatoes and onions were soft and tasty while small chunks of garlic added to the flavour.

Once the meal was done, Thomasyn's speech did not slur as badly, but there was still a running of certain words together. Sandra went to the pantry and came back with a plate of yellow cakes. She put them on the table and took away the pot, placing it to the side.

"I found these in the market and thought it would be a good way to finish the meal." Sandra's smile lit the room.

Bethany recognized the treats from years ago. "Lemon cakes?"

"Yes," Sandra smiled. "They had others, but I heard you loved these ones."

The cakes did not last long, and Bethany felt guilty having eaten three. But no one said anything, for each had their fill. With a sigh, Thomasyn leaned back, as did Mitch and Barrion.

And with the meal completed, Bethany rose to clear the dishes, but Sandra only jostled her out of the kitchen to the main hall with a new cup of tea, while Mitch and Barrion cleaned up.

Sandra accompanied both Bethany and Thomasyn to the hall and sat with them. Bethany noticed how Sandra leaned toward Thomasyn, and he leaned toward her as well.

"I want to come back here when we are done with the Dwarves," Thomasyn said to Bethany. "The town is nice, and it's warm here."

"Really?" Bethany asked. "Are you sure this is what you want to do?"

"Why can't you just be happy for him?" Sandra turned to face Bethany.

"I would be, if he was thinking straight." Bethany took a deep breath. "You've only been here for a few hours. We have three weeks to get to Capital and then the Dwarf King wants us back with the Realm's response. Also, we have to find out what happened to Jon."

"Jon left." Thomasyn leaned forward. "And when we get this contract back to the king, he will probably send someone else to negotiate the terms."

"But he may send us," Bethany said.

Sandra glared at Bethany. "You still hate me."

"No."

"Yes, you hate her," Thomasyn said.

"What would you know?" Bethany yelled. "You drove Jon away from us. He's out getting killed or something and all you want is to play with the blonde girl's breasts."

Thomasyn blushed. "You're not going to turn this around. This is not about–"

"Sandra's always wanted to be with you. Now, on our way back to Capital, she has the chance to take you away from everything."

"I'm not trying–" Sandra started.

"Yes, you're trying to take him away from the Realm." Bethany stood, shoving the chair back and causing it to topple over. "I'm not going to be a part of this." She turned and stomped toward the door.

"Wait!" Thomasyn said.

"No, Thomasyn," Sandra said. "Let her go. You just shoved this on her. Now she has to realize that you need to be free."

Bethany slammed the door behind her, cutting off any more of the conversation. Sandra had just started to wiggle her way back into her heart and now this was disclosed. Thomasyn wanted to come back here. It was infuriating. She lost Jon and now it seems that her only friend, Thomasyn, was about to be taken from her as well. They had a duty to the Realm, and that was about to be thrown away.

The Realm would lose two. Thomasyn and Sandra. They would not be Spears after this; how could they? The fact that he even thought of coming back to this little town instead of somewhere along the coastline truly baffled her. But not just the coastline. He could live anywhere in the Realm as a Spear. Being as good as he was, he could almost name the place that he wanted to live and it would be his. So why this town in the middle of nowhere?

It was because of Sandra. He wanted to be with Sandra, and she wanted to be with him. Well, she wanted to be with him right now. Who knew what she would want whenever he returned. Maybe in the next few weeks, she would move on to another person after experiencing him. There had to be some way for Bethany to make him understand this. Sandra was the type of person who only wanted to experience people. Once that happened, she grew tired of them and moved on. She was always like this.

Then it hit her. Sandra had tried to get Bethany on her side. She played her when they first arrived. Treated her special and then took him. That's why she gave up and told Sandra to try with him. It was all her own fault for befriending the girl. She had fallen into the trap.

Bethany found herself in the centre of town. She did not know how she got there, but many things were transpiring around her. Then she noticed one little action that most people would not see. Even if they did, they would probably not know what happened. A small child, no older than five, cut a small slit in a man's purse and took a coin from it.

At first, she could not believe the child did it. Here, in broad daylight, in front of a Spear. Then she realized that her tunic and cloak were back at the Outpost. The child may not have known she was a Spear.

Bethany reacted. The child, just a few feet away from her, was moving with the man. The child kept dipping his fingers into the purse, pulling out a coin each time. Bethany grabbed the child's shoulder in a vice grip, then tapped the man on the shoulder.

"This child has stolen from you." She was happy for the chance to deal justice, something she had not been able to do for a long time.

"What?" The man turned. His small shoulders were hunched forward and wild hair whipped in the wind.

"Let me go!" The child struggled, but could not free himself from her.

"He cut your purse and has been taking coins from you."

The man reached for his purse and fingered the hole. His eyes narrowed and face flushed in anger. "You little urchin! I'll kill you for that!"

"No! He will pay you back the money, and I'll take him to his mother." Bethany pulled the child behind her. "This is the way."

"Let go!" The child still struggled.

"No, he is mine to deal with. We have a way of treating such small thieves here that will stop him from doing this in the future." The man pulled a dirk from under his cloak.

SEVEN

Thomasyn stared at the door with his mouth agape. He did not expect anything like this when he started to tell Bethany of his plans. She was unpredictable, and something really made her angry about his wanting to stop travelling so early in his life as a Spear.

"That did not go well," Sandra said.

Mitch entered the room and stood there, hands on his hips. "What was all the screaming?"

"Bethany." Thomasyn stood and walked toward the corridor. "I have to change. Is there a tunic and pants I can wear?"

Mitch motioned to the rooms. "At the end of the hall, you'll find a closet of clothes. Just pick what fits. Your cloak is already dry."

Thomasyn nodded, then walked down the hall. He did not know what to do about Bethany, but he had to do something. Catch up with her. Explain why he did not want to keep running around the Realm. It was time to think about settling down, becoming a family man. Maybe raise a family. The time with the dwarves had revealed to him that there was more to life than just doing what everyone expected.

He found the closet and picked out clothes that looked to be his size. With a quick look, he found his cloak in the last room, which was the one thing that he cherished almost as much as the sword the dwarves had given him. He dressed.

Sandra and the two men looked up as he entered the hall. Barrion smiled and nodded with approval. Sandra winked, and Mitch patted him on the shoulder.

"Most people have a hard time admitting that they did not think before acting. Don't push the subject with Bethany. Just bring her back and we'll talk with her." Mitch nodded to Sandra. "She told us what happened, and it is something that all of us go through. It is the need to settle down. Sandra understood this very early, and requested permanent posting here with us just a few months ago, and was granted it.

"If you wish, we would be happy to have you here as well. The town has grown much over the last ten years, so another Spear would be greatly appreciated." Mitch dropped his arm.

Thomasyn nodded. To admit they had a shortcoming and needed support was something he hoped to be able to do when he got older. But for now, his sixteenth birthday was approaching, and it was time to think about family. Not the family he was born into, for he never knew his father, and his mother passed away bringing him into the world. He imagined Master Chail and Nanny Tess, wondering what they would say about his desire to start a family of his own.

Sandra was beautiful, smart, funny, and he enjoyed getting to know her again. Mitch had walked in as she pulled the plug in the tub. He never saw such a look of surprise and shock before. Shock, yes, on Master Chail's face when they practiced the training Master Dress performed on Michael so many years ago. He did not realize what it was back then, but he did now. And Dress paid with his life. Michael killed himself after the molestation became public.

"I'll bring her back," Thomasyn said, and he walked out the door.

At first he did not know what direction to head, but that soon sorted itself out. There was a gathering of people down near the centre of town. Something was happening.

Thomasyn jogged over to the crowd. And once there he asked, "What's happening?"

An old, balding man mumbled something through a mouth missing teeth, and with a quivering finger, he pointed to the crowd's centre.

"That girl there is claiming to be a Spear," he said. "Nera is going to teach her a lesson once he cuts off the hand of a thief."

Thomasyn's mouth dropped open. The punishment for theft is repayment and servitude for a year, and that would depend on the Spear who served justice, unless the theft was repetitive. To cut off someone's hand would be mutilation. He pushed through to the centre of the crowd and broke out into the clearing. The scene stopped him. With eyes wide, he watched as Bethany stood there, an iron clamp hold on a small child no older than five, and she held out her free arm to hold back a middle-aged man wielding a dirk with an evil curve to it. The man was shaking in anger and yelling at her. His face, red as scarlet, and veins stood out in his temples and neck.

"You'll release the boy to me, and I'll gut him for stealing. He must be the one taking from everyone around here. Times are tough enough without someone taking from you when your back is turned." The knife wavered in front of him, and he jabbed it toward Bethany to punctuate his angry words.

"No," Bethany said. "You'll not kill this child. Spears will serve justice to him, and since he was seen doing what he did, the justice will be solid and true. You will not mutilate this child."

"Revenge is mine to have, not some little girl who thinks she is one of her betters. Step aside, or I'll claim you kept me from my justice and take you as a prize as well."

Thomasyn stepped forward, tossed back one shoulder to reveal his sword. The hilt glinted in the fading sun, and the ornate carvings sparkled. "She is a Spear. Stand down, citizen, and I will not hold your actions against you. It is the anger of being wronged that heats your blood and makes your words unjust."

The man wavered for a moment, hearing Thomasyn's words. His eyes bulged in their sockets, and he stepped back slightly. Then he held his ground and firmed up. Shoulders straightened and resolute anger filled his face. "You're trying to trick me. You're no more a Spear than she is." His dirk flashed again toward Bethany. "I'll teach you to claim what is not yours after I taught her a lesson."

He stepped toward Thomasyn, his knife high to strike it down into the Spear's head.

As the man approached, Thomasyn crouched. He waited until the attacker swung down with the blade and saw he was off balance.

Thomasyn rolled forward. He kicked out his foot and hit the man's kneecap. With a scream, the man fell forward and landed hard on the ground.

With a glance at the man, Thomasyn stood and walked toward Bethany. "Are you alright?"

"Fine. I could have stopped him. I just didn't want to cause a scene like you did." She still held the child.

"I never meant to–"

"You never mean to, you just do." She turned and saw the crowd about her. "I'll take the boy to the Outpost. Mitch and Barrion can figure out what to do with him."

There was a gasp from the crowd. "He's dead!"

Thomasyn turned.

Several of the crowd had come forward to help the man. But upon turning him over, they saw the dirk firmly lodged between his ribs and into the man's heart. A pool of blood soaked into the sand and many of the people pointed at Thomasyn.

"He killed him."

"I saw it! Attacked a man who could hardly hold his knife."

"Why would you kill Cast? He was one of the biggest landowners!"

"He always gave to the people!"

The crowd kept calling out praise for the fallen man, and some even called for punishment. The words crescendoed into a hollering mass of words, no longer intelligible.

Thomasyn turned to Bethany. She stared at him, wide eyed, with her hand still holding the child.

The crowd contracted about them, pressing bodies closer together. Thomasyn felt claustrophobia set in. With a hand on the hilt of his sword, the Spear rose and turned to the crowd.

"There is no justice here. Back away and we'll have the other Spears here to judge what happened." Thomasyn held out his hand, motioning the crowd to stop their advance.

"We know what Spear justice is when they stand over their own," one large man said. He held up a stump instead of an arm. "They are never the ones wrong, but are wronged by others."

The crowd grumbled its agreement. Others spoke accusingly about the Spears taking, instead of asking, for what they wanted. The sound of such animosity was disturbing, and Thomasyn glanced at Bethany.

They could fight their way out of the crowd, harming or even killing those whom approached them. It would be a bloodbath if they did. Bethany shook her head, and Thomasyn knew that she thought exactly as he did. They must not fight.

The bellowing voice of Barrion thundered into the crowd. "Stand aside!"

With looks of concern, the crowd stopped its advancement and glanced about, trying to find the source of the command.

Mitch was not far behind, and his tenor voice rung out as well. "You will disperse, now!"

Sandra ran up to them and hugged Thomasyn. "Are you well?"

"They did not harm us," Thomasyn said. He motioned to the body of Cast. "He wanted to take the child and cut his hand–"

"Thomasyn!" Sandra said. "He has that right. The law was passed not two months ago. Children stealing can be claimed by the one they stole from and have their hand removed to keep them from doing so again."

This revelation surprised him. Children were never treated in such a manner before. Even the ones who turned bad. Now, with this new law, children could be removed from their family and mutilated for life.

"This law was ratified by the king?" Bethany asked.

"The king and council," Barrion said.

"We did not know," Bethany said.

Thomasyn stood tall and spoke to the crowd more than the other Spears. "Ignorance of the law is no excuse. We have wronged Cast, and in seeking to protect the one whom he was rendering the law of the Realm on, we cost him his life." Thomasyn unbuckled his sword and laid it on the ground.

Bethany pushed the child to Sandra and unbuckled her sword as well. "It was my fault. If I had not interfered, Cast would still be alive. Justice would have been served."

Barrion and Mitch entered into the centre of the mob to stand beside the three of them. Mitch glanced down at Thomasyn. "You didn't know about the change in the law?"

"No."

"There are several other changes the new king pushed through. I don't know where his head is." Mitch shook his head.

"We need to get back to the Outpost," Barrion said. "The crowd looks disorganized. Sandra, get Cast's body to the Wooder's home. We'll take care of the crowd."

Mitch nodded, drew out his sword, and pulled a short spear with his other hand. "Move aside," he said, pointing his spear at the crowd.

The crowd milled apart, allowing the Spears to make their way back to the Outpost. They left as Sandra lifted Cast to her shoulders.

"She's stronger than she looks." Barrion smiled at Thomasyn. "That's one of the reasons we don't want to lose her." The last part he spoke to Thomasyn.

Mitch kept his weapons drawn as they escaped the crowd's grip. He only sheathed his sword halfway back to the Outpost.

"What made you go out in the afternoon anyway?" he asked Bethany.

"I needed to get out." She scanned the way they came. Not one person followed them.

Once inside, the two older Spears relaxed and bade the two to come into the hall. Sitting down with their two visitors, Mitch sat opposite them as Barrion went back into the kitchen. He soon returned with tea for all of them and sat beside Mitch.

"What is going on?" Mitch asked.

"How should I know?" Thomasyn said. "Bethany stormed out when I told her what I wanted to do after we returned to Capital."

"You said you wanted to leave me. And that you didn't care what happened to Jon."

"I didn't say that." Thomasyn stared agape at Bethany.

"Yes, you did. 'I want to come back here' is what you said." Bethany's face started to turn red. "I would be left to return the contact to the Dwarf King and find Jon. No one cares that he's missing, maybe dead or being tortured."

Mitch held his hand in front of him. "What makes you think he's dead or being tortured?"

Her lower lip trembled. "I've been having dreams."

Barrion let out a bark of laughter, but stifled it when Bethany glared at him.

"Barrion," Mitch said, turning back to the young Spears. "Look, have your arms grown warm?"

Both Thomasyn and Bethany looked confused at the question. They did not get the reference.

"I don't think they know," Barrion said.

"Obviously." Mitch took a deep breath and rolled up his sleeve. He pointed to the scar on the inside of his bicep. "This scar. You both have one, right? Show me."

They did as they were asked. Both rolled up their sleeves and showed him the small scar they received when they were just one-year-old. Barrion nodded.

"Good. You made me think they stopped using the discs." He rolled his sleeve back down. "The discs join all Spears together. It is how the Seers contact us. They have another effect as well. If anything happens to, say, Barrion. If he is in a great amount of pain, I will know it, for my arm will grow warm." Barrion nodded, as if to confirm the statement. "Likewise, if anything happened to me, Barrion would also feel it."

"These discs– are they only for clutch mates?" Thomasyn asked.

"No," Barrion said. "They actually grow linked the more time you spend with a Spear. We can tell if something happens to Sandra, but because you have been away from her for a long time, your connection to her will be lessened."

Thomasyn nodded. The understanding of how the Realm was able to contact the Spears started to make sense. He realized the rituals they observed while training were not done just to have them carry on traditions, but also to join them with the others who went before. The link they must have formed with Shail and Garrion would be there for a long time, and this is what they alluded to in their teachings.

"Thomasyn, have you had any dreams about Jon?" Mitch asked.

"No," Thomasyn said. Then his mind wandered, and thoughts of Sandra with her long blonde hair came forward. The real reason he did not want to keep moving. The feelings for her came to the surface and excitement crept forward. He wiggled in the seat to try to adjust himself.

"Are you here, Thomasyn?" Mitch asked.

"Sorry, I was–"

"Not thinking of now," Barrion said. He smiled and winked at Thomasyn.

"Look," Mitch said. "There are some things that can stop the discs from working, but not much. They can be taken out of the arm, but usually that will cause heat to clutch mates that have been in close contact with that Spear like you two have been. If the arm is severed from the Spear's body, the disc only sends out a sharp pain, then nothing. If the Spear dies, the disc will flash between hot and cold when the link between them and another is strong."

"So, he is still alive," Bethany said.

"I would say so." Barrion stood and collected the cups. "I'm getting more. Do you want more?"

Mitch nodded, and Thomasyn mirrored him. Bethany shook her head. "I'll be back." She stood and headed to the kitchen. Barrion followed her.

When the two were out of earshot, Mitch turned his attention to Thomasyn.

"Did you hear how she was speaking?"

Thomasyn nodded.

"All she heard you say was you were leaving her." Mitch kept his voice low and stared at Thomasyn. It made him uncomfortable.

"You like Sandra," Mitch said. "And I bet you want to spend time with her. I can understand this. If I was younger, it would be what I would be thinking. She's beautiful. Nice on the eyes, and probably would make a great wife and mother. But remember, she is also a Spear, and may not want to settle down and have children yet."

"But I'm sure she feels the same," Thomasyn said.

"Are you?"

Thomasyn thought about that question. Sandra always wanted to be around him when they were training, and seeing her reminded him of it. And the way she greeted him.

"Yes, I'm sure she feels the same."

"That's a definite statement. Have you talked to her about it?" Mitch glanced away.

"No, but she's been telling me about the time we spent together since we've been here."

"Maybe she was just catching up with someone she likes? Maybe she sees you as a friend, and nothing else."

"No. If that was so, she would not have hugged me like she did. And I don't think she would have spent as much time with me while I bathed." That last part made his face burn.

Bethany came back into the hall, dressed in a tunic and cloak, followed by Barrion. The tension in the room elevated from the silence that took over.

"Sorry, too much water," Bethany said. She stopped, her mouth opened.

Each one of them stopped, and Barrion dropped the tea cups.

"Mitch," Barrion cried. "Sandra!"

Bethany started to cry.

Thomasyn grabbed his arm.

Mitch stared into the air.

Each one felt the discs in their arms pulse hot and cold. They each knew what it meant.

EIGHT

Thomasyn shook. His arm flashed from cold to hot and back again. It was just what Mitch had described. But with everyone here except Sandra, the flash of warning could only mean one thing. Sandra was dead.

How could this have happened in the town? The people did not seem so hostile toward anyone but him because of the old man's death. Sandra was only taking the body to the Wooder's.

Barrion was the first to react. He sprinted to the door. Bethany followed Barrion as Mitch and Thomasyn followed. The four sprinted down the street with only one thought in mind.

They ran past where the confrontation had happened. The crowd had dispersed, but there was still blood on the ground where Cast had laid. Down the lane, many of the town gathered around a large building.

The Spears pushed through the crowd, into the building, and then the main room. A large framed man bent over a body that lay on the ground. He appeared to be wrapping something and humming a soft tune.

Mitch stopped short. "Clay?"

The humming stopped, and the man lifted his head. "Mitch? Barrion, you're there as well, but who are the other two?"

Clay stood and turned to face the Spears. They saw Sandra laid out on the floor. Thomasyn saw her chest rise and fall, and he sighed with relief. She was still alive.

"What happened, Clay?" Barrion asked.

"She fell. The town's folk brought her in, jabbering something about elves. Not sure if they are right of mind. No elf has been on this soil for centuries."

"But Clay," Mitch said. "What happened to her arm?"

"The disc has been cut from her arm. I felt it. Thought that she was dead." Clay turned back and bent over the still unconscious form of Sandra. "She lost a lot of blood. The wound was deep, but she will survive. Another disc will have to be implanted soon. She should go to Capital for this, but not until she has had three days of rest."

Barrion breathed. "Thank the Five."

"Thank the people for bringing her to me. She would have died if they didn't." Clay stood with Sandra in his arms. "I'll take her to a room." He walked through the room and into a hall. As he passed, Thomasyn saw the Wooder's eyes were almost completely white.

"Can he see?" Thomasyn asked Mitch in a hushed voice.

"See? He is a bat," Mitch replied. "Never bumps into anything. Knows who's around or close by. If he's introduced to you once, he'll always know when you are around."

Barrion bent over. "They say he can feel you through the disc. That he's in tune with you, and the Five smiled on him as they took away his sight."

Mitch shook his head. "That's nonsense." He pulled up one of the chairs and sat down heavily. "That settles it. You two are staying for three days and then taking her to Capital with you."

Three days crept by. Thomasyn spent most of the time at Sandra's bedside, holding her hand, talking to her.

Sandra squeezed his hand.

"You're awake," Thomasyn said.

"Yes."

"How do you feel?"

"My arm is sore." Sandra started to sit up, but Thomasyn pushed her down gently. "I want to sit up."

"Clay said you are to stay in bed. Are you hungry?"

Sandra nodded.

"I'll get you something to eat," Thomasyn said as he stood.

"Wait," she said, and pulled on is arm. "I need to tell you something."

Thomasyn sat back down on the side of the bed and looked into her eyes. He could become lost in those eyes if he did not concentrate.

She took a breath and looked away sheepishly. "A few years ago, I would have given anything to get you into my bed. I always wanted to be with you, but..."

"But what?" Thomasyn asked.

Sandra blushed. "You and Jon were always protected. Not just because you were special. You know, the best of us. Bethany kept the other girls away from you. Some of us coupled when we came of age, just like the Wooders talked about outside the town of Salman."

"We were still young back then."

"But that is when we learned about it." She squeezed his hand again. "And that day when we were bawled out by Master Chail for copying Master Dress. If we had known–"

"We would not have done it." Thomasyn stood, the heat from his face hidden from her. "I'm going to get you something to drink and eat. Just lay still and I'll be back soon."

He left for the kitchen, picked up some cheese and water, and returned to Sandra. She was propped herself up on the bed, examining the bandage on her arm. She pointed to it. "What happened?"

"You were attacked by elves, and they removed the disc from your arm."

"Disc?"

"Yes, the disc." Thomasyn pointed to his arm. "The one they implanted when we were less than a year old."

Sandra closed her eyes for a second and let out a breath. "Oh, that was interesting." She opened her eyes. "The room spun for a second."

"I'll get Clay." Thomasyn stood.

"No," Sandra said. "I'll be well. The spinning has stopped."

"Good," Thomasyn said. "We leave tomorrow for Capital. We need to get another disc inserted into you right away. I'll leave you to sleep a little more. Eat up, food will help."

"Thomasyn?"

"Yes?"

Sandra sipped at the water. "How long have I been sleeping?"

"Three days."

She glanced down, her face turning crimson. "Who changed me?"

"Bethany."

Sandra smiled. "I guess she forgives me."

Thomasyn nodded.

"Are you really going to return with me? I mean, are you really interested in starting a family?" Sandra bit her bottom lip.

"I wouldn't have said it if I was not being truthful." Thomasyn stared at her. "Are you sure you're well?"

"I'm fine, just a little lightheaded." Sandra closed her eyes, then opened them again, looking at Thomasyn with her head tilted forward. "I wanted to know about the future we may have. What would we do?"

"We are Spears. We would keep the peace." Thomasyn smiled. "Did you think we would become farmers or something?"

"I don't know. But if I become heavy with a child, would I still be a Spear?"

Thomasyn averted his eyes. "I don't know. Maybe Master Chail would be able to tell us. I don't see any reason why you wouldn't, just not actively fighting." He swallowed. "I'm sure that would be the order."

"I want to be a Spear. I enjoy being a Spear."

"I understand." Thomasyn nodded. He could not figure out where this conversation was going.

"Good, as long as we both understand." Sandra drank down the rest of the water and handed the glass back to Thomasyn. "I'll eat when I wake up. For now, I'm still a little tired."

Thomasyn nodded as she lay back down. He wanted to help her, but a glare stopped him in his tracks. But she did not stop him from pulling up the covers and tucking her in. He leaned over and kissed her forehead, then left the room.

Walking into the kitchen, Thomasyn sidestepped around Clay, giving him a wide berth. The Wooder pulled out the crane from over the fire and lightly touched the meat on the spit. He nodded and pushed the crane back.

"Almost done," he uttered.

Clay ate well. And while Sandra was there, he made sure Thomasyn and Bethany ate well, also. Every meal contained meat and fresh bread. The meat was dropped off by the townfolk, even though Clay never asked for it, or Thomasyn never heard him do so. The man never turned away from anyone looking for healing, even if they came in the middle of the night. He would just bundle up and follow the person without asking questions.

"I really like bear," Clay said as he walked back to the table. "The meat is so tender and tasty. The drippings are really nice also." He reached out and took the loaf of bread. With a sure hand, he cut it into slices just under an inch thick. "Thomasyn. Can you get some of that soft goat cheese out of the pantry, please?"

Thomasyn had stopped wondering how Clay could tell who walked into the room. The Wooder never stopped them from doing anything, and he could tell both Bethany and him apart even when he just walked into the room.

"Sure, Clay. Any special one you want?" Thomasyn entered the pantry and stepped up on a stool to reach the upper shelf where the goat cheese was kept. His hand hovered there, waiting for a response.

"I think the one with blueberries in it. That would go well with bear, don't you think?"

"Yes, that would go well with bear," Thomasyn said. He glanced around the top shelf and found the package. The rough drawn picture of a goat in blue chalk told him it was what he wanted. "Got it."

"Bring it here, will you?" Clay dragged a chair across the room. "I need you to do something else for me, Thomasyn."

With cheese in hand, Thomasyn returned to the kitchen and placed it on the table. He looked over at Clay to see the man gesturing to him to sit in a chair. He did so.

"Now that you are here and see that Sandra will be well soon, I want to talk to you about her." Clay smiled, his cloudy eyes locking on Thomasyn.

"About what?"

"About your future."

Thomasyn nodded.

Clay stared at him with those unseeing eyes of his. The Wooder laughed without a warning. "Did you nod your head?"

"I'm sorry, Clay. It's just that you seem to be able to see everything all the time."

"Don't confuse sight with knowledge and awareness. I know you are there in front of me, and that you held cheese in your hand."

Thomasyn sniffed his hand. "You can smell the cheese?"

"No, silly young Spear, I asked you to get it for me and you always do exactly what you are asked to do without fail." The Wooder laughed again, shaking his head.

"Is that how you could tell I carried wood that one day?" Thomasyn asked.

"No, I could tell that because your arms did not swoosh against your cloak and the wood you picked was cedar, a very pungent wood to pick. It makes the most wonderful fires, and smells very nice when burned." Clay reached back and grabbed another chair, then sat down.

"You are an amazing man." Thomasyn said.

"No, just trained. When my eyes went dark, I had to do something, or live hoping others would help take care of me. I thought, Clay, you old bugger. Stop being sorry for yourself and make sure you are not a burden to anyone. So I did just that."

"How long did it take you to learn?"

"Years. At first I could still see a little. Maybe two or three years. My eyes failed a few months after that. Only shadows for a while, then total darkness."

Thomasyn leaned forward. "It must have been upsetting."

"No, not really. I was aware it would happen. I am happy with the time I had with sight. But the Five have blessed me with the ability to hear and smell. With that, I can know what is around me, and realize what is happening. Anyway, the town folk supply everything I need

76

without me having to ask. I take care of them, and they take care of me."

Thomasyn started to nod but stopped, knowing it would be silly to do so. "And what did you want to tell me about Sandra?"

Clay took a deep breath. "I know how you feel about her. Anyone could tell. You, out of all the men, have stayed by her bedside the most. You wiped her face when it grew wet and put extra blankets over her when the night grew cold. You love her, don't you?"

Thomasyn glanced at the ground. "I believe I do."

Clay let out a guffaw at Thomasyn. "Either you do or do not. When it comes to love, you either love someone or you don't love them. Think about this, young man. Your answer will affect two people, not just yourself."

With more to think about, Thomasyn grew quiet. His thoughts revolved around what he had experienced in life and the feelings that resurfaced when he encountered Sandra for the first time in almost two years.

The knowledge of all those things, and the desire to actually have a family, made him answer. "Yes, I do love her."

"That is a good thing to know," Clay said. "For a while, I was concerned. So, have you decided what to do after you marry?"

"What we would do? We are going to continue being Spears."

"Two of the order may marry, that is correct, but when children start to come, one will have to leave the order, and that usually means the woman."

"Sandra will not like that. She already said continuing as a Spear was important to her."

Clay nodded, then laughed into his hand. "I did it that time. At least you can see me nod." Clay stood. "Look, Thomasyn. There are women out there who would be happy to marry a man like you and raise many children, but Sandra would not want that right away." He put his hand on Thomasyn's shoulder. "Don't be disappointed when she finds out what will need to be surrendered in order to fulfil your dream." He took away his hand. "And decides it is too much to ask of her at this time in her life."

Thomasyn stood as well. "I don't think that will be an issue."

"You don't?" Clay laughed. "Well, just make sure I'm not nearby when she is told about it. Or better yet, if she does not think it will happen, when she is pregnant and told to sit aside while you go off to protect the Realm, I suggest wearing some armour when you do."

"I would not leave her," Thomasyn said.

"But if the Realm calls, the Spears answer. You would have no choice." Clay sighed. "Come; let us finish preparing the dinner."

And so they worked on finishing the dinner. Clay tested the mead and proclaimed it cooked. Thomasyn peeled potatoes and carrots to boil over the fire. With the manual work done, they sat once again and discussed how Sandra had recovered. Clay wanted to know if they would start their travel back to Capital tomorrow. Thomasyn answered affirmative. He outlined the rest of the journey and how quickly they hoped to be back home. His desire, though, was to resume the search for Jon, and hopefully reunite all of them in some way.

Clay warned Thomasyn the possibility of an attack from the elves would hinder their progress and that he should stay off the main trails. Walk through the forests was his advice. It was good advice, but would add almost a week to their travel time.

"And Sandra may not be able to handle the rough terrain until she is properly healed," Thomasyn said.

"Don't worry about that. After this sleep, she will be healed. Sandra is young, and the young are strong." Clay put the meat on a tray and started to slice it. "Be handy and get some of the ground radish root from the larder there."

The spicy ground root reminded Thomasyn of Jon and how he loved to eat such things. He promised himself that Jon would not be forgotten. They would need to talk to Master Chail in order to have permission to search for their friend.

He glanced up from his meal to see Sandra standing in the doorway to the kitchen. She was braced against the frame with her good arm. She took a breath and her face went ashen. "I was a little hungry."

Thomasyn was by her side immediately. "You shouldn't be out of bed."

Clay stood as well. "Little one, you still have half a day to heal before moving about. And then you are returning to Capital. Save your strength and return to bed."

"I will, but first ..." She motioned toward the meal that was almost laid out. "I would love to have some of that meat."

"That is a good sign. Your body wants to replenish itself after the ordeal," Clay said.

Thomasyn took Sandra's arm and guided her to the table. "I'll get you a plate," he said and grabbed one from the pile. "A little meat and vegetables."

He returned with her plate in hand to see Sandra's head on the table. Thomasyn dropped the plate as he rushed toward her.

NINE

Pin stared into Danton's eyes, which once belonged to Jon, looking for anything that should not be there. The Hobs scratched the man's head and smiled. "I think I see you in there."

Danton slapped the Hobs' hand away from his head. "Stop being a fool, Pin. Tell me what happened. Last I knew, the child fell on me and now, here I am."

Pin let out an echoing laugh. "Remember the last spell of rejuvenation? Even when you said no, I pushed you to do it. I am the Master of Magic and know what to do all the time." He grabbed Danton's hand and held it up. "See the ring? It holds back the child's mind and allows you to control his body." He let go of the hand and grabbed the sword. "Your sword was the key. If they hadn't taken it, you would have been lost.

"Look at the hilt," Pin said and pointed to the end of the sword hilt. "See the gem? It was hidden while you were hidden. The gem allowed your mind to talk to the child and drive away his grasp on reality. When that was done, the ring forced his mind away from the head and loosened his grasp on reality so much you could take control." Pin tapped Danton's head. "The child is now trapped, and as long as the ring is worn, he will not come out again."

"Which of the children did I get?"

Pin's smile split the side of his face. "The one you fought."

Danton smiled. "He was strong, but there is something wrong with this body." His hand went over to cover his stomach. "I feel hunger and a need to eat. Do you have any food that is edible for humans?"

Pin opened his pack and rummaged through it. Danton watched as the Hobs pulled out an upper arm, leg of a small child and several other things he could not recognize. "Smoked deer? I have smoked deer! You like deer, right?" Pin held out a slab of meat toward him.

Danton looked at it, his mouth watering at the sight. He grabbed the slab. It was a large piece of meat. He bit into it and chewed, leaving only half of it. Then he swallowed and ate the rest.

Once finished, his belly felt better. "Where did you get that, Pin?"

The Hobs scratched his head, then snapped his fingers. "In the little house where I found the child and man. It was on the way here. The man was not old, and the child had great innards." Pin licked his lips.

"You are disgusting, Pin. Was there any problems getting me away from the others?"

Pin shook his head. "The boy had an elf with him, but the creature was easily dispatched." Pin drew his finger across his neck.

"And why didn't you take any of him?"

Pin stuck out his tongue. "Elves taste funny. They are old, and the older the meat, the stranger it tastes. Humans only live so long before they die, and even in old age, they are still tasty. Elves live twenty times longer than man, and even when they are young, they taste foul. Must be something in them from birth. Old bones, old juice. Rank."

Danton's stomach stopped complaining. The body was well taken care of. Even with the sudden hunger that took him, there was nothing wrong. No aches. No pains. He decided it was a good thing that Pin took care of him. Yes, Danton was once again alive.

The cloak of a Spear felt comfortable. It had been a long time since he wore one. While flexing his fingers, Danton grabbed the sword at his side and smiled. The jewel glistened, throwing off brilliant colours. This was be a good body to have.

Pin smirked.

"What is it, Pin?" Danton asked.

"You." Pin bit into the forearm. "I remember the first time I rejuvenated you. Do you remember that day?"

Danton searched his memory and found the time Pin talked about. It was over 400 years ago, and it was fuzzy when recalled. The ceremony, a tedious ordeal, left an itching feeling all over his body. "I remember it."

"You almost look exactly like you did that time." He reached out and jostled the tunic. "There is still more growing to be done for this body."

Danton smiled. "I will work to make it stronger." He would make a heavy wood sword with a lead core. It would be used to bash against a thick wooden post until his arm bulged. Running with a pack filled with sand would make the legs stronger than they are now. So much work and so little time to do it. The training would have to wait until he made it home.

"Pin, there is one more thing to do." He had to hide himself from the Realm.

"The disc?" Pin asked.

"Yes, the disc. It must come out as soon as possible. We cannot waste time. Can it be removed now?"

Pin shook his head. "No. It is too soon since you took the body. Too much pain could loosen your grip on the mind." He took Danton's right arm and held it out straight. "Yes, the arm is strong. See the skin over muscle? There is no fat on the body, like it feeds itself before keeping anything."

"But did the boy eat all the time?" Danton asked.

"I saw him eat several times every day. I followed him for weeks as they travelled. I think he ate a lot." Pin stroked his chin. "Yes, he ate all the time, and did not turn away anything. How come the body is not fat?"

"There could be reasons. Maybe he ran a lot." Danton didn't know what caused the need to eat so much food, but something was truly wrong. "We must move."

"Yes. Come, I know of a secret way to the underground that will be easy for us to traverse and is away from prying eyes."

Pin led the way, and after a short time, they came upon a rock face stretching twenty feet into the air. He stopped and examined it.

"What is taking so long, Pin?" Danton asked. He was bored. This was not the life of a commander. The army of the Hobs Queen needed him, or they would disband and become animals, like the time he formed the army centuries before. Already he could imagine what damage the incompetent fools were doing.

"The way is masked magically. I will need to find the smallest trace of it again and then remove the guise." Pin's hand moved across the surface of the stone, disturbing leaves and dislodging twigs.

Danton watched the Hobs' brow furrow as he concentrated on the task. He could barely see the creature's hands moving across the rock face now. Pin was taking his time in the search. It irritated him that he was reliant on the Hobs for escape, and owed his continuing life to it.

Just when Danton was ready to suggest they continue their journey overland, Pin let out a howl of delight. His one index finger disappeared behind the rock and a great door materialized in the cliff face. Pin grinned with triumph as he pointed to the large barrier.

"What now?" Danton asked. The door was not really there from what he could see, just an outline of an opening with runes adorning the outside. He believed the writing to be dwarven at first, but then the unmistakable scrawl of the elves showed in one section. This confused him, for dwarfs and elves do not usually build together. And this door led underground, where most elves fear to go.

"This is the way. I knew it was here when I passed over it. The magic in this area is formidable, but not indestructible. This will take time." Pin stepped back as if to study the runes. "Dwarf, elf, gnome, human. They all had something to do with this. How to open..."

Danton stared at Pin while the Hobs examined the outline. He started to grow impatient, for as a onetime Spear and Master of Armies he would usually give the orders and had others carry them out for him immediately. Now he waited for someone he would normally command. Frustration boiled in him, and he started to feel the nibbling pang of hunger.

"I need food." Danton backed away from the wall of rock, wondering if Pin had heard him.

"Arms and legs in my bag, but I wouldn't advise you eat them. They have grown soft with age, just right for a Hobs' tender stomach." Pin kept studying the wall. "I have much to do here. Go hunt for the food to feed your human stomach. I will still be here when you get back."

With a humph, Danton turned and walked away from the one Hobs he could turn his back on. He tracked into the deep forest, crouched and hunted. Bird would be good and easy to find. Something that he could cook on a fire and feast. Something else would need to be gathered as well. He searched for tubers and other wild plants. The time of year would be right for blueberries, and such would flavour a fowl quiet well.

He discovered the berries first and gathered handfuls of them for several minutes. They were almost too ripe, and several burst in his hands. This did not dissuade Danton. It became a game to see how many he could pick without turning his hands completely blue.

Once enough had been gathered, he turned his attention to hunting once again. Wild turkey would be easy in the field before him, and he listened for telltale signs of the birds. After waiting for several minutes, he heard a soft cluck, followed by a tree call. Scanning the tree line, he found his prey. Two large female turkeys pecked at the ground while a male, black and ugly, stood guard.

With practiced ease, Danton took out a short throwing spear, reversed it, and aimed. With a flick of his arm, the spear hurtled through the air and struck the male in the chest, causing it to reel.

Danton was on his feet, running toward the dazed creature. He came upon it just as the bird regained its senses. He scooped it up and broke the bird's neck in one swift motion. Danton would eat well now, and not have to worry about Pin and his spoiled meat.

The ground showed signs of roots, and he recognized the plant leaves. Danton would have sweet roots with the bird. He dug with his dirk and pulled forth a tuber in triumph, and gave it a quick wash from his water bladder before putting it with the blueberries.

On his way back to the rock face, Danton gathered wood for a fire. If he had to wait until Pin unlocked the door, he might as well be comfortable and well fed. He found fallen dead branches. He picked them up and snapped the wood into usable length. And when he returned to the doorway, Danton was not surprised to see Pin still standing there, hand on chin, stroking the small hairs in deep thought.

"I killed a turkey and have a tuber for eating. Also found some blueberries. Are you interested in them?" Danton asked Pin.

The Hobs just waved a hand at him, still in deep thought and staring at the door. "I have part of it translated, but it is an ancient text. Well before my time, and I am old. A mixing of the languages before they were separated into their racial parts. Interesting. One word here says to hold back, while another says through the Earth. Don't know what they mean together..."

Danton built the fire and lit it with his flint and dirk. The musings of Pin no longer interested him. At one time he could easily have sat and listened to the Hobs talk, but that was well before the first recovery of his youth. After many years, the grating of Pin's voice wore on his nerves. The creature was smart, smarter than most humans Danton had known, but the most idiotic things escaped its mouth from time to time.

He made a small circle of stones inside the fire and placed the tuber inside it. The root would take the longest to cook, so he waited for a while and amused himself with plucking the turkey. Once bald, he removed the innards and washed the carcass. Most of the blueberries went inside the body cavity, while others went under the skin.

With the bird ready to cook, Danton wandered a little until he found a small stream. The water was cold, as if from a mountain, but none were present. He surmised it came from a spring deep underground. One that bubbles to the surface in order to escape the cold of the depths. He washed his hands, and when finished, gazed at the reflection staring back at him.

Yes, this was the man-child whom he had fought. The short blond hair, ratty from being unwashed, stuck out in many different directions. The eyes, blue as cold steel, stared back unflinchingly. The nose was just right for the face, something you didn't see much of in this day, but the blood under it was confusing. Why didn't Pin say anything about the blood?

He washed. First the hair, then the face. He gathered sand to scour away the blood from his face. Once he was done, the hair looked presentable. Almost human. There was no need to wait any longer. The tuber would be ready soon and the turkey still needed to be cooked.

Pangs of hunger bit at his stomach, making him wince. Something was definitely wrong with this body. He should not be so hungry after eating a large piece of smoked deer meat, but he was. Pin would have to be advised of this, and they needed to figure out what was happening to him.

Pin still stared at the rock face when he returned. The Hobs had a single-mindedness about him when confronting a problem. Stare and stare until he figured it out. Danton did not interrupt him this time. Better to let the thing stand there all night if he had to; the answer would come sometime. Pin would find the answer and never give up until he had it figured out. Even if they travelled above ground, the Hobs' mind would not leave this problem until he solved it.

Once, many years ago, Danton had given Pin a riddle to solve. One he thought was quite smart. He smiled, thinking back to that day.

"Pin," he had said. "What has four feet in the morning, two feet in the afternoon, and three feet in the evening?"

"What is this you give me?" Pin had responded. "There is no such thing."

"I assure you there is," Danton had replied. "In fact, I can name several of them without even trying."

The challenge had infuriated Pin, and for days on end he just stood there staring into the heavens, trying to figure out the riddle. At the end of the fifth day, Danton had come to Pin, and interrupted his thoughts.

"Pin, you haven't eaten or drank anything for days. You need to drink."

"I have not solved this riddle of yours. In fact, I believe there to be no answer and challenge you to prove otherwise."

Danton had sighed and gave the answer. "Man."

"You take me for a fool?" Pin exploded. "Man has two legs from birth to death. Hands are on his arms, not feet."

Danton explained. "When man is born, he walks around on his hands and feet, thus he has four feet. When he has grown, he walked on his two feet, not needing the support of anything else. As he ages, his two feet no longer can support him, so he uses a cane to walk around. Thus three feet."

"You take me for a fool! This is not an answer. You said feet, and man only has two feet, no matter what time of day it is." Pin turned and grabbed the water Danton had. "I shouldn't expect anything more from a man than trickery. No, leave me, Danton. I don't want to see your duplicitous face for a long while."

And he honoured his request. But their friendship always placed them together, even to this day.

"I have it," Pin called out just as Danton sliced into the turkey. "I have figured out the door."

"So what does it say?" Danton called back, slicing a piece of meat off the bird.

"The door seems to be a warning. 'Through the Earth into the depths of Kalagarar, beyond the stream of ice, you will enter the trap set in place to hold back the beast of Scars, trapped to never enjoy the light.' The whole thing is written using runes from the dwarves, humans, and elves. This is what took so long to translate." Pin came to the fire. "But it is still something to read. Opening the thing will take a long time still. I have to figure out what is holding it closed."

Danton chewed on the bird meat. His stomach complained that its emptiness would take much more than one bite to fill.

"So how are we going to open the door?" Danton asked.

Pin shook his head. "I don't know. The runes say something about asking permission to enter, but I don't know what that means. How can you ask permission to enter something when you need to talk to someone in order to get that permission? This is very confusing."

Danton stood, walked over to the door, pulled out his sword and knocked against the barrier with the hilt.

The door slid open.

TEN

"I'm alright," Sandra said as Thomasyn lifted her head off the table. A small reddening of her forehead marked the otherwise unmarred face. "I just... Well, the world spun for a second and that's when things went dark."

"You scared us, child. All I heard was your head striking the table and Thomasyn dropping plates. I knew something was wrong." Clay's unblinking eyes stared at her, his brows pulled together. He reached out to Sandra and Thomasyn noticed a slight shake in his usual steady hand.

"I've got you now," Thomasyn said, and Sandra leaned on his shoulder. "I don't think we'll be leaving tomorrow morning."

"I think not," Clay said. The Wooder rose and went to the pantry. On his return, he placed some twigs and leaves into Sandra's tea cup and swished them about. "Drink the tea, but mind the bitterness. No honey in it, for that would take away the healing power."

Sandra brought the cup to her mouth and grimaced. "This is very bitter."

"It has to be." Clay reached out his hand and touched her arm. "No sweet can be added to it. The leaves can only give their healing to you in the bitterness. Thomasyn, make sure she does not have anything sweet until the sun drops."

"I will, Clay. What was it you put in the drink?"

"Bay Rum leaves. They help with pain." Clay pulled back his arm from Sandra. "Sometimes I mix them with a nut that grows near here, but that will spoil a stomach that is not used to it."

"We learned something of the herbs you use," Thomasyn said.

"In your run with the Wooders? Before you were paraded in the town of Salman? I remember that run very well. I had a young Spear named Chail with me that day."

Both Thomasyn and Sandra stood with their mouths wide open. "Master Chail?" Thomasyn asked. "You did the run with Master Chail?"

"Why, yes," Clay said, rubbing his chin. "But we didn't call him Master at that time. He was a surprisingly smart boy. Always learning from and listening to others. I believe he questioned me about everything we passed those three days."

"Master Chail taught our clutch," Sandra said. "He's well respected among the Spears."

"He would be." Clay chuckled. "I surmised he would go far. Knew just when to speak or when to listen, that one. Will he be at Capital when you return there?"

"I believe so," Thomasyn said. "He was promoted to Master of Spears just after we left. I think the king did it to make sure Tess would not leave him, or he did not leave her."

"He married? Good for him. We always need great men like him to have children."

Thomasyn swore Clay smiled directly at him, but could not be sure.

"I'll take Sandra back to the bedroom." And with that, he guided her out of the kitchen.

Thomasyn knocked on the door to the bedroom. "Are you ready to go?"

"Not yet. Come in, if you want," Sandra called out to him.

He opened the door and saw chaos. One pack, half-filled, sat on the bed and clothes were strewn about the floor.

"I can't decide what to pack." Sandra dropped a small shirt on her bed.

"Three changes of clothes." Thomasyn picked the shirt, glanced at her and raised an eyebrow.

Sandra reached out and snatched it from him. "For sleeping." She stuffed it into her bag.

"You'll be sleeping in your clothes just like we did during training." Thomasyn picked up another very light shirt and repeated the same expression.

Sandra snatched it out of his hand. "For when I bathe."

"You'll not need it. Streams don't care." He counted shoes of varying size and colour. "Ten?"

"Look, if you're not going to help me get out of the way." She put three pairs of the shoes in the backpack and hefted it. With a satisfied nod, she put it down and put another two shoes into the pack.

"It would be better to leave some room for food."

Sandra turned on him. "I don't eat like you and Jon." She slapped a hand over her mouth. "I'm sorry. I didn't mean that." She reached out and took his hand. "You'll find him. I'll help."

Thomasyn shook his head. "You'll need a week or so to heal from the disc."

"I can catch up," Sandra said, looking into Thomasyn's eyes. A swelling of tears threatened to erupt from her sparkling, ice-blue eyes.

He looked down at her face and fell into the blue orbs. There were few things he was sure about in life. He was trained well. Few people or creatures could best him in a fight. No evil touched his heart. And he realized he wanted to be with this woman.

"We don't know how far we'll have travelled when you're able to follow." Thomasyn reached up and stroked the side of her face. "There is not much left to do but get to Capital and report to the king. I'm sure Master Chail will allow us to search for Jon, but he'll want you to return here to finish your assignment."

"And you think he'll agree to assign you here?" Sandra asked.

"I don't see why not. I've been north to south and as far west as the Teeth. This is east, so maybe he'll want me to touch the compass on all points." Thomasyn took a deep breath. "Master Chail is a great man and I'm sure he'll agree with the request and we'll be together here. And the Outpost is large for just three."

"Mitch said this is an old outpost built way back when the elves wanted to invade." Sandra backed away and resumed packing. "I think Barrion is missing the open space of travel. He may want to ask for reassignment. What are you thinking of, Thomasyn?" Sandra asked.

"I was just thinking of you and me, living in this town. Maybe having a few children and settling down."

She chuckled. "We're only 15 years-old, Thomasyn. Maybe next year, when we are older. Yes, next year."

"Then next year it is," Thomasyn said.

WITH BETHANY ON ONE SIDE AND SANDRA ON THE OTHER, HE waved goodbye to Mitch and Barrion. The two Spears had supplied four days of food for them. Each carried packs full of food, water and clothes along with their meagre belongings.

The town's folk just went about their day as the three Spears walked to the outskirts of town and then into the field, heading south. Children followed behind them, asking if they could join the adventure and become Spears as well.

But when Thomasyn asked if they had parents, most nodded and left the group. All had left but three before he decided to talk with them about the seriousness of their request.

They were all young, no older than five. When Thomasyn explained they were too old to become Spears. The children dispersed, swearing they would go to Capital when they were older to start their training. The Spears smiled.

The road allowed them to travel at their own pace, faster than most, but not as quick as those riding. They did pass those on horseback before the end of the day. A horse can run fast, but it must also eat and drink often.

They spent their travel time mostly in silence. Sandra reached out and took Thomasyn's hand. They held hands until mid-afternoon, when they started to encounter caravans heading to and from Capital.

Bethany did not comment on their handholding, she just shook her head and ignored them. Thomasyn glanced at Sandra and shrugged, knowing that it must be their small sign of affection that bothered Bethany. He would have to discuss it with her later, when Sandra could not overhear the conversation.

For the most part, they agreed on the speed of their gait along with which roads to take. Years of training together had them fall into old habits, and the walk became a game of spotting as many different birds as they could.

At the end of the day, Thomasyn called a halt to their walk. He did not want to push Sandra's recovery. Bethany excused herself, mentioning firewood, so he started to pitch the tents. Sandra busied herself with the fire area.

"We need food," Sandra said as she built up some rocks for a fire pit. "I don't want us to eat the supplies Mitch gave us unless we need to."

"I agree," Thomasyn said. "I'll find something."

He left her there and headed off into the forest to hunt. It did not take long for him to find a rabbit and kill it. One would be enough, but two would be better. He continued to hunt.

It was as if wildlife warned one another of his presence, but within an hour, he found another rabbit and killed it.

With supper in hand, he made his way back to the camp. Bethany and Sandra sat around the fire with a man and woman in their early twenties sitting with them. Bethany introduced the two as Jillian and Roger. They clung onto rags that wrapped their bodies. Both faces, covered with dirt, were gaunt, eyes and cheeks sunken in on them.

Eyes of faded green glanced up at Thomasyn as Jillian lifted her head and averted her gaze quickly. The disturbing thing was the woman had beauty, but that was hidden by what he could only see as starvation. The man was just as emaciated. Little flesh hung on his bones.

"We offered to feed them," Bethany said, her eyes puffy and wet. "They've been through a lot, Thomasyn. I think something has gone wrong back home."

Thomasyn sat down at the fire and proceeded to skin and clean the rabbits. "I only found two. If I had known…"

"We can share," Sandra said. "There is always game to catch for a good hunter."

He glanced up at the two visitors and then over to Sandra. Her smile was forced, without much joy upon seeing these two people. Thomasyn knew it was not an issue with feeding them. They travelled with more food than they needed, and he could hunt for more if there was a desire. No, she did not like the story they probably told her, and he needed to hear it as well. The two girls would be put through whatever heart wrenching problem the man and woman went through, but that could not be avoided.

With a sigh, Thomasyn nodded, and Bethany reached out and touched the woman's hand. "You need to tell Thomasyn what you told us."

Her voice was soft, barely audible to Thomasyn, so he leaned forward in order to understand what she was saying. Still, it took much to hear her words, and once she started, he did not want her to continue. But he listened in order to understand what brought these two people to the wilds of the road.

"Roger used to work in the butcher's as an apprentice, cutting up meat and making those little sausages for sellers." She paused, looking at the rabbit still in Thomasyn's hands. He passed the other one to Roger, who took it and started skinning it. "We didn't want for much, just wood for the fire and food for our bellies. Life was good until last year.

"It was the Hobs invasion that changed everything. Once the Spears marched out, the militia that was left filled their ranks."

"I thought all the militia marched the forced march." Thomasyn said.

The woman fumbled in her speech, not knowing how to answer the question. It was Bethany who interjected. "Just let her tell you the story."

Thomasyn nodded, and the girl continued. "The first few days, there were no changes. The militia kept the peace in the town and Roger went to work. I stayed home and made our meals. You see, I was heavy with child. The Wooders said he was healthy, and would make a fine butcher if he pleased." The woman's hand went to her belly. "That is until the fighting started.

"The militia started to demand money from the people. A tax, they called it. We already had a stipend set aside for the church and crown, but when they came and said it wasn't enough, well, we worried. Roger didn't make a lot, being a butcher. And all we had after paying out for the church and crown went to food, clothing and the rent. The militia men demanded almost as much as we paid our landlord. Three silver points, nothing less. They said it was because I was with child. If the child was no longer in me, then it would be less. They said it was because of me needing the Wooder and a mid-wife."

The woman's eyes bulged with moisture. She grabbed Roger's arm and wept into it.

Roger let her grieve and took up the story. His accent was strange to Thomasyn, for the man did not pronounce any H sounds in his speech. "You see, when Jillie told them the money was not here, they took it out on her. Beat her because I was not home, you see. When I got home, she was lying on the floor, belly all bruised and such. Blood about the floor told me something was wrong here."

Jillian patted his arm as she looked up at Thomasyn. There was a new resolute in the eyes, and her voice was much firmer. "They beat me until I lost my boy. They said if I couldn't pay, I wouldn't be allowed to have the child. And since we were still alive, the Spears would not have it either.

"They took my locket and wedding ring and still demanded the three silver points! It was back pay for having to beat me. They said it would help pay off what we owed.

"When Roger came home, my child had already come out. He was strong and lived for a few hours after being in the air too early. Only five months, that's how long I'd been heavy with my little boy."

Thomasyn nodded, not knowing what to say.

Sandra was the first to speak. "Do you know the names of the militiamen?"

"Terron, Bail, and Seron." Jillian spat out each name.

"Are you sure of those names?" Thomasyn asked as softly as he could.

"They joked with each other, saying if I wasn't so heavy with child, they would take me as payment." Her lower lip quivered. "Yes, I'm sure about those names. They are burned forever in my mind."

Roger put a stick through the rabbit, then over the fire to cook. Thomasyn did the same with him.

He thought about the issue before him. There was a true violation of the law here. These two people only wanted to live in peace in the Realm as members of a society of peace. Nothing seemed wrong with them. They were not angry or belligerent. Even during the telling of the story, neither of them showed any illness of mind, only hurt and despair. It was something that a Spear does not want to have happened to anyone.

"Did you approach the Spears when they returned?" Bethany asked.

"No, the militia did not allow it. They guarded the training grounds. There was one Spear we were told would help if we found him. Someone who trained the Spears." Jillian wiped the tears from her face, leaving streaks of clean and mud.

"Must be Master Chail. He would be one of the few Spears able to enforce the law, and no militia has the right to stop them," Thomasyn said.

They sat in silence for a while. Thomasyn worried about the Realm and needed to understand what was happening to their world. Jillian and Roger stared at the rabbits.

After a short time, Thomasyn interrupted the silence and, knowing that the dinner was almost ready to eat, spoke his mind. "I don't want you to answer until after you have eaten. This way you will not feel pressured into agreeing to something, thinking that food would not be shared unless you do." He looked over at both Bethany and Sandra, who nodded in agreement. "What is here we freely share with you, regardless of how you answer this question. Think long and hard about the answer that you will give, and speak between yourselves before giving it. Understand that no harm will befall you as long as we are here, and none of us will harm you regardless of your answer."

He took a deep breath and glanced once again at Bethany and Sandra. Bethany had a stoic look on her face, completely unreadable to anyone who saw it. Sandra beamed with pride as she looked back at him.

He was sure she knew what he was about to ask of the two, and knowing that it was something she agreed to made it all that much easier for him to say. He glanced back at Jillian and Roger. The two waited for the question.

"If you were under our protection, would you travel back to Capital in order to confront the people who did this grievous wrong to you?"

ELEVEN

"I need light," Danton said. He waved his hand in front of his face and was still not able not see anything. The door had closed behind them once they entered the cavern. Now he was engulfed by a black darker than squid ink.

"Open your eyes," Pin said.

"They are open. I can't see in the dark like Hobs' can. I need light."

There was a brief flicker, and soon a cold white light bathed the inside of the cavern. Danton relaxed, now that he was able to see in front of him. The cavern, with such a high ceiling, evaded the light, but the walls were not so lucky, nor far away. He estimated the corridor to be no more than twenty feet wide and well over that in height.

"How old do you think this cavern is, Pin?" Danton reached down and touched the rough-hewn stone beneath his feet. Moisture, but no moss. Strange indeed.

"Centuries old. The races have not mixed their runes like that for many years before you were born. Even before I was born! There seems to be a problem with this cavern." Pin took a few strides down the slope. The light bobbed up and down just inches over his head in a perfect sphere and stayed with him as he walked. It did not falter like a candle would.

"We need to stay together," Danton called to Pin, but the Hobs did not stop. With a deep breath, he followed the foolish creature into the heart of the hill.

What confused Danton most was the way at which the ceiling disappeared. The height of the rock face did not appear very far above him, but the light could not touch the ceiling here. How could that be? He did not know. Maybe Pin would be able to figure it out, but that could take a long time.

They walked down the corridor in silence while each mused over their own thoughts. Danton's head filled with thoughts of getting back home to his queen. She must be furious with him, having taken off without telling her what he was doing. But their cave was filled with children and grown Hobs. They needed to get more food for their entire population and expand. The tunnels they lived in could not be expanded fast enough for their people.

He could stop coupling with the queen, thus ending the birth of children. They tried it one day, but because of how Hobs were built, she could hold his seed inside her for decades. She did not stop giving birth for many years, and each new brood grew their family and population by thirty souls every three months.

Danton also wanted to increase the size of her throne, for it grew dismal and tight. That caused him to extend the reach of the Hobs, and why he ordered the small army to follow him to the surface.

If they attacked the surface again, he would not take the young soldiers with him. Instead, he would take the trained ones. The ones he spent the time to instil discipline on. The well-trained protectors of the caves.

Pin let out a squeak. The Hobs stopped and stared forward into the darkness.

"What is it, Pin?" Danton asked as he came forward to stand beside the Hobs.

"Do you not smell that?"

"I don't smell anything except musk. This place needs fresh air."

Pin sniffed the air. "There is more here. Take small puffs of air into your nose and let it swirl around inside you."

Danton attempted to smell what Pin was talking about, but all he got was a lingering stale odour of earth mixed in with rocks. Nothing seemed out of place for this type of cavern, except in their caverns they had ventilation that would help a person survive under the ground.

"I don't smell–" He stopped. It was there. Something under the smell of rock and dirt. An odour that lingered there in the back of the nose and now that he recognized it, the smell caused Danton to gag.

"Even the droppings cave does not have a smell like this." Danton took out a rag and tied it around his nose and mouth. It did not help.

Pin smiled. "That will do nothing to disguise the smell. Here." He reached out his hand, a small tied bundle in it.

Danton took the bundle and opened it. The white goo's smell of pine overpowered his nose.

"Put it under your nose. Just a small amount. You won't be able to smell what permeates the air here."

Dipping his finger into the goo, Danton dabbed a line under his nose. Just like Pin said, it stopped the smell from making him gag. He tied it up and handed the bundle back. "Thank you."

Pin nodded as he put it away. "We should start moving faster than we are. There is a lot of distance to cover and very little time to do it in."

"Are we heading in the right direction?"

"Yes, I can tell where the brood nest is." Pin tapped his temple with a finger. "All Hobs can tell which way is home."

"I know," Danton said. "I just wanted to make sure the space had not confused your direction."

Pin snorted, but led the way.

The floor kept sloping down, and Pin walked without a pause. The glowing orb above the Hobs head stayed with him, unwavering in the light it gave off.

Danton saw some drawings on the wall and stopped to examine them. The figures, little more than lines, adorned both sides of the cavern and continued as far as he could see. Every figure carried what he assumed were spears, pointed in the same direction, down the cave.

As they continued, the figures grew in number. Soon it appeared as if armies of fighters moved in the same direction they did. Danton lost count of how many were represented but estimated there must be thousands, if not hundreds of thousands.

Soon the figures changed. Not only were there the ones rushing forward, but some appeared to be hurtling through the air away from the rushing throng. It was disturbing to imagine what would cause someone to build such a record, for that is what he saw it as, a record of history. Why would it be hidden away behind such a masterfully locked doorway?

And then the drawing changed. Great tentacles reached out across the wall. Hundreds of limbs covered in suckers grasped the fighters rushing forward. Some of the figures, in a deadly battle with the tentacles, were raised, or thrashed against others. The battle must have been bloody.

Finally, the end of the army came to a head. Before them stood a wall with a small doorway set in it tall enough for Danton. A great mosaic of bones littered the ground before the door, and upon inspection, Danton discovered they were real. The picture painted on the wall was impressive. A great eye took up most of the wall, and a yellowish coloured body encircled it.

Pin stood there, staring. The Hobs' body shook, and great beads of sweat stood out on his brow. One arm raised and a shaking finger pointed at the eye. "The one of evil!"

Danton had never heard of the name and was curious about what it referred to. "Pin, what is the one of evil?"

The Hobs' bladder let loose, and urine ran down his leg to puddle on the floor. The usual dark green of Pin's skin lightened to the colour of pond scum. He just kept on muttering, "The one of evil! The one of evil!"

"Pin!" Danton yelled. When the Hobs did not answer, he shook it by the shoulders.

"Danton, I did not know. We must escape. There is little time for us if we want to survive."

"Pin, I don't understand why you are so worried. It's only a picture drawn on a wall."

Pin swallowed. "It is before the time of us. When all the races lived here, where the Realm is now. Together, on the surface of the earth."

Danton waited while Pin paused. Soon he realized that the Hobs would not continue unless he prodded him for the answers. "Pin, tell me more."

"The one of evil. It was uncovered when all the races toiled together to get the riches of the land from the heart of the earth." Pin ran his hand through thin hair. "The humans talked the elves and dwarves into digging down deep. They had found a vein of gold that became thicker as it went down. After two hundred feet, the gold was thick as an elf's arm. Finally, they all agreed to help dig the vein from the earth. It went well for them, and more labour was needed. The Hobs were asked to join in and share in the spoils if they helped. And we did. We dug the ground fast.

"Before they knew what happened, the hole was hundreds of feet deep; deeper than any hole the Hobs had dug before. Even deeper than the home we are travelling to.

"Once they had dug so deep, they started to smell the evil in the ground. Once they smelled the evil, it was too late. The evil came through and destroyed them all."

Pin was able to move now, and his hands became very animated as he spoke. "They told stories before you came to us. The large head of jelly with an enormous eye that stared without blinking. Its arms crushed all who came close, and hurtled the bodies through the air. It took almost every soul to fend it back into the ground and, once there, they sealed the way, they placed warning glyphs at the entrances. We saw no glyph? Why did we not see a glyph?"

"How long ago, Pin?" Danton asked, concern now making him uncomfortable in the space.

"Many centuries. They say it was over five thousand years ago." Pin scratched his head. "The glyphs, even with the power of all those mages, would only last a century if at that. No wonder we didn't find anything."

"Can we go back?" Danton asked.

"The evil was caged inside by magic infused in the earth. I am not that powerful. The old magic would be beyond me, I'm afraid. The only way to go is forward." Pin started to shake once again.

"We can move forward. How could such evil live for five thousand years without being fed?"

Pin shook his head. "The evil had survived for millenniums before being uncovered by the races. Do you think a few thousand years would be anything to it? How does the bear live through the winter? How does it know when to wake and eat? When the food is there for it."

"We are not talking about a bear. Only the two of us moving around. I'm sure it will not notice if we slip past. It may not even be in the place we need to go."

Pin still shook, but Danton knew there was only one way to go. Forward. A nibbling at the back of his mind was the only thing that gave him pause. There was nothing he could do about it but soldier on. He squared his shoulder and walked toward the door. The opening, blocked by a wall of bricks created by the rock itself, stood before him.

Wondering if it would work a second time, Danton drew his sword and rapped the hilt against it three times. Nothing happened.

"Did you think it was going to be that easy?" Pin asked.

Danton stared at the door, sword in hand. Something had to give, and he knew Pin would be the best to discover it. He stepped aside to let the Hobs examine the door.

Pin came forward with trepidation. He lifted his arms and waved them about, muttering words of power. Lines formed on the wall surrounding the door. The lines came together and became symbols and ruins.

Danton did not think much more would happen until the runes formed the same pattern that adorned the other door they had already entered. He believed he could recognize some of them, but others did not seem to make sense. Soon a whole littering of letters and words coloured the wall, engulfing the display of the one of evil. But it did not stop there.

Glancing about, Danton noticed how some of the figures seemed to move. He watched them, and yes, he could see them move as Pin chanted. One threw a spear, and it struck the jelly of the one of evil's body. A tentacle reached out and squeezed the life out of the fighter, throwing it away. Others, grabbed still alive, were tossed into a gaping beak of a mouth to be swallowed into darkness.

With every one that was swallowed, the one of evil grew another tentacle. That tentacle then reached out and grabbed another figure, this time one of a man, and tossed it into the mouth.

The sound of feet rushing forward to battle filled the space, and battle chants surrounded them. Nothing could prepare him for the death he saw. Even the battle between the Spears and Hobs just last year was nothing in comparison. He remembered the first battle he fought that involved death, the one when he first marched against the Hobs, before he was smitten. Even then there was not so much death, even though he had killed hundreds during his attack.

No, this was death on a major scale. The thousands who threw themselves into the path of the one of evil did so, knowing they would not return. Their sacrifice, long forgotten by man, was not in vain. They did so in order for those after them to survive. And one large creature, one Danton did not recognize, moved forward with a large gleaming, golden axe in hand, and sliced off tentacles faster than they grew. Soon, the one of evil only had a few tentacles to fight with, but they were not enough.

Then an elf came forward, one with golden hair and arrows with diamond heads, and shot the eye. The one of evil screamed a blood-curdling scream that made Danton stop. His stomach tried to jump from his throat and air escaped his lungs.

That is when the nibbling at the back of his mind became a headache, and he wanted to run from the spot. But he held his ground, knowing that Pin would soon have them free. And the battle fought on before him. The army, now advancing without the tentacles waving about, poked their spears at the one of evil, driving the creature back. As a man or dwarf or elf came too close the one of evil would pounce and swallow, a tentacle thrusting out from the body once it was done.

The dwarf with the golden axe swiped the tentacle away, and the one of evil screamed that monstrous screech. The men pushed, the dwarves marched, and the elves advanced. Spears thrust out, axes swung, and bows twined. The one of evil was backed into a large cavern and down into the earth once again.

Magic flashed, and wise mages made the rocks melt to form an entrapment for the one of evil. Other mages drew glyphs of power over the rocks and charged them with magic. The last mages created spells of protection and sealed the stones against the tentacles of the one of evil.

The world was safe, and the three heroes marched back to the world, never to tell about their deeds again.

Men, elves and dwarves confronted the Hobs and drove them from the surface into the depths of the earth. They chastised them for not fighting alongside the other races. The Hobs, doomed to be under the earth, pleaded, but the pleas fell on deaf ears.

Danton awoke from the vision. He glanced around to see Pin, shoulders slumped, standing there before a door partially opened.

"Pin, how long was I out?"

"An hour," Pin said. "It took that long for me to open the door." The Hobs turned to him, the usually smiling face gaunt with exhaustion. "I need to rest, Danton."

"Why didn't the Hobs help with the fight against the one of evil?"

"They couldn't," Pin said. "The queen of the Hobs, the only queen at that time, didn't want to have her children slaughtered."

"There was only one queen back then?"

Pin reclined on the ground. "Yes, Danton. We are a young race compared to elves and dwarves. We have only been on this world for a few thousand years. And our race does not build as fast as others. Only one has children, even though a brood can be thirty children."

"And that is why all the races hate the Hobs?" Danton asked.

"Yes. It is well founded. The Hobs should have helped, even if it crippled us. Now, with this ancient knowledge eating away in their mind, all the races see us as cowards, and not worth allowing to live. That is why we have acquired the taste for humans, for they are the ones who championed the other races to drive us underground."

Danton thought on this for a while and finally decided that his friend needed time to rest from all his exhaustion. "I'll keep watch, Pin. Sleep, and I'll wake you in a few hours."

TWELVE

With the evening meal finished, Thomasyn glanced up from the fire. He centred his attention first on Roger and then on Jillian. He hoped they would understand this was the only way to fix what was going on in the Realm.

"Have you decided?" he asked.

Roger looked at Jillian, and she nodded. "It appears we will go with you," Jillian said, lowering her eyes.

Sandra smiled and stood. She took two steps and sat beside Jillian, placing her arm around the woman. "Nothing will happen with Thomasyn and Bethany beside us. We'll make sure you're safe. I trained with them, and they are the best of the Spears."

Thomasyn's cheeks heated up. When he looked over at Bethany, he saw that her cheeks were burning bright red. But this did not discourage him. Helping the two people here was the basis of why he was brought up a Spear.

"You two are very brave." Bethany said. Thomasyn nodded his agreement. "To agree to face the people who wronged you is important, but to do it after they caused you to lose what you loved is an act of bravery beyond what most could muster."

There was nothing to add. Sandra and Bethany said the right things, strengthening the resolve of the couple. Upon glancing at Roger, he saw the man watching him. With the women talking, Thomasyn motioned Roger aside.

"Why did it take so long for you two to leave Capital?" Thomasyn asked.

"Well, it was not easy to decide what to do. Jillie really didn't want to leave." Roger kept his gaze down while he spoke.

"There must have been more to it than that," Thomasyn prodded.

"Yes, but it's the usual stuff."

"And what is that?"

Roger glanced away. "You know, the usual."

"But I don't," Thomasyn said.

Roger took a deep breath. "Jillie doesn't know, but the butcher job was not a paying job. I had to work at two places just to get the money to pay for the apprenticeship. And then I had to pay off the butcher once that was done." He looked up at Thomasyn. "One of the things we really needed was time. I had the butcher paid and was making money working there. Just needed to stop one job ta start making money when the new king started the new laws."

"Most of the debt was paid off, and we were just about to start a life. Then the baby was killed, and we had to pay for the funeral. That put us behind again, and I was in debt to the butcher once more.

"I was taking the last of the payment to him when I was jumped by the militia. The same guys who attacked Jillie. They took the money, ten silver points. That is when we decided to leave."

Roger leaned back on his hunches.

Thomasyn waited for an eternity. Then, after what he believed was enough time, reached out and placed his hand on Roger's shoulder. The man flinched, almost jumped, and Thomasyn realized he would have to guide the man in order to slay the devils that haunted him. If he did not, those demons would haunt Roger for the rest of his life.

"Roger," Thomasyn said. "We will protect you against the militia. Master Chail will bring justice to the men who wronged you and Jillian." He stood, and the women were still talking. "But now we have to make a decision."

"And what is that?" Roger asked.

Thomasyn smiled. "Do we go back to the girls, or do we hunt and find tomorrow's breakfast?"

<hr>

They hunted until the light of day sunk below the horizon. Not for meat, but eggs. They found a dozen of the little jewels in nests scattered throughout the trees.

Once they had the eggs, the men made their way back to the camp. The three women still sat around the fire, but their conversations had quieted.

Roger went over to Jillian and put his arm around her. The woman leaned in and kissed him.

Thomasyn looked about the camp, then noticed something was missing, something that had not been there from the start. He could not believe the absence of it did not show itself when the camp was set, so he made the decision to find out what happened.

"Roger, where's your tent?"

The man flushed and made a waving motion with his hand down the road. "All our belongings were stolen."

Sandra glanced up. "You mean there are bandits on the road as well?"

"Yes," Roger said.

Thomasyn could not believe how many bad things had happened to these two. "You can have my tent. The blankets are already laid out."

"No," Bethany said. "You can have mine. I'll sleep in Sandra's tent with her. This way, you two can have privacy." She stared at Thomasyn. "You will just have to sleep alone."

Sandra smiled, and Thomasyn blushed. He did not plan on sleeping with either of the girls, but stand guard due to the new information about bandits wondering the road.

"I'll stand watch for bandits," Thomasyn said.

"You can wake me for the second one," Bethany volunteered.

"And I'll take the last," Sandra said. "That way I can get the morning meal ready."

Thomasyn laughed. "I think you better take the first watch and I'll take the last. We know how well you cook." He coughed into his hand and held his stomach with the other.

Sandra picked up a pebble and threw it at him. He ducked, and the small rock went over his head with a lot of clearance. There was no worry about another rock being sent, so he smiled back at her and winked.

"It's dark, and we have a long road ahead of us." Thomasyn stood. "I'm turning in. Night."

He went to bed and laid down to sleep. His mind swam with what happened through the day and the information that they had gathered. Not one day of travel and two weeks left. What more would they find out about the new king and the laws that he had changed? How could they keep up with the changes if they travelled throughout the Realm to enforce what no longer was correct?

There needed to be a change in the world, and now was the time for it to happen. He puzzled over how to bring about change and restore order. And that is when sleep took him.

<hr>

BETHANY WOKE HIM WHEN IT WAS TIME FOR HIS WATCH. THE night was still dark, without any glimmer of starlight. His breath frosted in the air, and when he came out to the fire, it blazed to keep the cold at bay.

"Keep the fire going. I'm off to bed. Wake us when the light starts to open the day." Bethany stood and went to her tent. "And make sure breakfast is ready when you wake us."

Thomasyn nodded and threw more wood on the fire as Bethany headed to her tent.

The night did not hold any surprises, and he kept the fire going to keep off the cold, just as Bethany had done. It left him with time to think.

If they did find out about the two returning, then everyone would know. That was the best way to protect them. Make sure many people knew about the return as to cause issues if they didn't. The finger would point at the ones who had the most to lose. The people they were accusing of wrong doing.

With that resolved, Thomasyn glanced about. The morning light started to make an appearance, but not enough to wake the others. He decided they needed more than just the eggs, so off to the field he went.

Blueberries were common at this time of year, and he set out to find them. He searched for signs of old fires. Rocks, placed in circles to protect against the wind, were the clue. Along with the blueberries, he found wild garlic, and this he pulled out of the ground with pleasure. The meal would be a delight for the butcher and his wife.

Back at camp, he started to prepare the meal. Rocks in a circle would hold the eggs until they were cooked, but placing the onions in the fire would burn them. So he built another round of rocks just outside the fire, allowing the stones to heat while he busied himself washing the berries. He finished before the sun started up the horizon.

Thomasyn woke Bethany and Sandra, and explained his plan to ensure they could get their two charges into Capital. Not an elaborate plan, but Bethany agreed some of the simplest plans were the best. No one would challenge three Spears bringing forth witnesses with a valid accusation of a crime.

Roger and Jillian joined them soon after, and together they ate the morning meal. Thomasyn passed out the eggs and garlic, and the two became overjoyed at the flavours.

With the meal completed, the Spears broke down the camp. They left the area exactly as they found it. No proof of their overnight stay remained at the side of the road.

They walked soon after.

The next few days did not bring any issues. They stopped when they found water and filled up their skins. When they needed, they halted and took care of their bodily needs. And as the sun dropped below the horizon, they ceased walking and setup their tents in order to sleep.

Thomasyn took Roger with him to hunt for their dinner that first day and found the butcher very keen to learn how to fend for himself. Sharp eyes, that is what Thomasyn noticed of Roger. And once the man noticed tracks that Thomasyn overlooked, and it was a personal triumph for the man.

On the second day, Thomasyn took them a little further into the forest than the last. He showed Roger the tracks they followed and explained why.

"These are wild pig tracks. If we catch one, it will feed us for several days and we won't need to hunt." The reasoning was sound, but what Thomasyn did not tell the man was he wanted him to spend a full evening with his wife.

They found the swine, pushing its snout into the dirt, trying to root something out. There were several rooting marks in the dirt, and some black marks around the holes. Something special lay under the earth here, and the pig was trying to get at it.

He pointed to the holes and motioned Roger to be silent. The man nodded his understanding and did not move or make a noise.

Thomasyn hefted a short throwing spear and tested the wind. He was upwind of the animal, and he did not want to scare it. So in a crouch, he circled around, not closing the distance, but moving around the beast. It did not notice him, even when the creature moved about to root more of what it was looking for.

Once he was more downwind of the pig, Thomasyn readied to throw the spear, but hesitated. They heard rustling, and Roger stood. The pig froze, and the spear flew through the air.

Thomasyn retrieved his spear from the side of the pig, and Roger started the butchering of the animal. Thomasyn watched and made notes on how the man removed the insides. But he didn't discard anything.

As the man finished, he took the small intestines and squeezed out what was inside them. He did the same with the large intestines. Soon, a small pile of steaming mess was to the side, but Roger kept the intestines with the other parts. And once he was done, he used the small intestines to bind the front legs together as well as the hind.

"We can lift the thing better this way." He took a branch and removed all the twigs, then ran it between the tied legs.

With Thomasyn's help, the pig was hefted on their shoulders and Roger picked up the innards in a sack. This confused Thomasyn at first, but Roger explained they tasted the best when cooked.

Roger was correct. The evening meal was cooked over the fire with more blueberries and the last of the garlic Thomasyn had found the day before.

With the meat cooked and their bellies full, they laid down to sleep. Each Spear set to watch the camp while the others slept. And in the morning, Thomasyn made sure all the meat was cooked and ready to carry for the next few days.

The preparation was well timed, for during the afternoon of the next day, large thunder clouds moved in from the west. Thomasyn called a halt to the trek, having a feeling the weather was about to turn to the worst. They hurried to put the tents up, but not singly. The tents went together, allowing for everything to be housed under covered.

They did not put out a watch. Instead, each Spear slept near an opening, with the two charges in the centre. Once they ate, they slept, paying no heed to each other. The night stormed and wind threatened to rip their tents from the ground. But the Spears had set them properly, and only a small amount of wind crept under the slats.

The next day, rain still emptied from the sky. Nothing seemed to let up. Thunder echoed and lightning brightened the day in short bursts, but the sun did not show itself. They judged the time by the passing of hunger. The meat from the pig pushed that hunger aside, and only when the needs of their bodies cried for relief did they venture outside, and quickly returned.

At the end of the next day, the rain lessened, and they hoped that the following morning would bring the warmth of the sun at the start of the day. The sun did not come.

Neither did the rain. So the Spears broke camp and returned the land to the way it had been. No one could tell they had been there. Not a person or an animal. They left the site perfect and seemingly undisturbed.

The next week, they did not see anyone else moving on the trail. In the evening, the women would set the camp and Thomasyn would take Roger to the forest to hunt. At times, he would let the man track their prey. Mostly they only tracked pheasant or quail. Thomasyn explained that now they approached Capital, and large game would be scarce. He also did not want to waste anything they killed, so just enough was all they took.

And at the end of the second week, the high walls of Capital came into view. They stood at the top of a large escarpment and looked down. Off in the distance, no larger than their fingernail, the walls created an oblong structure of defence on the cliffs of the coastline.

Thomasyn looked upon the sight of his home, the place he grew up and trained with fondness. He wanted not to just return to the old barracks, but to see the ones whom he loved. Master Chail and Nanny Tess. Thomasyn missed them, not having set eyes on them for a year. It was the separation of a child from their parents, for both Chail and Tess acted as and protected each child as such.

Thomasyn stared out at the great city of the Realm and sighed. There was nothing left to do but proceed forward, and reclaim the city for the people that it had protected for so long. To remove those whom caused harm to the two people they protected, and possibly others, those people have been taking advantage of those weaker than them.

Yes, they were almost home, and Thomasyn wanted nothing more than to run the rest of the way.

Sandra's hand found his, and she squeezed. A smile lit up her face and Thomasyn fell into her eyes once again. Bethany squeezed his other hand, and she as well smiled at him. He was a rich man, with two women whom he could rely on.

"Let's go home," Thomasyn said.

THIRTEEN

Bethany did not realize she had grabbed Thomasyn's hand. With a nervous smile, she released and stepped away. It would not be appropriate for her to rekindle the old feelings she had felt about him a year ago.

She did not mind Jillian so much, but Sandra, with her smirking smile and blonde hair that appeared to always be just perfect no matter what happened, got on her nerves. Not just sometimes, all the time. But it was more than her perfect hair, or large breasts, that she paraded around. The smile was what drove her anger the most. Those perfect teeth under soft pink lips. Yes, she hated that smile, for it came with such a positive outlook.

Still, Sandra seemed to like Thomasyn enough to want to keep him happy. And Bethany truly wanted for him to be happy. No, who was she kidding? She wanted to be happy. At first she thought Thomasyn would be with her, but he became distant even when she was the only one in his sight. And then, because he did not show the same attraction, she turned her attention to Jon. Now, with Jon gone, she looked at Thomasyn once again for some reassurance.

Bethany turned from the view and walked past Jillian and Roger. Something disturbed her more than her dislike of Sandra, but she could not figure it out. She wanted to have the love Sandra received, but did not know how to get it. There was more. Something about how all of Thomasyn's attention seemed to go to Sandra when she wanted it.

No. Bethany shook her head and decided there was more to life than the attention of some boy. She needed to have more of a reason to keep going.

"You don't rejoice like the others," Jillian said.

Bethany felt the woman's hand on her shoulder and shook it off. "I'm fine."

"No, you're not." Jillian came up beside her, took a hand, and pressed it against her heart. "All of you have been so supportive of us. I don't know how to repay you."

"We're Spears. You don't have to repay us." Bethany pulled her hand back and started to walk away.

"But we want to," Jillian said. "And more." She caught up to Bethany and kept pace with her. "There has to be something you want."

"There's nothing you can do." Bethany glanced back at Thomasyn then quickly brought her eyes forward.

Jillian followed her gaze. "I don't think I could do anything about that."

Bethany's brows came together.

"Oh, don't get me wrong," Jillian said. "If I could do anything to help you, I would. But it seems they are starting a relationship. Something strong that may blossom into a beautiful thing."

"Into something... Don't tell them," Bethany whispered.

"No, it wouldn't be my place. But you are also beautiful, Bethany, inside and out. There are a lot of men out there who would want to be with you."

Bethany glanced at the ground. "Not like I am. Look at me! I'm built like a boy. All muscles and no curves. How can I get a man if I don't have a body that would entice him?"

Jillian grew silent, but kept up with Bethany. After walking for a while, she broke the silence. "Have you had a lot of time to get to know people?"

"Yes," Bethany said. "I spent all my life in Capital with thousands of people."

"No, not there. You spent a lot of time training in Capital, not mixing with people. Did you at least get out into the actual city and meet the people?"

"Of course not. We spent all our time training and sleeping."

Jillian snapped her fingers. "That's what I mean. You didn't spend time with people. What good is it to be able to knock a fly out of the air with a spear if you don't know how to talk to someone? Did you get to go to other cities?"

"Salmon, once. We had free time there as well." Bethany smiled at the memory of lemon squares.

"How long ago?"

"Oh, it feels like a thousand years ago. Maybe five, six years ago."

Jillian shook her head. "Too long ago."

"But I was in the Town of Lands for a while."

"That was the town you helped save from the Hobs, right?" Jillian asked.

"Yes. I had to run from that town all the way back to Capital. It took three days without sleeping." Bethany remembered the pain in her feet from the run, and a tear formed remembering Brand. Even though she had only known the retired Wooder for a day, she still missed the way he talked with her.

"There was no time for you to meet someone then. What about after the battle?"

"There was a feast for the Spears, and a dance!" Bethany tried to remember who she had been around besides Thomasyn and Chail. "I danced with Master Chail and then Thomasyn. Something happened and we ended up in a field together. We didn't have clothes on." She blushed at the confession.

"Did you two... umm..." Jillian raised her eyebrow and inclined her head at Bethany.

"No!"

"Are you sure?"

"There was no blood, and I didn't feel any different. I would feel different if we did anything, right?"

"Yes, you would have been sore." Sandra blushed and shook her head. "You would know."

"Then we didn't."

"You do know that riding a horse can make it so you won't bleed, right?" Jillian asked.

"I didn't know that." Bethany wondered if she would bleed, but it was of no concern. "But that was when I thought we would be together. Then he grew distant."

"Do you know why?"

"I think it was because of Jon."

"I think you mentioned him before, but who was he?"

Bethany snapped, "Not was. Is!" She immediately regretted saying the words like she did. "I'm sorry, Jillian. I didn't mean to snap that way. Jon is... well... he's like a brother. Once I would have thought otherwise, but no, nothing more than that now."

"Is there a chance you'd get together with him in the future?" Jillian was smiling again.

"No, I'll never be with him." Bethany knew that to be true now. Jon was lost. Even if they did find him, there would be nothing left of the one they once loved. "Jon's... broken."

Jillian nodded. At first, Bethany thought the woman would say something, but they walked again in silence.

"I hope you find someone like Roger," Jillian said.

"As long as I can understand him," Bethany muttered.

"I heard that." Jillian was smiling again. "Sometimes I don't know what he is saying." She laughed. "Yes, his accent is really strong."

"Where is he from?"

"Fishery. He said that's where he gets his accent, but I don't think so."

"That's where Thomasyn is from. He was brought to Capital for training when his mother died."

Silence followed. Bethany did not know how to explain to the woman how a Spear felt when they found out where they had come from. What feelings of loss they had or disconnection from the people? Bethany still felt a loss from not knowing her mother. She knew they found her in a town on the outskirts of the desert. A collapsed hut and the Wooder luckily found her three days after her mother had died. The

Wooder named her Bethany, meaning strength of spirit. Bethany did not want to let that Wooder down.

"Did you ever meet the Wooder who found you?" Jillian asked.

"No. We don't usually get the chance. The Wooders who find the Spears are always out wandering the Realm, helping others and finding more Spears. If we are lucky, we will meet one of the Wooders who is taking a child to be trained, but that would only be a wish."

Jillian looked behind them. "The others have almost caught up."

"We'll talk later, then," Bethany said.

"Yes, later."

***

Night quickly approached, and the Spears decided to set camp one last time before making the final few miles to Capital.

Bethany took this time to show Jillian how to build a firebreak with stones. Then she taught the woman how to build a fire using the wood that they found around the camp. Thomasyn and Roger went off to hunt together for the last time, and upon their return, they carried three rabbits.

Sandra had gathered wild radishes and onions. These were put aside for the meal. Roger butchered the rabbits and stuffed the radishes and onions inside. Once they had fully cooked, each ate in silence.

The last of their food was put aside in order to supply them with a meal over the last of their journey.

Bethany looked forward to seeing Master Chail and Tess one more time. She was homesick, and wanted to see home again before striking out to search for Jon, or return to the Teeth.

There was the other reason for wanting to be in Capital again. This had to do with Jillian. The woman was set on finding someone for her. Someone who Bethany could enjoy being with and would enjoy company as well. This was a high order, and Bethany would not wish the woman ill on finding her someone, but it was not going to be easy. Men, Bethany knew, found her intimidating. Every one of them stayed away from her, except Thomasyn and Jon. Those two were able to keep up, and in some ways, surpass her. This was why she liked being around those two, and for some reason when one went missing, they all felt lessened.

She did feel a connection between the two boys, and she hoped that they felt the same connection with her.

Jillian broke her out of the melancholy. "Bethany, is there anything that you really want? I mean, you are a Spear, and from what everyone says, you're really good at being one. But is there anything else you wanted out of life?"

Bethany thought about his question. There was something she wanted besides being a Spear. Just a few years ago, she would not have felt this way, but now she did. "I want to have children," Bethany said.

Thomasyn spat out the water he was drinking. "With who?"

Bethany threw a pebble; it did hit Thomasyn in the chest. "Not with you! Ew!" She looked away to see Jillian trying to stifle a laugh. "Sorry, Jillian. I know you think you'll find someone for me when we get to Capital, but look! I get angry when someone pokes fun at me. Even when that person is as close to me as a brother." She shook her head. "I don't know what to say."

"Bethany," Jillian said. "I know a few people in Capital who would love to get to know you. My cousin, for one. He's dated both strong and soft women, and he says the best time he's ever had was with women who challenged him. So I'm sure you'll like him for what he is."

"I don't know, Jillian."

"What have you got to lose?" Jillian asked.

"What happens if I fall in love with him?" Bethany asked.

Thomasyn raised his hand. "The sun will stop rising in the east."

"Thomasyn!" Jillian said.

Sandra punched his arm.

"He's right," Bethany said. "No one will believe it. They'll wonder if I cast a spell or bewitched him or something."

"Or maybe they'll think you're in love," Sandra said, her voice soft. "I agree with Jillian. You should let her introduce you to her cousin."

Bethany was still not convinced. "But we don't have the time." She took a deep breath. "First, we have to make sure Jillian and Roger are delivered to Master Chail. Then we have to give the contract to the king.

And once we've done that, we have to look for Jon and take the king's response back to the Teeth."

Thomasyn nodded. "Yes, we need to look for Jon."

Sandra glanced between the two of them. "This is important for you. I'll ask if I can join you as well. I'm sure Master Chail will approve. Three is the luck."

"Are you sure?" Thomasyn asked. "I didn't want to volunteer you for it. It will be a hard road. We'll have to get back to where he was and figure out which way he went."

"Someone will have seen him," Sandra said. "If I remember, he used to walk around like an elephant."

Bethany laughed. "Yes, like an elephant."

They fell silent again, and did not speak until the sun set for the evening. Jillian excused herself and Roger. They entered their tent and soon the three heard the sounds of kissing. No one said anything; they just got up and went to their own tents to sleep.

Morning came and Thomasyn made breakfast once again. Sandra and Jillian broke camp. Jillian asked if she could return the land to the way it had been before they stopped. Once she was done, Jillian asked Bethany to make sure it was completed to her satisfaction. Bethany inspected and agreed that she did a good job. Jillian was very pleased, and hugged both girls, thanking them for teaching her how to honour the land.

Roger voiced his thanks to Thomasyn for showing him how to hunt. Thomasyn thanked Roger for showing him how to use the entire animal and not allow anything to go to waste.

With the camp cleared and packed, the five travelling companions made their way toward the gates of Capital.

The fields they passed were full of farmers reaping the harvest for the year, but they did not look as happy as they did just a year ago. Bethany noticed many bent their backs with pain, not desire. No songs rung out in the fields. Happiness was no longer steadfast in Capital, and it was something she had looked forward to hearing.

Thomasyn and Sandra looked as concerned with as she did and decided to stop one of the walkers to find out what was happening. The Spears could not believe the answers they received.

"We are leaving," one group said. "They taxed us so much we could not afford to live here anymore." And another group answered, "This is a crime, and it's the militia causing it. I wouldn't be surprised if the whole Realm is feeling the pain."

"Where are the Spears? Are you not protected by them?"

A woman, no older than Jillian, glared in disgust. "They parade around in their compound and do nothing. What good is it having them train here and do nothing but eat our food and demand more and more from us each day? The militia collects our copper and silver and if they think we didn't pay enough, they beat us. I'll not be beaten again. Salmon is a good city, and I'm making my way there."

It was a disaster. The Spears no longer loved by the people. What could have caused this to happen? The king could not disband the protectors of the Realm. It was an inherent right for the people to be protected. The Spears could not be kept in the training compound, and the people needed to have a voice.

Bethany, Thomasyn and Sandra agreed. They would be that voice. They would find out what happened. Master Chail was the one in charge of the Spears. He controlled them, directed them, and trained them.

With their purpose in place, the three marched to the front gates with Jillian and Roger in tow.

At the gates to the city, stood three large men. Their armour bound in place and helms down, covering their looks. Something was wrong with this, and Bethany glanced at Sandra and Thomasyn, moved her hand in a signal to keep an eye on how the men moved, and answered.

"Sandra, hold back with Jillian and Roger. Make sure they are protected," Bethany said as they approached the first guard. The helm of the man followed her, even though she could not see the eyes hidden beneath.

When she was within two paces, Bethany stopped and stood with hands on hips. She examined the man, but did not flinch. He stood over six feet tall with arms as thick as a birch tree. The pike he held gleamed with a serrated edge on one side of the blade and the other looked sharp enough to cut metal.

Not to be intimidated, Bethany stared into the man's eyes and spoke. "I am Bethany, a Spear. Me and my fellow Spears have urgent business with Master Chail and the king. Stand aside and let us enter."

The man's chest heaved, and she could all hear the deep rolling laughter from within. Bethany felt her cheeks heat, and she raised a hand to cover her nose from the stench of the man's breath.

"No one sees the king unless he sends for them. And as for Master Chail, well, he retired after the Hobs incident. Now, if you are really Spears you would know this, so stand aside! You are not welcome in Capital."

FOURTEEN

Danton stared at the opening and wondered at the strength it must have taken to build such a barrier between the world of man and the world that held the One of Evil. It was beyond his comprehension.

Pin slept to the side, a stone in the hand under his head. Using such as a pillow confused Danton. How could any creature sleep in such a way?

He sat with his back to Pin and stared at the door. The slight crack was the only sign that it was open. Danton stayed in that position for two hours. He chewed on dried meat and waited for Pin to recover from the ordeal of casting his magic. This was different than the other form of the dark arts the Hobs' had performed for him. Pin never showed how strong a mage he was, even after the centuries they had known each other. The first clue happened when Danton first joined the Hobs over 400 years ago.

Back then, he was a pertinent man with dreams of conquering the Realm. It was the Hobs blood that affected him back then. Why he had licked his blade in a blood lust he never knew. But it caused a change in him. Now, centuries past and a new body later, he could understand the power it gave him.

Blood, just like the magic Pin had used to keep him alive, was power.

It tied them all together. Even the gift of his own blood in a jewel given to the Hobs queen bound him to her beyond question. He would have to do another blood gift, knowing the gift did not contain the blood this body held.

The queen may be upset with the change, but nothing could be done about it. This man-child that he now possessed was strong, and could sire thousands of children with the queen. The strength of their bloodline would increase. The Realm would be theirs; it was just a matter of time.

Danton felt concern for Pin. The mage expended himself too much, forcing open the door with magic. Hopefully, the beast within did not know about the prison breach. If it did, how could they hope to get past what took thousands to cage? Maybe there was still magic around them to help ward off the One of Evil.

With a grunt, Danton stood. The damp of the cave made him shiver. He glanced about, but there was nothing to burn. Maybe if Pin could conjure up the light, he could also bring forth something to warm their bones. No, he did not want to wake the creature. He would let him sleep.

Images of the weapons used by the heroes came to his mind once again. Did they leave them here, in case their cell did not hold back the One of Evil?

Danton examined the part of the wall painting depicting the heroes and their weapons. The figures looked larger than the others. The men around them were drawn with only lines, but the heroes were actually full figured men, dwarf and elf. Upon closer examination, he could see the whiskers of the dwarf, and pointed ears of the elf. They appeared perfectly natural and lifelike.

"What stories you could tell," Danton said in awe.

The face of the man turned to him. Danton jumped back while drawing his sword.

The face turned away. Magic.

Danton sheathed his sword and stared at the figure. It was a silly thing to try, but he decided he would. Taking a deep breath, he addressed the figure directly.

"What secrets do you hold?"

The head of the man turned again and faced Danton. Great chasms went from the corners of his mouth to the sides of his nose. The eyes, with dark circles under them, did not blink. Danton watched as the face became more and more like a man than a drawing. When the mouth opened, he could almost feel the brush of air against his cheek and the pungent odour of a man's unwashed mouth several hours after eating.

"I am the one they left behind to guard the door." The voice did not echo like Danton's did. The apparition's deep bass shook the rocks without causing dust to fall.

"What is your purpose here?" Danton asked.

"I am the one they left behind to guard the door," it said once again.

"This is ridiculous. Why did they leave you here?"

Images moved on the rock. A play of lines formed and the voice spoke. "Eons ago, man dared dig for the Heart of the Earth. They employed men and dwarves and elves and Hobs. Upon digging deeper than any had before, they uncovered evil. It did not have a mind, it could not be reasoned with, it only fed on whoever approached." The wall played out, all the races digging into the ground and coming upon the tentacles of the beast. "We battled it and lost." The picture changed to the One of Evil escaping the ground and roaming the land, eating anything it could. "The battle between the living and the evil went on for years. Many died." The picture changed to show a forge and a dwarf with a large hammer, making an axe grander than any Danton had seen in his long life.

"The dwarven smiths forged the axe of the mighty from metals unknown to man." The dwarf plunged the axe head into a tub of water and pulled it out. "Elvin magi infused the metal with magic and locked it in place." The picture showed elves bent over the axe, waving their hands in intricate patterns. As they waved their hands, lines appeared on the head of the axe, making the weapon look like a piece of art instead of a tool of destruction.

"The weapon was given to a man," the figure said, and a young man who resembled the figure held the axe high in the air. Lightning struck the head, but the man was not harmed. "The Gods touched the weapon. We were ready.

"All the races save the Hobs marched on the evil and drove it underground here, to be forever guarded. One man, one dwarf, one elf, sacrificed themselves to guard the door to the evil. We waited for years as people brought us food and water. We never wavered. Soon, many years passed, and we still waited, watched, and stood guard to protect the land from the One of Evil, but man forgot. In time, no food came to us, but we still kept our pledge to protect."

Danton, fascinated by the pictures, listened carefully to the figure.

"The elf perished first, for they are creatures of nature and there is none down here. The dwarf went second, for his hands were idle and they needed to work with metal and rock to keep his mind alive."

The image grew silent, and the pictures changed to show just him standing before the door. "I alone persevered. Man has a presence of will, a single-mindedness to sacrifice himself for the better. Here I stand. Here I stay. Here I protect."

Danton waited for more, but none came. The figure started to turn back to the way it was before. "Where is the axe?"

The figure turned back to Danton, filling out with life once again. "The axe of power, the one weapon forged with the blood of all the races. The rock that moves mountains. My hands hold the weapon and will only release it to youth and age. One who seeds both worlds of light and dark. The one who brings forth children in both worlds."

Danton stared as the figure formed back to a drawing, and then to nothing more than a rough outline carrying the shape of an axe.

"What are you doing?" a voice behind him asked.

Danton jumped. Placed back against the wall as he drew his sword. When he noticed it was Pin he relaxed. "Pin, don't ever do that again. Why would you sneak up on someone like that?"

"I didn't sneak up on you." Pin pushed Danton aside and examined the pictures. "Crude. Why would someone draw such a thing on a wall?"

"Didn't you see what happened?"

"What? You staring at a wall?" Pin reached out and touched the rough surface. Nothing happened.

"Pin, the wall showed me what happened here all those centuries ago."

Pin turned to Danton. "The wall showed you what happened? How? It's just a drawing."

"The pictures moved. They told me about everything. How the One of Evil devoured the land. How the dwarves created the axe, and the elves imbued it with magic."

"And what else did it tell you?" Pin's tone mocked Danton.

Danton reached out to the wall. "It said it holds the weapon and will only release it to youth and age, and one who seeds both worlds of light and dark. I really don't understand what this riddle has to do with an axe."

"It is a clue," Pin said. "Something to make the mind question what is around it." He scratched his chin. "If it told you something, then you would have the ability to answer the riddle. Old and young. I could surmise that would be you, maybe. Your mind is old and the body you are in is young."

"But what about the last part? The seeds light and dark?"

"You are human, and they are in the light, but you married the queen, and she is in the dark. Light and dark." Pin snapped his fingers.

"Then I am the one?" Danton asked.

"Yes, you are the one."

"Then I should be able to do this." Danton reached out to the figure and grasped at the wall where the figure's hand touched the axe. His hand passed right through the rock and the smooth surface of an axe handle greeted him. He grasped the handle and pulled out the axe created by dwarves imbued with magic from the elves and wielded by man.

DANTON STARED AT THE WALL UNTIL THE STING OF A SLAP woke him from his trance. Pin stood over him, concern etched his face.

"Never do anything like that again!" Pin screeched. "Stupid. Never play with ancient magic. You never know what will happen."

The ringing in Danton's ears started to die down. He heaved himself into a sitting position. The world spun for a second before righting itself. "The answer was obvious. You couldn't get it and I think we'll need it."

Are you sure?

A chill went through Danton's back. The voice was inside him.

"I don't care if you think we need it or not. If I don't get you back to the queen, I might as well try to mate with a human for all the good it will do." He stood and went to the wall.

"Sorry, Pin. I won't do it again."

But you will. We both know this. You'll do something stupid again and lose your life to some better fighter.

Danton froze. Pin just stood there beside the wall, trying to put his hand into the wall like he saw Danton do to get the axe.

"What are you doing?" Danton asked.

"There may be more items hidden in another catch somewhere." He stepped a pace to the left. "Maybe some potions or something that will allow us to pass undetected."

"Do you really think there is anything else around here?"

He is delaying, trying to make you out guess what you need to do.

Danton shook his head and tried to get the voice out of it. "Pin, did I hit my head just then?"

"You're fine." Pin kept searching.

"For a moment I thought..."

Thought you heard the voice of a god?

He stopped rubbing the back of his neck. No, this was not normal. And if the gods wanted to talk to him, Pin would hear it as well. There was no God down here, only Pin.

"Have you eaten?" Pin asked.

"Huh?"

"Have you eaten? Remember, there is something wrong with that body and you need to eat more often, and larger amounts." Pin stopped searching. "If there is more, it is well hidden."

"Pin?"

"Yes, Danton."

"When I was hidden in the sword–"

"You were not in the sword," Pin said.

"Where was I?"

"Inside the head of the boy."

Danton took a deep breath. "And where is the boy now?"

"He is gone."

"Gone?"

"Yes," Pin said. "Gone. When the ring went on the finger, it cleared out the mind of the child in order for you to take over."

"Are you sure he is gone?"

"Yes, I'm sure."

"How sure?"

"Positive. His mind was tortured by yours for a year. His grip on the body was loosened by the sword as well." Pin glanced at him. "Why do you ask this, Danton?"

Yes, why do you ask, Danton? Could it be because you are losing control?

"I'm hearing voices."

"What type of voices?" Pin asked.

"I'm not sure. It seems to know what is happening."

Pin shook his head. "Is your mind loose?"

Danton stared at Pin.

"I guess not." Pin poked his finger into Danton's stomach. "You seem good, but maybe there is something about this that should be looked at. Too bad we don't have much time."

"There is nothing here in this cavern. Why not try and figure this out?"

You'll never figure it out!

"Did it talk to you just then?" Pin asked.

"Yes."

"What did it say?"

"It said 'You'll never figure it out'."

"Humph. Maybe we won't, but we can give it a try." Pin looked around the cavern. "Not here, though. Let us get out of this tomb and investigate when we are closer to home."

Danton nodded, then they walked to the door. It opened at the worst part of the wall. Nightmares would surely ensue if they walked through the door. It was right where the monster's mouth was. He could not help but feel as if they were walking into the gaping mouth of the One of Evil itself.

They stepped forward. Danton realized the door was not opened far enough for any of them to pass. They would have to force it open further. With a glance at Pin, he grabbed the edge of the door and pulled. It moved ever so slowly. Soon, Pin was able to place himself between the wall and the door. The Hobs steadied himself and pushed as hard as he could. Danton watched as the veins stand out on the Hobs' forehead.

The door swung open enough for them to squeeze past. Pin entered first. He made a waving motion with his hand and the ball of light dimmed to twilight. Danton needed that light.

With a grunt, Danton squeezed through the door, following Pin, making sure he did not touch anything.

The door started to close, and he hesitated, then turned to find something to jam it open. Pin's hand stopped him. When he looked at Pin, the Hobs shook his hand and closed his eyes, then made a motion to stay as quiet as possible.

They made their way down a small corridor. It did not slope at all, and no echo came from their footfalls.

The journey through the darkness was slow.

"I can hardly see," Pin hissed quietly to Danton.

"Why? I thought all Hobs could see in the dark," Danton asked, knowing that Hobs could see heat on anything.

"Everything is the same colour, except us and where we touch. But even that is hard, for the walls are about the same. Do you not feel it?"

Danton had not felt the wall, but now he reached out and placed his hand against it. The wall was the temperature of a person half a day dead. Still warmer than most things, but less than his hand was. "You can still see, right?"

"Not without the orb." Pin pointed to the floating light.

"Then keep it and let's move forward."

As they progressed, Danton could feel his stomach knot. He was not really hungry, and his stomach did not grumble for food. Every part of his body wanted to be somewhere other than here. He did not know why. Even Pin seemed to be on edge.

"Pin."

"Yes, Danton," Pin whispered.

"I don't like it down here."

"Neither do I."

You are a coward.

Danton ignored the voice. "How much further?"

"Not much. The walls are opening up and that would mean the end of the tunnel. We should be out soon."

Danton nodded, even though Pin was not watching. He did notice the walls stretching away from them, but it did not take away the sickness he felt. The hairs on the back of his neck stood on end, and coldness grasped his fingers. He had the feeling they were not alone, but he could not say why. The feeling of loathing spilled forth, and the unmistakable urge to urinate swelled in his bladder.

The last of the tunnel finally gave way, and the two pushed toward what Pin identified as a door. It was much smaller than the other one. This door did not have any special features, just a pulsing around the edges that Pin reported.

Pin motioned Danton to stand a small distance away and thrust his hands into the air. The Hobs mumbled soft words in an ancient language that Danton did not understand.

Danton glanced about, not knowing what he was looking for. He studied the darkness just a few feet away from his nose. He gripped the axe hard enough to cause his hand to cramp.

Movement caught his eye, and he turned to face it. Darkness stared back, then he realized it was a large floating eye.

FIFTEEN

Thomasyn saw Bethany's fist ball up as she glared at the guard. Sandra cleared her throat behind him while Jillian and Roger stood silent. The guard stood there, staring down at her from his station. Something was going to give, and it was not the way he wanted to see this play out.

He reached out, took Bethany's hand, and whispered into her ear, "Not here."

Her head dropped, hand un-flexed, and she dismissed him by turning away. "He's not worth the effort."

"Hear that, Gorg? You're not worth the effort!" the man's companion said with a laugh.

"She's still not getting in." The man stamped the pike's end into the ground.

Thomasyn nodded to Sandra. They turned away from the guard and all of them headed down the path that stretched along the exterior wall of Capital.

"Master Chail stepped down?" Sandra asked. "We never heard that."

"Something is wrong." Bethany glanced back at Thomasyn and he nodded. "He would never have stepped down."

"Wait," Jillian said. "What does that mean for us? The militia is still there and now we've been turned away."

"Don't worry." Thomasyn rubbed the back of his neck. "We'll think of something. Until then, let's get to the field house."

Bethany nodded. She took the lead, and they followed her to the field. From there, they walked around the exterior of the city wall until they were almost a mile from the main gate. The walls were not guarded there and in disrepair.

Roger plugged his nose. "Why does it smell 'ere?"

Sandra giggled.

"Where," Thomasyn said, "do you think they dispose of waste?"

Roger shrugged. "Most people just throw it into the slug out back."

"Not that waste," Thomasyn said.

"I still don't understand," Roger said.

Jillian leaned over and whispered in Roger's ear. He squinted, then frowned. Roger started to watch the ground, minding where he put each step.

"There!" Thomasyn pointed to a section of the wall. "They haven't used that section for a while."

"I would have figured you'd pick the cleanest part," Bethany said. She jumped to a dry hump of dirt.

They made their way through the field and came to the wall. Thomasyn judged the height to be about eight feet. He braced against it and Bethany used his knee and climbed atop his shoulders to reach the top of the wall. Sandra climbed next, and then Jillian.

When the woman stepped on Thomasyn's knee, she lost her balance. With quick reflexes, he steadied her and his hand touched her belly.

Jillian stared down at him while he moved his hand off her stomach. She mouthed the words "Don't say anything," and he nodded a silent promise.

Once Jillian was over the wall, Roger climbed, and then Thomasyn jumped up. He grabbed Bethany's hand and together, she and Sandra hefted him up and over the wall.

When he hit the ground, they got their bearings. Satisfied,

Thomasyn pointed down one street, and they all headed in that direction.

Thomasyn scanned the crowded market and waited with the group for Bethany to return. She had not wanted to remove her cloak and weapons. She complained that the last time she had left friends on a mission, she returned to Jon broken, and did not want to risk such a happening again.

Sandra promised she would take care of Thomasyn, and Jillian did likewise for Roger.

Dressed in a white cotton blouse and loose green skirt taken from drying lines, Bethany was able to wander into the crowd and toward the barracks.

It confused Thomasyn that the people stared at them. Spears usually walked openly in the city streets. But when they saw them, the citizens openly talked about how strange their appearance seemed. The behaviour caused concern, and before charging into the barracks, they needed information. The plan formed, and Bethany was the only one who could be disguised accordingly.

Now Bethany walked toward where they hid in a small alleyway. A scowl crossed her face while she crossed the market square. Several vendors tried to stop Bethany to sell her food or trinkets, but these were shoved away.

Once with her friends, Bethany grabbed her sword and dirk from Thomasyn. "Next time, you wear the dress."

"He has the legs for it," Sandra said, sending muffled laughter among all of them.

"What did you find out?" Thomasyn asked.

"Master Chail supposedly stepped down a month after his return. There were rumblings of culling the Spears prematurely because there were only light injuries suffered by them during the Hobs' incident and no militia men fell. They say the Spears are really not needed now. A Master of Spears who I never heard of. They call him Ze... Zeam... Something strange like that. I can't pronounce it." She adjusted her cloak. "Definitely something wrong. The Spears have not left the training grounds since Master Chail returned."

"What about the Wooders?" Sandra asked.

"They've been coming and going without issue," Bethany said.

"Have they been bringing Spears?" Thomasyn asked.

"No. The ones I talked to said there haven't been any Spears brought for a year. And the Spears haven't opened the doors to hire any wet nurses either." She glanced nervously behind her.

"What's wrong?" Sandra asked.

"I think someone noticed me asking questions."

Thomasyn glanced at the square, but did not see anyone paying them heed.

"Did you see anyone following you?" Thomasyn asked.

"No, just … it's just a feeling. Is anyone watching?" Bethany glanced over her shoulder.

"What else did you find out?" Sandra asked.

"Not much more. It's like everyone is scared to talk." She turned to Jillian and Roger. "Why didn't you tell us about Master Chail?"

Jillian shrugged. "He's a Spear, right? How could we know what happened? Everything is behind the training walls of the Spears."

"The shop I worked," Roger said. "It's just over to the 'Olt district. Other side of Capital."

Thomasyn nodded. The inner workings of the Spears would be unknown to anyone not involved with them. A lonely butcher would have no way of hearing anything, especially since he lived and worked on the other side of the city.

"I'm sorry," Thomasyn said.

Jillian turned to him with a raised eyebrow. "Sorry? About what?"

"Thinking you could be holding out on us." Thomasyn glanced down at her belly. "We've been travelling together for a while now, and I should have known."

"I should have said something," Jillian said, and turned to Roger. "I'm pregnant."

Roger's eyes went wide, and then a smile pulled at the edges of his mouth. "'Ow long?" he asked, reaching out his arms to hug her.

"Three months now. I was scared to say anything."

The embrace lasted a long time, and when they released one another, tears rolled down Roger's face. He kissed her hands.

"We don't have time for this," Sandra said.

Thomasyn glanced at the crowd and saw several of them looking their way. They were in the open and needed to get under cover. He tried to remember the area from all those years of living in Capital, but it was hard. Most of their time involved training in the grounds sectioned off from the rest of the city. And when they did go out, it was to make their way into for the surrounding countryside for more training.

"Thomasyn?" Bethany said. "Do you remember the older ones who came back for advanced training when we were only ten or eleven?"

"Barely. They didn't stay long in the barracks, if I remember."

"Do they know why?"

"They didn't want to be around children?" Thomasyn said.

Sandra smiled and winked at Bethany. "Not really."

Bethany nodded. "No, they had other things on their mind."

"Nanny Tess told us about them," Sandra said. "She told us to stay away, that what they did was not right."

"I still don't understand why," Thomasyn said.

Sandra smiled at Bethany and Jillian stifled a smirk and said, "If you don't know what men and women do together by now…"

Thomasyn felt his cheeks heat. He did not think about that, and most of the boys back then did not either. The Spears who came back for advanced training were just under twenty, and their thoughts could have been on women, and that is why Tess would warn the girls about them.

"Near the outer training area," Sandra said, "there is a brothel. Most of the city knows nothing about it. They don't try to get just any men. They want Spears with new coins in their pockets and don't beat them."

Thomasyn shook his head. He had the urges, yes. But he ignored them and thought others did as well. "I really don't want to know about it either." Thomasyn motioned for them to start following him, and then he turned to Sandra. "You know how they got in and out of the training area?"

"Yes, I followed one once. Thought it would be fun to surprise them. But he found me just before he went outside. I did see his friends go over the wall, though." Sandra walked past Thomasyn. "I'll show you where they went over."

Sandra led them through the city and around the back of the training area. The homes started to give way to shops and multi-family buildings. Signs, painted with symbols and pictures, disappeared to be replaced with words. Sweet Shop, Dress Maker, Cobbler. Each one was more elaborate than the last as the buildings became larger.

Looking toward the wall while walking, Sandra counted the grates and stopped. "Here," she said.

"Where?" Bethany asked.

"We have to wait until dark, but there is a mark here and a place to put your hands into the space between a few stones." She went right up to the wall and studied it. "But they just don't show up in the sunlight for some reason."

"But if they can be seen by the moonlight," Thomasyn said. "Why didn't others climb into the grounds and steal what they can grab?"

Bethany tapped her temple. "Think, Thomasyn. Who would break into the Spear's training ground to steal anything?"

He thought about it and realized his question was not well founded. "They would be caught by Spears, or at least the Spears in Flight."

Sandra and Bethany nodded.

"He's not too bright," Bethany said. "But at least he's pretty to look at."

Sandra laughed. "And fights well."

They laughed at Thomasyn's expense. He suggested that they wait for the evening. It was the only way he could divert their attention away from him and to the task at hand.

***

THE BUILDINGS BLOCKED OUT THE SUN BEFORE IT SET beyond the horizon. Tendrils of light stretched out, trying desperately to keep the world alive. And as they failed, the bright face of the moon hanging high in the sky reached out to illuminate handholds sunk deep into the wall.

Bethany pointed to them first, and Thomasyn nodded. They decided that Jillian and Roger would wait outside the barracks, not entering the training grounds, in case there was an issue.

They scaled the wall. It was easy, up and over, then down to the ground on the other side. The dirt stirred as they hit, and with their knowledge of the layout. They made it past the obstacles strewn about and to the inner training area. The one young Spears would practice in daily.

Weapons lay strewn about on the ground, and they made their way around the small piles. The footprints of many showed up in the ground as if the keepers did not sweep the dirt after practice. The grounds were dismal.

Thomasyn motioned to the others. They lifted the hoods of their cloaks, blended into the shadows. They could just make each other out as they moved toward the barrack's door.

Thomasyn reached it first and took hold of the handle. With a shove, he opened it. He looked back and motioned Bethany forward. She disappeared through the door, followed by Sandra and then himself.

The corridor was dimly lit, but they could still navigate with ease. Thomasyn crept low to the ground, followed by the others. They passed the newborn chamber. Only the sound of sleeping children could be heard.

"Where are the wet nurses for these children?" Sandra whisper.

"Best not to ask," Bethany said.

Thomasyn hushed them, hunched down, and walked quietly down the corridor. His target, the office of the Master Spears. Master Chail's office. Two more doors down and he was there in front of it. He pushed open the door and the well lit room flooded the corridor in brightness.

There was a scraping sound of a chair against stone. A shadow crossed the doorway and Con looked out.

"Master Con?" Thomasyn said.

Con looked down, squinting. "Who's there?"

Thomasyn stood and pulled back his hood.

"Thomasyn?" Con said. He reached out and placed a hand on the Spear's shoulder. "Who else is with you?"

Bethany and Sandra pulled back their hoods, but stayed crouched in the shadows.

"What's happened, Master Con?" Thomasyn asked.

"Not here," Con said in a hushed tone. "Come. Come inside. It is not safe for you out there." He backed away from the doorway and motioned the three Spears inside.

When the last of them entered the office, Con closed the door and put a locking bar across it. The man let out a breath and turned to look at them. "You have grown."

Thomasyn scanned the office. It was still the biggest single room in the barracks, not meant for more than one person. A cot to one side and the desk covered in papers showed it had not changed much.

"Where is Master Chail?" Sandra asked.

"Sandra? I thought Jon would be with you." Con touched the girl's cheek, eyes soft with recognition. "It is a joy to see you alive. All of you."

"We've came from the Teeth. The Dwarven King wants a new contract with the Realm." Thomasyn pulled out the contract from his pack. "He told us to give it to the King, and that is what we are trying to do. What happened to Master Chail?"

Con took the contract from Thomasyn and walked around the desk. He pushed the papers aside and examined the contract. "Just like the king said, the dwarves will rebel if not rewarded for the work they do."

"They only want a fair share," Bethany said. "And their smiths make better weapons and armour than ours. They are willing to make them for us also."

"Master Con! Where is Master Chail?" Thomasyn asked, hoping to get through to the man.

Con sat down and leaned back in the chair. "The king had him arrested two months after the battle."

"Arrested? Why?" Sandra asked.

Con stared at her for a second. "There was an uproar from the people. They said Chail would be a better king than the son of Savoy. So he was charged with rebellion under an old law and jailed. He has not yet been sentenced."

Sandra approached the bed and sat down. A tear slid down her cheek. "All is lost. The king is mad."

"Don't say that," Thomasyn said. "We'll figure a way to get Master Chail free and your disc replaced."

Con looked over at Sandra. "You've lost your disc?"

"It was cut out of my arm three weeks ago." Sandra rolled her right sleeve up to show the bandage.

Con came to her side and removed the bandage. He touched the scar softly, not going near the last piece of scab that was still formed on the inside of her arm. "That can be dealt with easily." He motioned to Thomasyn and Bethany. "Come here and take Sandra behind the desk. Cloak yourselves until I tell you to come out."

They did as he said. Soon, Thomasyn could hear the bar coming away from across the door. It opened and then closed. They all waited.

A few minutes later, the door opened, the sound of two distinctly different footsteps entered, and the bar was lowered back in place.

"Con, I still don't understand why you would wake me at such an hour to come to your office."

"As I said, Master Jerek, all will be revealed." He came around the desk. "Come, it is good now."

The Spears stood, and the Master Wooder Jerek, an old man dressed in night clothes sporting a long white beard, took a step back, then he stopped. "Is that... No, I was told they were assigned to the North."

"I assure you it is." Con smiled.

"Bethany?" Jerek said. "Is that really you?"

Bethany's cheeks reddened. "Yes, Master Wooder, it is I."

"You are supposed to be up north. Why are you here?" Jerek asked.

"Enough of this," Con said. "Sandra, come here." Sandra came over to Con and he took her arm. "See? Someone cut her disc out. Did you bring one like I asked?"

"Well, yes. But this is not right. If someone cut out her disc they could track the comings and goings of the Spears and Wooders across the Realm." Jerek drew out a small silver disc with etching on it. "I don't have the knife, though."

"Any knife will do," Con said.

"True, but there is the ceremony of replacement. We should do that to ensure a perfect bond to the child."

"I'm not a child," Sandra said. "And all I want is to have my disc replaced."

Jerek shook his head. "This is highly irregular."

"Can you do it?" Con asked.

"Of course I can," Jerek said.

"Then do it," Thomasyn said. "Please."

Jerek examined Thomasyn, then let out a long breath that made his moustache hairs quiver. "Very well. Come here, child."

Sandra came forward, holding her arm out for the Wooder.

"I don't know who did this to you, but they cut very poorly. This will hurt." Jerek took her arm.

"I'm ready," Sandra said.

"Con, get her something to bite down on," Jerek said. "Unless you want her to scream and wake the whole barracks."

Con pulled out a writing nub from inside the desk and handed it to Sandra. She put it in her mouth and bit down just as Jerek cut off the scab. Blood flowed and he placed the disc against the cut and held it there.

SIXTEEN

Thomasyn watched as Jerek held the disc against Sandra's arm for several minutes. He hummed, but did not say a word. He nodded to Thomasyn and Bethany with a slight smile. When he let go of Sandra's arm, the gash no longer flowed with blood. The edges of the wound were knitted together, and only a small bump showed where the disc infused itself into the flesh.

"You are still pure of heart," Jerek said, smiling at Sandra. "That's good. You will need to be in order for the disc to take hold and fully function quickly."

"Maybe that's why we don't know what happened to Jon," Bethany said.

"Jon?" Jerek asked. "What happened to him? I thought you three travelled together."

Thomasyn told him about what happened to Jon during the battle and trip to the North. When he started to explain the problems during the Southern march, Jerek held up his hand.

"No, that would not stop it from working. The disc was in him for a long time and you would know if anything life threatening ailed him."

"Then how do we know what happened?" Bethany asked.

"We could check the Chamber of Seers to get the answer," Jerek said.

"I'm not fully familiar with that," Con admitted.

"I'm not surprised. The seers keep most of their secrets closed to outsiders. I only know of it because one day they called me there to administer healing on a seer they called a dreamer." Jerek looked over their heads for a few seconds. "It is deep in the centre of the castle. Not even the king knows of its existence. It has a vaulted ceiling with a map of the Realm, and every pinprick of light representing a Spear or Wooder."

"We could find out what happened to Jon," Bethany said to Thomasyn. "It might be helpful in finding him."

"First, we have to get Master Chail free." Thomasyn turned to Jerek. "Do you know where Master Chail is?"

"The old dungeon." Jerek shook for a second. "I was there when they took him. He did not look well."

"How long ago was that?" Sandra asked.

"Oh, several months ago," Jerek said.

Con glanced at Jerek. "Are you sure he's still there?"

"Why would they move him?" The Wooder just stared back at Con.

Thomasyn interjected. "Is there anything else you saw when you went down there?"

Jerek paused, his eyes glazed over. "When I was down there tending a Seer, the king came down. Yes, there was something strange. Not sure why, but when the Seer saw King Darious the man started to convulse. The king grew agitated and left. Something strange is happening to the king, and I don't know what it is."

Bethany stepped forward. "Could the Seer have seen something that you didn't?"

"I don't know what he could have seen." Jerek glanced at her. "Is there a problem?"

"I know Darious. There's no way he could have done all the things they say he did." Bethany stood there, hands on her hips.

"Yes, it was Darious." Jerek glanced at Con. "You can verify this. Darious is the one who brought the charges against Chail."

"Yes, he did. But for some reason Darious changed after the Hobs were defeated. It was so sudden, right after his mother passed away," Con said.

"Milon is dead?" Bethany asked.

"A lot has happened since you've been gone," Con said.

"Yes. I think we should visit the Seers and ask them why such would happen," Jerek said. "Maybe we should start with freeing Chail."

THOMASYN FOUND IT HARD TO BELIEVE THAT ANYONE could make more noise than Jerek did while walking. His footfalls hammered against the stone walls of the corridor and he cleared his throat every few minutes. Once, he even stopped, placed a hand on his back, and stretched. A popping sound echoed about them, and he sighed.

Bethany, Sandra, and Con moved quietly, so he did not concern himself with them. Soon, they were deep in the castle proper. Jerek commented that the dungeon entrance lay ahead, and last time, the militia had escorted him into the depths.

Before they turned a corner, Jerek stopped them and peered around. In a whisper, he said, "There are two guards. The corridor is over ten feet long before the door. I have an idea to get past them." He looked at Con. "It will involve both of us. Are you up to it?"

Con's eyes darted about. "I... I don't have formal training in fighting. What can I do?"

"Just come after you hear me call for you." Jerek started to take off his robe.

"Really? Why are you–" Con started.

"To give the illusion I'm sleeping." Jerek undressed to his small clothes. "Don't be too fast, though."

Jerek stood half-naked, his legs thin and white, hardly thicker than his arms. He handed his robe to Con, winked at Thomasyn and walked slowly around the corner on wobbly legs.

At first there was no sound, then muffled voices traveled from down the corridor. Jerek's voice then rang out.

"Con? Where am I, Con?"

Con took the clue and rushed to the corridor, Jerek's robe in hand. "I'm here, Jerek."

Thomasyn, Bethany, and Sandra waited. Mumbling from down the corridor erupted, and then the sound of bodies slumping to the ground.

"Everyone, come around," Con called.

The Spears came around and stopped. Two guards lay on the ground, Jerek leaned against the wall with his robe almost fastened. Thomasyn looked up at the man and gestured with and opened a hand to the guards.

"My training as a Spear was almost completed when I lost a finger on my right hand." Jerek held up his hand, the ring finger only a stub. "Enough to end my training, but not enough to stop them from indoctrinating me as a Wooder. That was many years ago."

"But the noises," Thomasyn said. "How could you be trained as a Spear and make so much noise when walking?"

"To keep the illusion. If I turned the corner and they didn't know I was coming, it would have raised suspicion."

Bethany tied the hands of both guards and Sandra took care of the feet. Once done, they gaged the two and smiled up at Jerek. Bethany waggled her finger. "You are a crafty old man, Wooder."

"You can call me Jerek, Bethany." He turned and opened the heavy door.

Torches lined a staircase leading down, the steps of each landing made of rough-cut stone. They walked silently down the stairs; once at the bottom, they encountered a corridor of barred doors. Each contained a small barred window with no light escaping from them.

Jerek grabbed a torch off a wall and thrust it into the holes one at a time, then looked inside. He did this for three of the doors until he stopped and motioned to the rest. "He's in here."

Bethany and Thomasyn grabbed the door first and pulled off the bar. With a tug, Thomasyn opened the barrier. Light flooded into the small seven foot long room and Bethany pushed into the room beside him. It was only five feet wide and on a stone bed with straw lay Master Chail.

Master Chail's dark brown hair lay matted against his skull with streaks of grey, and he was thinner than the last time they saw him. His eyes, usually bright and alive now, were sunk into their sockets and a ratty beard almost hid the smile as he raised his head. "Bethany, Thomasyn," he gasped, his breathing shallow and quick. One hand raised, then fell.

"Don't move, Master Chail. We brought a Wooder and he will help," Thomasyn said.

Jerek came forward. "He needs water."

Thomasyn glanced about the cell, saw a cup in the corner. He filled it with water and handed it to Bethany. She lifted Chail's head gently.

"Not too fast," Jerek said. "Slow. He's going to be thirsty and want to swallow a lot at once, but it will only hurt him and cause his body to expel it just as fast."

Bethany nodded and only tipped enough water to wet Chail's lips. The man's tongue whipped out and took the water. Bethany spilled a few more drops on his lips, and he repeated the action.

"You took your time," Chail said and laughed a little. The laughter turned to a cough, then to a wheeze. "We need to get out of here."

"You'll need food first," Jerek said.

"I have some food." Thomasyn reached into his pack and passed a little piece of bread and cheese forward.

"Slow. Wet the bread and have him nibble on the cheese," Jerek said.

"No, I need to get my strength back. The king needs us." Chail lifted his head again. "We'll also need a Seer. Only they can see what has happened."

"What happened?" Con asked.

Chail shook his head. "Not here. We need to take a Seer to the king. They can see what is happening and then we will be able to save him."

They fed Chail the bread and cheese, slow at first, but increased as the man sat up. They climbed the stairs slowly, and once at the top, Jerek led them to the castle grounds that held the Seers' living area.

Soon they were in a different area of the castle, and Bethany pointed to a tapestry hanging on the wall.

"I remember that," she said.

"Yes," Chail said. "This is the area where we talked to the council so many months ago."

The flickering light of a candle cast disturbing shadows of a moving figure. Thomasyn stopped and hugged the wall.

The shadows stopped moving, and the soft voice of a young woman floated down the corridor. "Who's there?"

Thomasyn rushed forward, hand held out in front of him, with one finger to his lips. A young girl stopped, looked him over. She took a deep breath, but before she could scream, he crouched a little.

"I'm not going to hurt you," Thomasyn said softly.

She studied him. "Isn't that what most men say before they attack an unarmed woman?"

Sandra came up beside Thomasyn with her hands out. "Yes, they do if they were alone. But as you can see, there are a few of us here. We mean you no harm, and the Wooder back there can attest to it."

The girl's shoulders dropped as she let out her breath. "What do you want? You know you're in the Hall of Seers. We are guarded here by the minds of those who weave spells and control the sight of the Realm. If you leave now, I won't say anything."

"Are you a Seer?" Sandra asked from behind them.

"She's not a Seer," Jerek said. "She doesn't wear the robes." He came forward and held out his hand. "Who are you, child?"

The woman took his hand. "Dallia," she said.

"Dallia," Jerek said. "What a lovely name. Why are you in this hall?"

Dallia straightened her back. "I'm here to visit my father, if that's any of your... Wait, you're Master Wooder Jerek, right?"

"Yes, that is me," Jerek said. "How do you know me?"

"You attended my father several months ago," Dallia said. "Papion, the Seer of the king."

Jerek stared at her, and then his face softened. "I remember your father," he said. "But I don't remember you being there."

"I was hiding in the back," Dallia said.

"I remember your father had a nasty cut on his arm, and he wouldn't tell me how he got it."

"It was the king." Dallia gritted her teeth. "He had come into our quarters and father went to him. That is when the king tried to stab him, but only got his arm."

"This may be interesting," Chail said. "But we have to get a Seer to help the king."

Dallia, upon seeing Chail, stepped up to him. "Master Chail? They said you died in jail last month."

"The news of my demise is a little premature. Can you take us to your father?" Chail asked as he reached out and steadied himself against the wall.

"Yes, this way," Dallia said, and motioned for them to follow her.

Dallia led the way through the corridor. And in a few minutes they came to a large door, and she opened it.

A dimly lit sitting room with an older man awaited them. The man stood and walked up to Dallia. "What took you so long?"

"Father," Dallia said. "I met these people. Master Wooder Jerek, Master Chail, and these three Spears."

Papion stood and bowed to Chail and Jerek. "I didn't believe you were dead, Master Chail."

"We have a Seer here, and I would like to know how he can help the king?" Jerek asked.

Papion sat down. "I cannot help the king."

Jerek stared at him. "Why?"

"He is under the control of evil," Papion said. "To release him, we will need to cut it away, and I cannot get close enough to do it."

"I can cut it away," Thomasyn said.

"Will he allow you to get close to him?" Papion asked.

"I don't know. I've never met him," Thomasyn admitted.

"He knows me." Bethany stepped forward and glanced at the floor. "Last year, he showed interest in how I was doing after running here…"

Chail looked up. "Yes, he did."

"Then you can get close." Papion sighed. "The evil is masked by a spell, but I can teach you an incantation that will unveil it. Be warned though, if you start it, the evil will know what is happening and may try to break free from you."

"I can get close to him. But the spell… is it? Don't worry about him breaking free. Show me the spell," Bethany said.

Papion took Bethany to a back room, and Dallia excused herself and returned a few minutes later with a change of clothes for Chail who slumped into a chair, eyes drooping.

Thomasyn wanted to keep him awake, but Jerek advised against it, saying the man needed to regain his strength, and sleep along with food would help him do that.

When Bethany returned with Papion, Chail was fully asleep.

"Should we get something for him to eat? Maybe his strength will return," Bethany said.

"That is a good idea, but I still think we should get sleep as well." Thomasyn glanced at Con. "I almost forgot. We have two citizens hiding outside."

"Two?" Con asked.

"Yes," Bethany replied. "Jillian and Roger. We need to get them to safety."

"Tess." Con stood. "Sandra, do you know the Lunday section of Capital?"

Sandra shook her head. "No. Most of Capital is a mystery to me."

"Then I'll have to go with you." Con walked to Sandra. "We could make it like I wanted to have an escort."

"Yes, but don't most know about..." Sandra started.

"About my condition? Not as many as you think." Con smiled at Bethany. "Most think it's a rumour, and it is something spread to just catch others off guard." He giggled a little.

"Then you two will get them," Thomasyn said. "Careful with Master Con, he is not trained like we are."

Sandra put her arms around Thomasyn and hugged him. "I'll be safe. You just make sure you get Bethany to the king, and help save us from the madness that appears to be running the Realm."

Dallia cracked open the door, then poked her head out. "The hallway is clear."

Sandra let go of Thomasyn, and Jerek put his hand on her shoulder. "We'll meet you there." He turned to Con. "And you take care to follow her lead."

"I will," Con said. "Take care of them as well. And him." He nodded toward Chail.

"Yes. I'll have to make sure he gets some more food. And soon."

Papion touched Con's arm. "Time to go."

Con and Sandra left, leaving the rest to plan what was needed. It was decided they would wait until the morning. Bethany was positive the king would recognize her, and that would be when the spell could be spoken. The incantation Papion taught her only took a few seconds to say, and he made her practice it. The Seer acted as the king and tried to push her away, or interrupt the saying of the spell. But to his amazement, Bethany was very adept at making sure she completed what was started.

They discussed how to get into the Royal Sleeping area and settled on delivering the morning meal. Thomasyn, not being known by Darious, could be a tester sneaking in someone known to the king.

With everything planned out, they only had to wait. Papion was busy during their planning, and when he returned to the room, he pushed a tray laden with fruit, cheese, and dried meat. Two large jugs of water also adorned the trolley, and they woke Chail, making the man eat and drink quite a lot.

Chail did look better after his rest, and ate well. He admitted, fighting would not be something he could do for some time, but he insisted on speaking to the king.

"Are we ready?" Thomasyn asked.

They all nodded.

SEVENTEEN

With hesitation, Thomasyn, Bethany, Master Chail, Dallia, Jerek, and Papion left the quarters and made their way to the northeast end of the castle. They walked past large corridors and through empty halls. Then, as if a bell had rung out in the air, the castle woke.

The empty hallways filled with people busy making the life of those around them easier. Maids busied themselves with cleaning and dusting, squires started setting out dishes and cooks could be heard clanging pots together.

Soon the aroma of onions cooking in butter and ham sizzling spread from kitchens along with breakfast sausages. No one challenged the small troop who made their way through the corridors toward the sleeping area.

No guards stood where they went, for the secret of the back corridors was only shared with those trusted servants and people bound by oath. Even the steps leading up saw little traffic.

Thomasyn worried they would be found out. Someone was bound to challenge them, but when one did, Jerek stepped up and insisted he was called to tend the king. It was a miracle the few who stopped them backed down so quickly. He would thank the Five for that later.

Jerek kept close to him, guiding the young Spear either left or right.

At one point, the man hesitated, appeared to be trying to recall something, and then motioned to the left of a fork in the hall. At the top of a fifth stairwell, he indicated they should all stop.

But Thomasyn did not want to stop. He motioned them to keep going and continue to the King's quarters. Jerek pointed to a window.

"The sun is starting to climb the sky," he said in a hushed voice. "We're a little early. The king will be surrounded by people getting him ready for the day. We wait a little, the servers will be attending him with food and that is when we can make our move."

It was logical, and Thomasyn, along with Bethany, nodded their agreement. No further discussion was needed, for just outside the door would be the king's chambers, and their ultimate goal, the king himself.

Both Bethany and Thomasyn pulled short, throwing spears from their holders against the packs and reversed their grips. They hefted them.

He was about to open the door when Chail reached out and took his spear. "Remember who taught you." Chail smiled.

Thomasyn nodded and unstrapped his last throwing spear from against his pack. He would either have to replenish the supply by raiding the armoury or fashion a few new ones in the forest later on. The spears, though tempered with fire and sanded smooth, did not last forever.

The sound of a trolley rolling across the stone floor carried through the corridor.

Thomasyn cracked open the door and saw the cart being pushed by a young girl. She was no older than 15, and her wide eyes stared at the door as she stopped pushing the cart. He knew she saw him, so, moving slowly, he lifted his finger to pursed lips and pushed the door open a little more. Chail threw the spear.

It struck the girl on the forehead. She crumpled to the ground.

Bethany dashed into the corridor and checked the girl. "She's breathing normally." Bethany turned the girl's head and Thomasyn saw a red circle start to form on her forehead.

"She'll have an awful headache when she wakes," Chail said.

Jerek rushed to the girl and applied a sweet smelling suave on the welt. "This will help her heal and take away most of the ache."

Dallia came through the door and stopped. "That was fast."

"The king's sleeping quarters are just beyond that door." Jerek pointed. "Bethany, I think this would be a good time for you to take the place of this young one. Are you ready?"

Bethany nodded and started to take the woman's clothes off. She hesitated and looked up. The men suddenly looked away.

Several minutes later, she said, "You can turn around now."

Thomasyn looked at the girl and then at Bethany. She had removed her tunic and cloak and placed them on the woman. The robe worn by the woman was now on her. "What are you doing?"

Bethany started to push the trolley. "You get under this and I push it into the chamber. If something happens, you climb out from under the cloth and help."

It made sense, but seemed childish. He could not think of anything better, so with a shrug, Thomasyn lifted the cloth and balanced on the wood, holding the wheels in place. No, this would not do. He got out from under it and stood there.

"No, how about you just go in without closing the door, and I'll cloak near the door. If anything happens, I'll be right there." Thomasyn waited for the negative response he knew would come from Bethany.

Chail put his hand on Thomasyn's shoulder. "Good plan. If I had my cloak, I would join you."

Bethany frowned. "Cloak yourself by the wall then. We need to get this done."

Thomasyn went to the door, pulled his cloak about him and allowed the material to blend with the colour and shape of the wall. He counted, stayed still to hold the blending, and watched through the slit in the hood as Bethany wheeled the trolley to the door. She knocked softly, and a muffled voice told her to enter.

The door opened into the chamber, and a large bed could just be seen from his vantage point. The room was a mess. Clothes strewn about the floor did not cover the dirt. A chair, shoved to the side and tipped, added to the array of chaos inside. Then the smell hit him. Rotting meat. Sour milk. He could not imagine living in such conditions.

Bethany stood just inside the doorway, looking inside. Thomasyn could not see her face.

"The food, over there," a deep voice said.

"Yes, Sire."

She pushed the cart forward and stopped just before she was out of his view. There was a rustling sound, and a phlegm filled cough. Bare feet slapped the floor and Thomasyn could see a shadowed figure approach Bethany. The man was slumped over.

"Nothing but food? Did you bring wine?" the king asked. A cane in his right hand shot out and lifted the cloth draped over the trolley. "No, nothing there." The cane tapped the silver dome covering the food. "Lift it."

Bethany lifted the dome, revealing bread and sweets. She lifted her head.

No, Thomasyn thought. Stay low and use the spell.

She did not, but instead reached out her hand toward the king. "Darious?"

The king stopped and looked at her. Light caught his face and rough stubble, flecked with grey, and showed the growth of a five day beard. Pale skin showed from behind long stringy hair that fell down over shoulders. Clouded eyes searched the room, through the open doorway and finally, to Bethany's face. His left hand reached out, fingernails long and dirty, and hesitated just before Bethany's face.

The hand came down. "Bethany." The king stepped back. "Why are you here?"

"Darious, what happened to you?" Bethany approached the king but halted when he held up his hand.

"Things have happened," he said. "The world is bigger than–"

His voice broke, and he winced. At first he started to grab at his neck, but stopped.

Bethany ran to him and flung her arms round his middle. "I missed you."

Darious started to return the embrace, but halted just before encircling her. "You should not be here."

"Then send me away."

Thomasyn did not know why she did not start the spell. Papion told her she needed to be close, and now she was. He wanted to shout at Bethany, tell her to start saying the words, but he could not without putting her in danger. Still, if he inched a little forward, he could have a better view but break the camouflage, and the king's back was now to him. He decided it would be best.

He uncloaked and moved a few inches forward. He watched and saw Bethany staring at him. Before cloaking, Thomasyn signed to her: Now.

Bethany shook her head slightly, and with one hand signed back: Not yet.

Thomasyn cloaked himself and allowed the magic to vale him once again.

"What has happened to you, Darious?"

"There is no time. You must leave, Bethany. Leave before it awakens." Darious pushed her away and tried not to look at her. "It sleeps, but it will awake soon."

"What will awake? Darious, you're not making sense."

The king turned away from her and stumbled back to the bed. He gripped the sheets and pulled them off, revealing grey and black stains. "It cannot stay awake in the sweat. It is drowsy around it." He wrapped the sheet around his body and neck. "But sometimes it fights through the slumber and sees what I see."

Bethany approached the king again, but he held out his hand to stop her. She signed the words: Get ready.

She was within an arm's reach of the king, and she started to chant.

"What are you doing?" Darious cried out. "No! It will hear the magic!"

Bethany kept chanting. A sing song of words Thomasyn could not understand. Darious flung the sheets off himself and toward Bethany. She ducked and kept on chanting the spell. Sweat started to drip down her face.

Darious screamed, and Thomasyn uncloaked. He stepped forward just as the king lunged at Bethany. She jumped aside. Thomasyn flung his body forward and tripped the king. The man went sprawling to the floor.

A small glistening shape of green tendrils like a misshaped squid hung around the king's neck. Two small black eyes squinted at him with anger and hate. A trickle of blood leaked from between it and the king.

The others entered the room and stopped. Papion entered last and pointed at the thing on the king's neck. "That is the evil controlling the king!"

Darious screamed in pain now, clutching at his throat as his face turned red. The scream stopped suddenly, and the king gasped for breath. His fingers clawed at the tendrils around his neck.

"Get it off him!" Chail yelled.

Thomasyn pulled out his dirk and scrambled to the king. He cut one of the tendrils and black fluid squirted out. The king's chest heaved, trying to take in air. Thomasyn cut another, then another and soon the thing had no more and Darious was able to breathe. The king was no longer conscious, but the creature was still attached and pulsated.

"Pry it off him!" Papion said, kneeling beside the king.

The creature's eyes focused on the Seer and a gurgling sound erupted from its body. It started to pulsate even more.

Thomasyn took his dirk and tried to pry it free, but could not get between it and the king.

Jerek shoved him aside, a smoldering cloth in his hand, and grabbed the creature using it as a shield between his hand and the thing. When he pulled away, the creature came with him. The gurgling sound erupted into Thomasyn's mind and he fell to the ground. Using the last of his strength, he lifted his head and saw Jerek throw the bundle of cloth and the creature into the fire at the other side of the room.

Thomasyn's eyes closed, and he lost consciousness.

Dallia's voice woke him, and the cloth against his forehead soothed the headache. He opened his eyes. He was not in the king's quarters, but a smaller room with several candles burning bright. The bed he lay in felt soft and warm. The odour of fresh baked break wafted into the room. She stood over him, cloth in hand, concern clouded her face. Finally, his head cleared enough to hear what she was saying.

"... the evil went into the fire. Jerek was able to grab an ember from the ashes and used it to pry off the thing." She dipped the cloth into water and resumed cleaning his brow. "It seemed strange that everyone dropped when the thing died. I was outside the room, and Father said that is why I didn't drop like you did."

"Where..." Thomasyn could not finish the question.

"The king?" Dallia raised an eyebrow. "He's sleeping. The poor thing was under the control of that monster for a long time. He was awake just in time to call off the militia as they broke into the chamber."

"Where is Chail?" Thomasyn asked.

"Still asleep. Jerek said he needed to sleep a little longer before eating and then after that he should sleep again." She sat back. "Thomasyn, what are you planning to do now?"

"We have a lost soul that needs to be found." Thomasyn sat up and rubbed the back of his neck. "Bethany and I have to find out what happened to Jon. See if there is any way we can bring him back."

Dallia ducked her head and stared into his eyes. Thomasyn glanced away, not wanting to see any reason not to find his friend. To compound the problems he felt creeping around in his mind was Sandra. The feelings for her bubbled inside him.

Thomasyn swung his feet off the bed, and he hunted around for his sword and spears. "Where is my stuff?"

"At the foot of the bed," Dallia said. "I gather Bethany will be just as anxious as you are to leave me here."

That stopped him. Thomasyn turned to her and watched how she stood, leaning toward him. The way she ducked her head and raised looked up at him. It reminded him of how Bethany used to look at him.

"You... I... Sandra wants to make a life for us when we are finished here." It was not the best thing to say, but it had to be done. He did not want to have her believe something could come from the feelings she was showing.

Dallia blushed, looked at her feet, and wrung her hands together. "It was just a thought." Her voice broke.

It was not going right. Thomasyn knelt in front of her and took a hand in his. "Dallia, we have only known each other for less than a night. Yes, there has been a lot happening, but Sandra... I've known her most my life. We grew up together. Trained, fought, and there has always been something about her that I liked."

"Do you love her?" Dallia asked, hope seemed to swell up in the words.

"Yes." It was certain that he did. The feelings he felt could only be that. He loved Bethany, but not in the same way. He wanted to be with Sandra. Meeting her on the road kindled the desire to be with her even more.

Dallia brushed a tear from her face and smiled at him. "I guess it is better that way. Father is training me to be a Seer, anyway. And that would be a hard thing for me to give up."

Thomasyn smiled, and then it hit him. "Didn't Con and Sandra come back from getting Jillian and Roger?"

"Yes, they came back just an hour ago." Dallia stood and dropped his hand. "I'll take you to them."

She walked to the door and opened it. The sound of voices, hushed as if taking care not to disturb others, drifted softly into the room.

Dallia motioned Thomasyn to follow her, then left. He rushed out the door and walked down a corridor lit by torches. Only a few yards out from the room, the corridor turned and then opened up to a chamber no larger than ten feet by ten feet. A large table sat in the centre. Con paced behind it, and Jillian sat at one side with Roger next to her.

Sandra looked up at the sound of their entrance and jumped out of her chair. She bounded toward Thomasyn and flung her arms around him. Looking into his eyes, Sandra said, "I missed you." And then she kissed him.

Thomasyn kissed her back and felt the warmth of her lips on his. It was pleasing to him to wrap his arms around her again. Once the kiss broke, they hugged, and Sandra buried her face into the nape of his neck. They stayed there for what seemed like an eternity.

Con cleared his throat. "There will be enough time for that later."

They released each other, but kept holding hands. Sandra blushed and Thomasyn felt his cheeks heat.

"Sorry," Thomasyn said.

Jerek entered the room with Papion.

"The king will recover," Jerek said.

"I'm not worried about his recovery," Papion said. "I'm concerned about his mind. That thing." He waved his hand to his left. "That thing fed on him, pulled his thoughts and made our king do things very out of character."

"But it is dead now," Jerek said. He reached for a chair and sat on it.

"Yes, and while we know its origins, there is no way to find out anything else about it." Papion sat beside Jerek. "So what did it really want to achieve?"

Con spoke up, "I think we must rejoice that we have our king back again. The Realm will be able to heal once all those silly laws are rescinded."

Bethany entered the room followed by servants pushing carts with cheese, bread, smoked meats and warm tea. Sitting across from Thomasyn and Sandra, Bethany nodded. "No one thought about food for us, so I had the cook put something together for us."

They all reached out and started to eat. The cheese disappeared first, along with the smoked meat. Both Sandra and Bethany grabbed a cup of tea and picked at the cheese.

"One question," Bethany said as she sipped her tea. "Papion, is there any way we can use the chamber to find our friend, Jon?"

EIGHTEEN

The eye hovered in front of Danton. He willed his legs to lift, but his feet remained stuck to the ground.

"Pin," Danton hissed. "Run!"

The scrambling of the Hobs' feet reached his ears. Danton held the axe aloft and the dying gleam from Pin's light glinted off its edge. There was a slight rumbling, and the eye retreated.

Danton turned and ran after Pin. He did not know how the Hobs could tell which way to go, but he followed him.

They passed through the doors, and now the floor slopped up. The walls still stood a great distance apart, and the ceiling vaulted overhead.

You are a coward. The axe could have defeated the One of Evil, so why didn't you use it?

He ignored the voice. Yes, he could have fought the beast. Yes, he could have been courageous. Yes, he could have died.

You could have won.

"Pin," Danton called out. "How much farther?"

The Hobs did not answer, he just kept running. The light bobbed over his head.

"Damn-it, Pin. Answer me!"

He is as much a coward as you are.

"I am not a coward!" Danton grabbed his stomach. A great grumbling sounded, and there was an emptiness within him. *This body will be the death of me.*

I will be the death of you.

"No, you will not!"

Danton swung the pack off his back while running. He scavenged some dried meat and bit into it. *This better quiet the stomach.*

No, no, it won't. Not for long. Not ever.

He glanced backward and saw the eye closing on him. There were only two choices: keep running or turn and fight. He decided to keep running.

The side walls slowly came into view. The ceiling, now mere yards above him, closed down on him. The corridor narrowed and he could see how the creature could become stuck, unable to pursue. Hope swelled in his heart.

No! You will not survive this!

A pang of hunger ripped through his guts. The world started to fade. *Damn this body! It needs so much and gives so little. There is not time to eat!*

Laughter echoed through his mind. *I told you. It is time to die!*

Danton doubled over.

<hr>

THE EYE STARED AT HIM FROM JUST FIVE FEET AWAY, ITS upper and lower sides wedged against the ceiling and floor.

A scream echoed through the air.

At least he thought it was such. Unlike the voice pushing in his mind, the scream seemed to be banging against the outside of his head to get in. There was something about it. Something that was not quite human or animal.

Inside his head, the voice shouted, as well. At first, unintelligible, but soon words took form.

No! You were supposed to die! It is not fair that you live! It is my body, and you stole it from me! Give it back or die!

Danton smiled.

The light behind him grew. He glanced back to see Pin inching his way toward him. The Hobs still shook, and his hands were pushing against either side of his head. Sweat covered the creature's skin.

"How did you get it stuck?" Pin asked.

"I just ran," Danton said. He stepped closer to the eye and examined it. The One of Evil vibrated in place, unable to either advance or retreat. Flesh, pale pink in color, surrounded it on the outside. No eyelid covered it. The thing could not blink, just stare. Behind it, he found a body of crimson, a bulge more than anything else, added to the appearance, making it look elliptical from behind. Stubs, where tendrils once were, surrounded a great beak like mouth very much like an octopus. The beak snapped closed when Danton approached, and the stubs wiggled as if trying to grab him.

"What do we do now?" Pin asked.

"I'm not sure." Danton came around to the front again. The bloodshot eye stared at him. The green of the iris contracted from the light.

"Kill it."

"Should we? It is obviously old. Much older than any of us. Killing it could upset the balance of life." Danton pulled out the axe. "Maybe just injuring it would be enough."

"There are things in this world that do not deserve to live. Something like this is one of them." Pin took out a dirk and approached the eye. "This thing killed thousands of Hobs as well as humans and dwarves. Killing it would be the best thing for the world, and a much needed revenge for the fallen."

Danton was not convinced. Wedged in place, the creature was more an oddity, a trapped animal unable to attack or defend. Killing it would not be sport, only a release from the pain. It did occur to him that revenge against the creature would be possible, but why should he seek revenge for something that happened many years in the past? Something he did not witness, nor felt the effects of.

Pin stepped closer to the eye and drove his dirk into it. The creature shook. And when Pin pulled the dirk out, nothing followed it. No fluid or blood. The Hobs leaned closer and stared at where he stabbed the creature.

"The skin is thick."

"It will take more than a mere dirk to puncture it." Danton stepped forward. The axe pulsated in his hands. He could feel the ache the weapon had for killing the creature. It wanted to strike the beast. Take chunks out of it. Kill.

Danton gave in, and with a large swing, the axe struck, and buried into the eye just outside the iris. Both of them fell, holding their heads from the pressure of the scream hitting them. A pounding, like a hammer, slammed into them from some unknown source. The eye pulsed, moved forward slightly, and stopped once again. It was now wedged even more from its attempt to attack.

With one hand reaching out, Danton used the axe to pull himself up. He yanked, and the head of the weapon came loose from the eye. A clear liquid smeared the edge of the axe. Gelatine oozed out of the gash, dripping on the floor.

The creature still lived.

Pin laughed without humour. "It is stronger than you thought."

One more swing. One more strike. Another force pounded them back.

Danton examined the slashes in the eye and decided striking the creature from the front was not the correct action to take. He scrutinized the stumps and beak closer. The crimson skin pulsated while he approached. Using the edge of the axe, Danton sliced one of the stumps close to the body of the creature.

The cut spilled a black liquid that sizzled and bubbled on the ground. Limp skin flopped as the remainder of the appendage wiggled at his feet. This gave Danton an idea.

Danton drew his sword, axe now in his left hand, then stepped forward. A slash of the axe against another wiggling mass which caused the creature to vibrate again, and this time Danton stabbed the sword into the thing's beak. Black blood gushed.

He continued to cut more of the stumps closer to the body. Each time he chopped at them, he thrust his sword into the beak. The work was laborious. Soon, the throbbing of the creature slowed. So much of the black blood littered the ground that Danton's feet slipped every few swings.

Danton stabbed the sword into the last of a stump and swung the axe between the two halves of the beak. The creature shuddered violently, then shrivelled into a pooled mass of flesh and fluid.

"You killed it!" Pin spat at the mess on the floor. "The One of Evil is dead."

With a sigh, Danton walked around the mass of flesh and cleaned the axe and sword using a cloth. Sweat littered his brow and dots of burns scared his hands and face from the splattered blood. He dropped to his knees in front of Pin, shook, and laid down his weapons.

"Pin," he said. "I need something to eat. This body is empty, and I will not be able to continue without nourishment."

The Hobs reached into his pack and pulled out more smoked meat. "I was saving this ..." He smelled it and frowned. "It has not soured from age yet. Perfect for human bellies." He handed the meat to Danton.

"Thank you."

Pin handed over a water skin. Danton felt strength return to his body as he ate and drank.

A smell emanated from the corpse. Not only did it turn Danton's stomach, but Pin started to complain as well. It surprised Danton, for Pin usually did not complain about the smell of rotting meat. He stood and walked down the corridor in the direction they came from. The desire to be as far away from the stench was overpowering.

"Pin, let's get away from here."

The Hobs stood and walked toward Danton. "We have time now. No need to hurry."

"I want to see the sky again." Danton kept walking, not hearing the voice in his head any more.

They walked in silence for a few hours, heading in the direction Pin indicated. There was no way he could tell if the Hobs knew the way to the exit of this cavern, but he did not waver in his direction. Nothing but carved stone decorated the walls. Soon Danton found himself wanting more than just the gray of solid earth.

A scream erupted through the air. The unintelligible sound split the air like a knife. Then the words followed, filled with anger and a desire for revenge.

"Who killed my child?"

Danton stopped. The hair on the back of his neck stood up and the blood in his veins turned cold. "I thought there was nothing else in here?"

"Was that not the One of Evil?" Pin asked and turned to Danton. "If this is really the–"

A scrapping noise echoed down the corridor. They both looked back and saw a head, mouth gapping open full of sharp teeth. The green skin, framed by fire red hair, inched forward. Long arms dug fingernails into the walls and pulled the creature toward them. It clambered through the corridor, head compressed and squeezed as it advanced.

Danton smelled the foul breath of the advancing nightmare. He could not tell what it was, just that the fiend was able to push itself closer to Pin and him. Nothing, not even the shrinking corridor, appeared to slow the advancement of the evil image coming toward them.

Pin did not move. Danton found that his feet were frozen in place. Ice coursed through his veins. With a force of will that came from an unknown place, he turned his head and grabbed Pin's arm. The Hobs' face, pale as a shallow pond frozen over in the winter, turned to him. A small line of spittle fell from the corner of his mouth.

"What is wrong with us?" Danton asked.

"The monster," Pin stuttered out. "It has magic."

"You have magic."

"I can't use it like this." Pin raised his arms to waist height, but they shook.

"Concentrate, Pin. Do something."

Pin fumbled in his belt pouch then raised his arms above his head, palms facing the wall, chanted and tossed some black dust into the air. Darkness formed before them, and blocked their view of the approaching terror.

Danton's feet came loose from the ground. It felt like he walked on needles, but he was able to move. He glanced over to Pin and saw his companion finally moving. That was enough for him. Without any more delay, he ran again.

Pin, already ahead of him by several strides, led the way that Danton hoped would take them away from their pursuer.

After the first five minutes, Danton stopped keeping track of his strides. Soon he lost count and could not tell how far they had run. The scraping noise still followed them, and every once in a while, the back of his neck itched.

There was less of an ominous presence now, and soon Pin slowed his run. Danton followed suit, wondering why they were slowing. And soon the limits of the light Pin had summoned revealed a wall looming before them, dark and unbroken.

When Pin stopped before the wall, he mumbled some words and tossed a white powder into the air. The powder floated down and then swirled as it fell. A line formed on the ground and ended at a small pile of the dust. Pin walked to the spot and ran his fingers over it.

"There's a slot here." Pin turned to Danton. "You may be able to pry it open with the axe blade."

Danton approached the spot. The tingling feeling grew in the back of his mind. The beast still approached. He hefted the axe and slid the blade into the slot. There was an audible click, and part of the wall moved inward.

Pin grasped the edge and tried to pull. It did not budge. Danton then grabbed it along with him, and still it did not budge.

"Try wiggling the axe," Pin said.

He grasped the axe handle and wiggled. The head creaked, and a circle glowed around the slot. He pushed the handle to the right, but it would not move that way. When he pulled it toward him, the handle came around.

"Keep pulling!" Pin said.

He pulled. Muscles flexed and arms strained. The body was strong, but the age of the device was great. The axe handle only moved less than an inch with each tug, and the effort tired him greatly. A creaking sound erupted from the device every time he heaved on it. Now the handle was almost level with the ground.

"It is open to the outside. We have almost escaped!" Pin kept trying to tug on the edge of the door. His fingers just made their way through the slight slit to the outside. "Pull harder!"

Danton grunted and heaved. He did not know a time that he worked so hard to move anything so little. And finally, after a great lurch, the axe head pointed to the ground, handle to the ceiling. The wall swung apart.

A scream of frustration bounced off the walls. "Killers! I will skin you alive. Grind your bones to dust. Chew on your still beating hearts."

With a glance back, Danton shoved Pin through the opening, pulled out the axe and dived through the door. The grinding of rock against rock rumbled and then came a slam. The door stood closed behind them. The sound of sizzling, like wet meat on a hot stone, resonated in the cave as the portal sealed itself. Magic flared around the seam and it disappeared into the rock.

The two laid on their backs, gasped for breath and stared at the moon high in the sky. Pin groaned. The Hobs sat up with great effort.

"We have travelled an amazing amount of distance in such a short time." Pin pulled out a water skin and guzzled from it. "But I would not want to do such again."

Danton turned his head to stare at Pin. At first he thought the Hobs joked. Making fun of the danger they had uncovered. With a grunt, he pulled himself up to a sitting position.

"Pin, you have such a poor sense of humour." Danton's stomach grumbled. The pain of the need for food erupted in his body once again. "Why does this body need to eat all the time?"

The Hobs put his hand on Danton's forehead. "There is nothing wrong with you. Are you sure you're hungry?"

Danton put his hand on his stomach. "Yes, I'm sure." He stood and took off his pack. With a fast movement, he turned it upside-down and emptied the contents. This was the first time he had looked into it and was surprised by what he saw. A few small items, hard black eggs and squares of paper. He reached out and picked up a square and sniffed it. Nothing. He unwrapped it.

A small jewel of food looked back at him. The cube, just a little smaller than his fist, was dark and tender looking. He put the cube in his mouth and chewed. Spices erupted in his mouth and the flavours made him smile with his eyes closed. There was pure joy in the dried meat. Nothing else could have satisfied him more than that simple flavour.

After the meat was finished, he picked up an egg and cracked the shell. It was hard-boiled. He shelled it and ate. For the first time in a long time, his stomach felt full. Maybe now it would let him rest in peace without bothering him to fill it again.

"I don't know how you can eat that," Pin said.

Danton looked up and Pin bit into a finger from a human hand. "This," Pin said, "is perfect for the belly. Flesh so tender and sweet. Nothing can beat the taste of smoked human flesh."

"One day, Pin," Danton said. "You'll choke on one of the small bones in a hand. That's when I'll clap in front of your face."

Pin barked out a laugh as he bit into another finger. Suddenly the laughter stopped, and the Hobs reached for his throat.

Danton rushed to Pin and slapped him on the back. Pin started to laugh again.

"I knew you would not let me die," he said. "Just like I would never let you die."

Just before Danton could respond to his friend, there was the thud of a huge weight hitting the stone somewhere behind the rock face. They both looked at each other, packed up their bags then ran.

NINETEEN

Pin and Danton ran for fifteen minutes, glancing behind often. They then slowed to a fast jog, not bothering to glance back. Now, after two hours, the two started to walk. There was no noise of pursuit.

Danton felt silly for running so long. The creature, stuck behind ancient magic, seemed unable to escape. And he now had an axe that was sharper than his sword. He took the weapon off his back and examined it again. The intricate pattern of lines with runes etched between was unreadable to him.

"Pin, can you read any of these?" Danton asked.

"No," Pin said. "They are of an ancient tongue unknown to me. I doubt anyone could read them."

"It would be nice to know," Danton said.

"Know what?"

Danton hefted the axe. "The name of this weapon. Every magically blessed weapon has a name."

Pin shook his head and muttered something under his breath.

"What?" Danton asked.

"Nothing. You humans have the strangest ideas. Naming your weapons." Pin pointed to a level part of the clearing they walked. "We should make camp before moving on."

Danton agreed, and once they made camp, he hunted for game. The fields supplied a fair array of birds, and he was able to kill several before returning to their camp. They cooked half the birds and Pin put the other three into his pack. The Hobs muttered something about destroying food by cooking it.

They settled down for the night.

The next day was the same, but the game changed from bird to rabbit. Flat ground was very easy to find in this part of the Realm. The winter pulled back its claws, and the days stretched into three weeks. The two did not talk much for the area seemed familiar.

The sun, two hours away from setting, hid behind light, fluffy clouds. Danton was about to call a halt to pitch camp when the trees opened and a large hut stood a few hundred yards before him. They were on top of a knoll, and two miles further on, he saw a town filled with people.

"I cannot go down there," Pin said.

"Of course not." Danton stared at the hut. "Why does this dwelling look so familiar?"

"You died here."

Then it struck Danton. It was the realization that his life had ended at one point. It felt so long ago that the memory was no longer strong in his mind. It was the hammering of a sword. Raised weapons. Sparks from magic. A pain under his chin.

He reached up and fondled his jowl. No scar. Nothing to show he was killed at one time. But this was not the body he died in. This was the body that had killed him. The one who had murdered him, tucked away somewhere. Safe, unable to cause any damage. A perfect end to the one who took his life.

"Do you think anyone is in that building?" Danton asked.

"I don't know." Pin scratched the back of his neck. "There was a lot of death there for the humans. Probably not. I don't see any smoke."

Danton looked up at the top of the hut. There was little wind, and what little there was brought no odours to him. Maybe it was empty. It would be nice to spend a night in a warm bed instead of just blankets on the ground.

He walked toward the hut.

"I don't think we should go there," said Pin.

"I want a real bed." Danton approached the door and pushed it open.

"Don't go in there–"

Danton ignored Pin. He walked through the open doorway and into the common room. It was a shamble of broken plates and overturned chairs. Even the table was broken in two. Another door at the other side of the room looked across at him, a door hanging on a thong hinge.

With a hope that the bedroom would be in better shape, Danton crossed the room and stopped. The bed, overturned and ripped apart, stood on end against the wall. A chest with its lid open stood in the middle of the room. It looked out of place in the destruction of the floors. A rough tunnel went down. He entered and took a sheet from the bed. Without hesitation, he wrapped it around the head of the axe and lit it.

"You won't like what's down there," Pin said from behind him.

"I need to look." Danton held aloft the axe and started down the hole. A large pot in the middle of the room stood there with arm and leg bones in it. Hooks attached to the wall, stained black with dried blood, clanked and echoed as they hit the wall from the shifting air. An image of people hanging on the hooks and watching as bodies were hacked up in front of them filled his imagination.

Yes, that was what it was like. You never saw it, did you?

"No," Danton said. "I never saw it."

What did you think they did with the people they found?

"I... I just never let myself imagine it."

"Who are you speaking to?" Pin's voice sounded miles away.

"Nothing. There's no one down here."

"You should come up. I have a fire burning up here."

Danton looked up. A fire? The Hobs were insane. It would smoke and tell the villagers someone was in the hut. This large building overlooked the structures of the town, and the sunset behind it compared to the settlement. If the residents discovered Pin and him here... he hustled back to the bedroom and into the main. Pin sat beside the hearth. A little fire flickered without putting much smoke through the roof hole.

"Were you worried?" Pin asked.

"Yes. I could see you lighting a high fire that put out enough smoke to preserve some meat." Danton walked over and sat beside Pin, facing the fire. "It has just enough heat."

"It should hold back the cold of the night. Just a little bit more." Pin grabbed a small piece of board and put it on top of the fire.

Silence grew. Each stared into the fire. Flames licked up a foot and dissipated. Light from outside faded, casting an array of dancing shadows against the wall.

Danton stood and covered the window openings with a few blankets from the bedroom. He went outside and made sure no light was seen from the outside world. His stomach grumbled. Food. He would need to eat once again. It disturbed him. The amount of food this body needed disturbed his thoughts. A grumble and pain lanced through him. Then a small cramp hit. Not only was he hungry, but he needed to void himself.

He poked his head into the hut. "I'm going to find something for dinner."

Pin stood. "I'll come with you."

"No!" Danton realized he had barked out the order. "No, Pin. I need to do this alone."

"But we are close to the town. You may run into someone."

"And your company won't cause an issue?" Danton asked.

Pin stared at him for a moment, then glanced down. "I was not thinking, Danton. Sorry."

Danton went to Pin and put his hand on the Hobs' shoulder. "Normally your company would please me, but not here. I don't want someone to come upon us and cause problems."

"And when we are travelling, I put up the tents while you hunt. We share the tasks." Pin smiled. "Maybe we need to bring another with us. Maybe the queen?"

Danton laughed. "When have you known the queen to leave the den?"

"Or pitch a tent." Pin laughed.

They laughed together for a short time. The pain became more urgent, and with the forest close and no out house present, he excused himself, pleading the fading light. Pin nodded in understanding and went into the hut.

———

With his small clothes in place, Danton pulled up his britches. The amount that came out surprised him every time, but this time it was more watery than anything else.

He noticed bird nests prior to entering the forest. In the morning, he would raid them for eggs. There would be a cooking pan in the hut somewhere; he would have to look for it. Now, he just went about with quiet footsteps, looking for anything to capture.

He was only concerned with how close the town was to the woods. Most of the easy game would have already been flushed out. A thought of raiding a nearby farm entered his head, but it was dismissed just as fast. He remembered the outline of this town and the surrounding farms. All of them would have dogs.

So he hunted. Wild turkey would be nice. And the meat could help the eggs along in the morning. With the thought of food in his mind, Danton's stomach grumbled once again. The emptiness bothered him. When they return to the caverns of home, he would get Pin to investigate what was wrong with this body.

Danton scanned the ground, looked for any signs of the birds, but none showed. Not even the scrape of a beak against a tree.

Ready to give up, he headed back to the hut in the dying light. There was a rustling sound to his left and Danton crouched with a throwing spear ready. He listened. There was no sound for almost a full minute, and then the bush ahead of him moved slightly.

Using the point of the spear, Danton thrust into the bush. A yelp erupted, and a young girl no more than nine jumped out. She wore a tattered light blue dress and leather slippers. From the tip of her head to her feet, dirt covered every layer of visible skin. Dark blue eyes offset her dirty blonde hair.

"Hey!" she yelled.

Danton laughed, then stopped as he realized the girl would be perfect for Pin's morning meal. "What are you doing out here this late?"

The girl, who was brushing leaves from her hair, stopped and glared at Danton. "Who are you pushing a spear into a bush?"

Danton glanced at the spear and realized the tip was levelled at the girl. He flipped the weapon, butt end up in the air, making the spear point came toward his body. He caught the shaft near the tip as it pointed downward. With a swift motion, he lowered the butt to point at the girl. "I asked you first."

Staring at what Danton had done, the girl pointed at him. "You're a Spear!"

Danton smiled.

"I knew it! Were you here last year for the big fight?" The girl put her hands up and punched at the air beside her. "I saw some of what happened. Lots of Spears and Hobs and men in armour fought. They said one of the Spears, a boy named Jon, killed the Hobs commander. They said he was a blond boy with a dark mind but fast sword. Strong and smart, they say."

He cleared his throat. "I think–"

"Yes, he has blond hair, probably like yours. And he took the sword of the Hobs commander right outside this hut. Do you know him? This Jon guy?"

Danton wanted to say yes, just to give the girl a story to tell her children in the years to come. He could not. Telling the girl would give too much information. She would want him to come to her home. Meet the town folk, celebrate, and stay for too long. It would also increase the chance of Pin being found out.

"No," Danton said. "I remember hearing about it, but I wasn't here." He realized something was amiss. "What is your name?"

"Missy. Mom called me little Miss when I was born and it just stuck."

"Missy. What are you doing out here?" Danton lowered is spear.

"Mom wanted me to hunt. I'm a good hunter. Always catch something." Missy winked at him. "I can always find something to eat."

"So, have you found anything yet?" Danton asked.

"No," Missy confessed. "I was hoping you were something, but you're too big." She giggled and pointed to him. "And you're skinnier than a sapling!"

Danton shrugged it off. His body was not skinny. Lean, yes, but not skinny. "My body needs a lot of food, and I'm between posts right now. That means I have to hunt as well." He waved at the deep forest. "I haven't found anything in here, though."

"There is game out here. You just have to figure out where it is moving. Do you want to hunt with me?" Missy smiled, letting the last of the light gleam off her teeth. She was a pretty little girl, and Danton realized he was already caught in the trap. Soon, if she caught something, she would ask him to return to her home and share the catch. If he caught something, he would be expected to offer to share it with her family and return to their home.

"We could hunt together!" Missy started to jump and clap her hands. "That way, we can watch both sides at the same time."

His eyes must have said something, for the smile disappeared off Missy's face and she stopped jumping. Downcast, she kicked at the dirt. "There's a reason." Danton said.

"My family's starving," Missy said. "I find what I can, but we have so many mouths to feed. Mom, Jilly, Sally, Bobby, Randy, Harry, Conney, Rory, Denny. We have so many and so little. I haven't caught anything in two days and all we have left are bones. We've boiled those bones for two days, and now they won't flavour anything."

"I'm sorry, Missy." And he did feel sorry. Especially with all those mouths to feed and no food to bring home. He would have to do something to make Missy feel better about what happened. If he found something, he would drop it off at the girl's home. If he could find out where she lived in town...

"I understand," Missy said, but her voice still held disappointment. "Spear secrets."

"Spear secrets." He held up his hand, palm level, and pointed to the ground.

"What's that?" Missy asked.

"A special shake used to seal agreements between people whom we, as Spears, feel a kinship to."

"What do I do?"

"Put your hand under my hand and slap it up." He illustrated the action with his other hand.

Missy nodded, then reached out and slapped his hand from underneath. He smiled.

"Now I'll tell you the secret, but you may not tell anyone else. Remember, you promise. Spear secrets."

Missy nodded, her head bouncing up and down.

"I need to find food for a Hobs."

"A Hobs?" Missy drew in a sharp breath.

"Yes, a Hobs." Danton straightened. "I have to take the beast back to Capital, but he eats strange food, most of it raw."

"They eat people," Missy said. The corners of her mouth turned down and young eyes grew wide.

"Yes, they eat people."

"Were you out here hunting people for the Hobs?"

"No!" Danton stared at the girl. How could she think that? A human hunting another human to feed to a Hobs? Their soul would be lost to the eternal darkness. "I could not imagine that."

Missy stubbed her toe against the ground and winced. "I hope you wouldn't do it." She looked up at him. "Is the Hobs whole?"

"I don't know what you mean, Missy." Danton glanced around when he heard the rustling of another bush. This time, the noise was not a person from what he could hear; it was too light a footfall.

"Does the Hobs have all his fingers and toes?" Missy asked. She held up her hand and wiggled dirty fingers at him. "You know fingers, like these."

Danton chuckled. The little girl was entertaining, and the interaction was very enjoyable. It was a shame that he could not spend more time with humans. He surmised Missy's family was nice, but he could not afford to leave Pin. The Hobs would get very upset and lonely. Then he would wander out of the hut and into town. Once there, he would be discovered and killed.

He needed Pin to live.

"Yes, he has all his fingers and toes." Danton located the rustling sound, a bush just behind Missy.

"I would like to see him."

"You would?" It was strange. Humans usually disliked the looks of the Hobs. They found them small and creature like.

"Oh, yes." Missy brightened up with the possibility of meeting a Hobs. "Mom said I should stay away from them, but I don't think they were as mean as she says."

"They are probably worse." Danton remembered how the Hobs had acted during the raid, and the time before that when they had overtaken a large farmer's home. "They eat people, but love to eat small children, for they find them the tastiest."

The bush behind Missy rustled a little more, and Danton was sure a small rabbit or turkey would come out of it soon.

"Oh, Mom said they eat people. That is why she said to be mindful when around them." She smiled even more. "That's why I'm the one who goes out to hunt them."

Danton almost missed what she said. Then it hit him. "You're hunting Hobs?"

Missy took on a shyness that was uncharacteristic of what she was like when he met her. She glanced at her feet for a second and then looked up. "Yes, I hunt Hobs. What else would I hunt in the Town of Lands? We hunt them, kill them, and then we eat them. They're really good once they have been roasted over an open fire."

TWENTY

Bethany stared at Papion, waiting for the answer to her question. Thomasyn nodded and Con cleared his throat. Jerek just stared at his plate. Sandra just waited.

Papion nodded to Bethany. "There is a way to find him." He put down his cup. "It is not something we talk about often to those who are not Seers."

Bethany understood. Each faction that protected the Realm guarded their own secrets carefully. The Spears had theirs, but shared them with the Wooders. The Seers, naturally, would have their own as well.

"It has to do with the discs, right?" Bethany realized she was rubbing her arm.

"Discs?" Dallia asked.

"You have not reached that point in your training." Papion looked down at his plate. "We don't share our secrets easily. Out of all the servants of the Realm, the Seers are the most vulnerable."

"The Spears protect everyone," Thomasyn said.

"Yes, everyone in the Realm. But the Seers are rarely outside the castle for long. We never see the Spears, only the militia. And we all know what they are like." Papion pushed away from the table. "I'm not allowed to take just anyone to the Chamber of Stars."

Bethany glanced at Thomasyn and mouthed the words "Chamber of Stars." He shrugged and turned back to Sandra.

With a Look at Papion, Bethany asked, "Where is this chamber?"

"In the domed tower," Papion said. "Not a place most would go."

Sandra turned to him. "Why?"

"It is kept dark for the seeing."

"But the dome," Sandra said, "it's made of glass. How could it be dark inside?"

Papion smiled. "How could the deep pool be dark when the water is clear? How is it the sky is blue in the day, but black at night?"

"Those are riddles that science could answer given enough time," Con said.

"Yes, and they have had a lot of time to answer them and still have not. But this is not science." Papion lifted his hand and waved it before him. He mumbled words in an archaic language and the air in front of him started to turn black. It started as a small pinprick, and expanded to the size of a dinner plate.

Con leaned forward, as did Thomasyn and Sandra. Bethany scowled. "Magic."

Papion dropped his hand and the disk dissipated. "Yes, magic." He dropped his head, shoulders slumped, and he took a ragged breath.

Bethany reached out and helped steady Papion. "Are you alright?"

He lifted his head. "I'll be fine. Magic takes from you when it is cast."

"I saw something like that," Thomasyn said. "Back at the Town of Lands. Danton went into a tent with a Hobs and I think a spell was cast. The Hobs came out frail and older looking, but Danton came back at least thirty years younger."

"Blood magic," Con gasped.

"Yes," Papion said. "One of the darkest forms of magic. The spell is a form of blood magic. It takes from you a toll for what you do."

Sandra nodded. "Mitch said he saw blood magic eat away someone when they tried to cast a spell of life."

Papion glanced at Sandra. "It would be interesting to know what happened to the caster. Most don't try such magic."

Bethany grew tired of the interchange. She wanted to find out what happened to Jon, and this Seer was holding her up. Pushing away her plate, she stood and walked away from the table toward the door. "We should go to this Chamber of Stars of yours. Maybe it can answer the questions I have about Jon."

Papion stood, a little shaky on his feet for a second and then steady. Dallia was at his side. "I'm all right, Dallia. It'll pass in a while. I haven't cast anything like that for a long time."

"You shouldn't test yourself like that," Dallia said.

"If you don't test your borders..." Papion said.

Bethany glanced at the door, then turned to Papion. "Can you lead the way?"

"Yes," Papion said. He drew a deep breath and straightened up. "Yes, I can."

With a nod, Bethany extended her hand toward the door. Papion put his arm around Dallia's shoulders and walked through the door. Bethany followed with everyone falling into step behind her. The corridor was empty, save for a few servants walking to and fro taking care of the castle. One old man swept dirt from the floor and a woman, behind him, scrubbed it with a brush and soapy water.

The palace's atmosphere changed, and Bethany could feel it. Her first thought focused on Darious, and she hoped that the king would survive. The citizens of the Realm were not happy with some of the changes he was forced to make in the laws. Hopefully, he would change them back.

Bethany glanced up. She had not been mindful of where they were walking. For some reason, there were few servants in the area. And those who were about did not look up or speak. It confused her, for she believed most people talked excessively when allowed. And it hit her again; she was not focused on her surroundings.

This time, taking great care to concentrate, Bethany stared at objects around her. She looked at the walls, the floor, the ceiling, and decided finding Jon was important to her. There was no real reason why, just that she needed to have him back in their group. It was the family again.

Not having the clutch around them was bothering her, so having Jon back again would complete the group.

She stopped. "Bethany, get a hold of yourself!" She dug flat fingernails into the palms of her hand. The pain snapped her out of the daydream. Again, she had wandered in her thoughts. How was this happening, and why was she not able to stay focused?

Dallia came up beside her, a worried look on her comely face. "You wander."

Bethany felt like laughing at the statement. She wandered worse than a cat trying to find a mouse. And it all came down to wanting to find Jon. The last speckle of hope to get her family together disappeared from her mind as she stood there.

She shook her head. It had happened again.

"Dig a fingernail into the palm of your hand," Dallia said.

A finger nail? She could not do that. For one, it seemed childish. She looked at her fingers, nails chewed down to the quick. It was like the journey she wanted to go on to find Jon. She knew it would take her out of the city and toward her friend.

A sharp pain in her hand brought her attention back to the present. Dallia held a spear head and pressed it into her palm. It was painful, but did not injure her. The point was not as sharp as her spears.

"Stop that," Bethany said, pulling back her hand.

"It is this place," Dallia said. "The whole area is controlled by others. You are wandering in your mind because of them."

"Foolish. I'm not keeping my mind on the task." But there it was again, the thoughts of Jon and trying to get her family back together again. The pain broke through, and this time Bethany did not react with a violent temper.

"Here," Dallia said, and pushed her hand closed around the spear point. "Hold it like that and the spells woven in the walls will not affect you."

Bethany stared at the spear point. A simple little thing, but it worked. Could all magic be dispelled by such actions? She did not believe it. "Can all magic be stopped like this?"

"Like what?" Dallia asked.

"By putting something like a spear point in your hand and causing pain?" Bethany looked at the others. Papion handed an object to Thomasyn and Sandra. Con stared at his hand with wonder.

She then saw Jerek. The old Wooder stood in place, frozen with his eyes glassed over. It was strange to see the old man not move, and if she was not concerned for him, it would have been interesting to do something. She could have mussed up his hair, or braided his beard. Anything to make the Wooder look more dishevelled or comical. No, that would not be right.

Bethany watched as Dallia went to Jerek and gently took his hand. She placed something in the old man's palm. The Wooder blinked and stared at Dallia, who instructed him on what happened and how to keep from falling into the delirium.

With everyone armed against the spell, they made their way deeper into the Seers section of the castle. Down this corridor, up a flight of wide stairs with a high ceiling, and finally through a corridor that bent in an arc like a pulled bow. They finally stopped before a double door. Three Seers sat on a bench in deep discussion. They stood as the group approached.

Papion held up his hand in greeting, and the others responded in kind, but did not rise. Each wore a similar dark blue robe as the Seer, but they had wrapped around their middles a sash of white. The end of the sash flared out to show an elaborate rune, each just a little different from the other.

"They are the keepers," Papion said. "The members of our order who care for the dreamers."

"The dreamers?" Thomasyn asked.

Jerek responded before Papion could. "The dreamers are the ones who watch our borders and send the messages to the Spears in dreams. They have to sleep in order to send the dreams."

Papion glanced at Jerek sideways. "Yes, they dream, but not asleep like most would think. They lay in a trance, staring at the movements of the Spears."

"The movement of the Spears?" Sandra asked.

"It's easier to show you then explain." Papion walked toward the double doors, but the three other seers stopped him. They talked in low tones, and Papion became animated. He indicated the group with one arm and pointed to the doors with the other. The eldest member of the group shook his head while the other crossed his arms. Only the third one seemed to be listening to what was being said.

After a few minutes, the one who listened turned to his companions and seemed to be pleading the case of the group. He became enthusiastic.

Bethany grew bored.

Papion left the others and headed back to the group. He frowned and was ashen. With slow steps he approached. And once within arm's length he stopped, raised his head, and spoke softly. "You are being allowed to enter, but remember, stay quiet regardless of what you see." He motioned toward the objects they carried in their hands. "You no longer need those. The enchantment ended several floors below."

Bethany pressed her lips together and shoved the spearhead into a pocket within her cloak. With a glance at the keepers, she followed Papion and the others to the large doors. The two seers who argued stood aside while Papion and the one who sided with him pulled. The two men struggled at first, then the doors moved with a soft gush of air. Then silence.

Papion motioned the group forward. Inside, the vast chamber stretched out before them. The lack of light surprised Bethany the most. Everything was dark, even the light that tried to enter the chamber was subdued by some force. The walls, she surmised, were painted black. Then she spotted them.

At first she thought bodies littered the inside, but then Bethany saw the rise and fall of their chests. These people were alive and lying on their backs on tables, slightly reclined. Each faced the ceiling.

When Bethany looked skyward, she took a quick breath. Above them, painted on the ceiling, a vast map of the Realm lay, with thousands of little white lights dotting its surface. She pointed to the lights.

Just as she was about to ask a question, Papion whispered in her ear, "You must not make any loud noises."

She stopped, tilted her head, and whispered back. "What are those lights?"

"Those lights, Bethany, are Spears and Wooders. This is the

Chamber of Stars, and each one of those stars represents someone with a disc."

"How can you tell which one is which?"

"We cannot, but if someone close to the person does the dreaming, they will be able to show the person who they are looking for." Papion placed a hand on Bethany's shoulder. "You will be the one who dreams."

The statement took Bethany aback, and she did not know what to say about it. "Why me?"

Papion smiled. "You are the woman. He is the man. Men have a hard time finding men when they dream, just like women find it hard to find other women. It is all about the opposite attracting. This is why you will do the dreaming." He motioned her forward to a table near the centre of the room. They all followed. Bethany stared at the table; it was seven feet in length and three feet wide. The incline would have her almost flat on her back. Even though she was tired, there was no need to lay down to sleep, and she did not think would come even if she tried.

Dallia took a cup from under the table and pushed it into Bethany's hand. She made a drinking motion. Without hesitation, Bethany drank down the contents and almost gagged. It was foul, bitter, hot, and smelled of boiled dung. She fought to keep it down.

Her eyes started to close.

"You must fight to stay awake," Papion whispered. "No matter what, you must stay awake and concentrate on the one you want to find. Don't let your mind wander. Keep it clear that you want to find this person."

Bethany nodded and yawned. She struggled to keep her eyes opened as she laid on the table. It was not comfortable, and this helped her keep her eyes open. Her left hand was taken by someone and she looked over to see Thomasyn holding it. Then her right, and Sandra was there looking down at her.

"Remember," Papion spoke softly. "Concentrate on the one you want to find."

Bethany concentrated. She stared at the ceiling. A voice to her left said, "Jon." Then another one echoed his name. Soon, every one of the seers said Jon's name. She stared at the ceiling, trying to figure out how she would find him. Then, without warning, she started to see the flat, green fields of the Town of Lands. At least she thought it was the Town of Lands. It could have been any town with a vast expanse of flat fields. But Bethany was sure of this area, having run through it over a year ago.

And the expanse of the town was unforgettable, even the large hut at the top of the hill. She remembered that well. The sun, setting behind a forest of spruce trees, gave long shadows that played nicely against the ground. Two figures, one a somewhat tall blond man and a small girl with wild eyes, walked among the trees.

Bethany could not hear what was being said, so she tried hard to figure out where they were walking to. The man had several rabbits slung over his shoulder and held the hand of the girl. Could they be father and daughter? No, she finally could make out Jon's unmistakably lean frame. His face was soft, softer than she had ever seen it before. But worry lines decorated his cheeks and forehead. Something was wrong.

With more than a quick thought, she reached out to him and found herself looking closely at his eyes. They were no longer an ice blue, but more green. This was confusing, but anything can happen when a magic wielding elf was your companion, she surmised.

The image started to fade, and she fought with it to stay and tell her every detail of the young man. Why was he limping slightly? Where was that smile? Did he still believe in their duty? These questions did not get answered in the dreaming.

The vision started to flicker, and soon she only saw the ceiling once more. It disheartened her, and then the sound of voices echoed through the chamber. She heard "Jon", and then "Danton" from different areas on the floor. Soon the vision came back, and instead of Jon holding the girl's hand, it was the face of Danton on his body. Her head whirled as she realized that Jon was not there anymore.

But to keep herself from worrying too much, Bethany tried to figure out what caused this change. He was still Jon. She could see that. It was as if a veil fell across his face and was replaced with that of the man he had killed.

Then the face was that of Jon again, and this confused her. Maybe it was the drink they gave her. Something in it caused hallucinations while awake. That had to be it. She was dreaming, and nothing would fix that but time. She would watch what played out.

Jon and the girl reached the large hut, and he guided her inside with a hand on the small of her back. She did not hesitate or recoil from the touch, so Bethany knew Jon was still a little tender toward people. The inside was in shambles, and she noticed that heavy blankets covered the windows to keep the light inside.

With a shrug, Jon tossed the rabbits to the side and called out something. A Hobs, the old one who had been with Danton, came forward and licked his lips. The girl, at first, went toward the Hobs holding a knife. She jabbed at the creature, but it danced away. This went on for a few seconds before Jon, looking absolutely bored, slashed the girl across the back with a spear shaft. The girl crumbled.

Bethany sat up straight. The speed of her movement caused Dallia to breathe in sharply. With a shaking hand extended, she mouthed the name of their missing friend. "Jon."

She watched both Thomasyn and Sandra shrug until they followed her pointing finger. There, on the map, only one light shown. It pulsated with a brilliance more powerful than any of the other lights.

"He's in the Town of Lands," Papion said. "But there is a problem. He should not be pulsing like that."

Bethany found her voice. "It is not just him," she said. "It is Jon, and it is Danton."

Twenty-One

Danton stood in the forest with Missy, shocked by the revelation the child had given him. He knew how much the Hobs had decimated the local wildlife with the raid last year, but this was unimaginable. Why would humans start hunting Hobs? Because of hunger? The blood of the creatures was toxic. He had no idea man could eat the flesh.

But there was the child, telling him they could eat Hobs flesh. He shivered upon hearing the information. Nothing could make him want to even attempt to eat a Hobs. Then it hit him. Pin. His friend, even hiding in the hut, could be at great risk.

Danton thought fast and realized there was nothing he could do to keep the girl from entering the hut if she wanted. So he was left with one option. With a straight back, he looked down at Missy.

"I should tell you something," Danton said.

She smiled. "I knew something was up."

"Yes, your intuition is well founded." With a smile, Danton held out his hand. "I'm on a mission for the Realm."

Missy clapped her hands. "I can help!"

Danton dropped his hand. "In a way. You need to witness

something. I'm not able to tell you what it is now, but after you see it, you can tell me what you think of the plan."

There was no need to convince the girl any further. Danton could see the desire to follow him through wild fire if needed. Her smile could light up the darkest night. The only problem he could think of is that she would be missed. So this would have to be handled quick, and without incident.

"Follow me," Danton said.

Missy kept up with his steady pace. Her head would scan the forest from the small path. Then she dodged into the thicket. A few seconds later, she came out with a small rabbit in her hand.

"Not a Hobs, but it'll do." She smiled and waggled the little creature in front of her as she walked backward.

Danton laughed. Missy appeared to have only one care in the world. She wanted to have fun whenever possible. It was hard to believe that beneath the smile, curly hair and crooked teeth was the heart of a killer. Even with an abundance of rabbit, she hunted Hobs. He thought of Hobs as human, in a manner of fashion, so eating one to him would be akin to cannibalism. Then again, Hobs ate humans, and he had no issue with that. Maybe he thought of himself as more of a Hobs. It was an interesting dilemma, especially with what he planned to do.

Missy spun and started to sing a little wordless tune in time with her steps. Danton had only seen such joy in children back home, and after two years they became full grown Hobs, only interested in food and blood. He wondered about the last brood he sired, and how much longer his queen could birth with the seed he left her. He wanted his legacy to live on.

"Be mindful," he said to Missy. The child laughed again and smiled a crooked smile at him. Ants marched up and down his spine as she headed off into the trees once more. He could not figure out what made him uneasy all of a sudden, but there was something about Missy.

By the time they made the clearing, she carried four small rabbits from her traps.

"They need to be hung out for an hour," she said, eyeing Danton. "How much longer?"

"Just a few more miles until we are at the hut." Danton saw the flash in her eyes.

"The hut? It's haunted." She held up her hands, rolled her head about, and made groaning sounds. "The ghost of the dark one will get you."

"The dark one?" Danton asked.

"Yes. He was the one who fell. They say some blond Spear killed him. The dark one was over 1,000 years old!" Missy, eyes wide, glanced around the field. "They say you can hear all the dead screaming on a clear night."

"Do you hear any screams?"

"No, but Mama said you can only hear them when they're hungry as well."

"And what," Danton asked, "do you think they would eat?"

Missy seemed to think about this for a while, but did not say anything. The girl shrugged.

"A ghost eats nothing," Danton said. "They don't have any teeth to eat with, and your hand goes through them like it goes through smoke." Then something came to him, and he could not resist. "But if the man was killed, that dark one you were talking about, he would have jumped to another at the time of death."

Missy's mouth dropped. "His soul would jump?"

"Oh, yes. He would have been protected by strong magic." Danton smiled. Strong magic indeed.

"They say their eyes flashed."

"Flashed?" Danton asked.

"Yes. Both of their eyes. Some of the town folk watched from behind the circle of Spears." Missy waved her hands, eyes wide as she told the part of the tale she knew.

"It was a fight," Danton muttered. "He was a strong opponent, but if the revitalization spell had been just a few weeks prior, it would have turned out differently."

"What?" Missy asked.

"Oh, nothing." Danton stared into the night as it fell across and hid the last of the fading light. "I was just thinking how strong the magic must have been to spark such a reaction."

"What reaction?"

"The flashing of the eyes." Danton continued to walk.

The last two miles disappeared under their feet faster than he cared to think. But most of the time he thought about the fight, and how hard it had been to defend against the onslaught of that Spear. Danton remembered the complicated attack he tried, and still did not get through. In fact, it was turned against him without effort, and that is what disturbed him the most.

He lifted his hand and stared at it. There was nothing special, nothing different. The hand, so much different from his own, was the same structure. Maybe a little thinner, but nothing else. Shaking his head, he thrust the offending limb into a pocket of the cloak. His stomach grumbled once again, and he knew food was needed... soon. At least the hut was closer now, and the fire where Pin would be standing.

The thought of what he was about to do caused his hands to sweat. Crossing a line like this could make returning something difficult to do. Why would he need to do this deed? What demons urged him to consider what he was about to do? Then the voice interjected in his musing, and caused the fine edge to cut through the shadow of doubt.

What do you think you are going to do with my body?

"It is not your body," Danton whispered.

"Your body?" Missy asked.

"No, that was not to you," he said.

It was to me.

Danton shook his head. He needed to exorcise this demon from his mind.

Not going to answer me? I leave you alone for a long time and you repay the kindness by ignoring me? I'm hungry!

"You'll get food," Danton hissed.

"Oh, yes. I'll get food," Missy said and held up her rabbits.

"Yes... yes, Missy. We'll cook them up on the fire." Danton could reply if it made sense to Missy, and then quelling the voice would be easy for the next few minutes.

I will kick you out of my body, the same way I took your life.

Ire built up in him on that declaration. This was his body now. Did the boy think he was a demon? A small minded fool like he was? No, he was Danton. He was a leader of Spears. It was his intelligence that led them to the Hobs underground caverns. It was his tactics that protected the Realm for years. And now it was his will to live, as well as the magic supplied by Pin, that allowed him to hold this body. It would take more than words to push him from it.

I have more than words.

A dull pain tickled the back of his right eye. It intensified exponentially, and soon Danton wavered, the ground almost coming up to him as he caught himself.

"Are you alright?" Missy asked.

Yes, are you alright? A laughter echoed in his mind.

"I'm fine." He looked to the hut, now only a few yards away.

What are you thinking of doing, animal?

"Animal?" Danton asked.

"Yes, I caught the animals," Missy said.

That is what you are. An animal. You take what you want and have no care about who you destroy in the meantime.

"I am not an animal," Danton sneered.

"Of course not, silly. These are." Missy lofted the rabbits in front of him once again.

They reached the door of the hut, and Danton turned to Missy, holding a finger to pursed lips. "I want you to be mindful. What you will see may disturb you. Do not be afraid."

Missy stared at him wide eyed. "I get to see a secret?"

"A big secret." Danton reached out and pushed the door inward. A small fire lit the inside with shadows. Pin had cleaned the place and righted some of the furniture. A pot hung on a crane, and water boiled in it. Impaled on the crane's end, cooked a haunch. It looked like meat from the leg of an animal, but he knew better. The Hobs had a particular taste for certain meat.

"It looks scary," Missy said.

"Don't worry," Danton said. "I'm here to protect you. The Spears are always here to protect you."

He entered the hut and beckoned her to follow. Once in the room, he went to the table and hastily covered the body of a freshly slaughtered young boy. The child was small, maybe seven. The neck snapped and head at an unnatural angel. Where Pin had found the child was a mystery. The Hobs could find food anywhere when he needed it. He glanced back. Missy still stood in the doorway. She apparently did not see the body.

"The fire is small. You should build it up." Missy came in, headed toward the fire, and sat on the hearth. She picked up a small knife next to her and started to dress the rabbits. "Is there any more light?"

Danton glanced about, looking for Pin. He moved to the bedroom, not there. Then he went to the back room. Pin was not there either. Wondering where the Hobs was, he walked back into the main room and stopped. Pin stood staring at the girl. Missy glared back, knife in hand, a skinned rabbit in the other.

Pin, holding his short sword with point angled toward the girl, grinned with his small, sharp lower teeth showing.

Missy's back was to him, but he could hear the sound of her breathing. It was rushed and must be through clenched teeth, for it hissed. She wavered, shook violently, and gestured with the knife.

"A Hobs with a sword? Your kind runs around naked, grabbing small children where ever you go."

To his credit, Pin did not lunge at the girl. Instead, probably due to an already sated appetite, he grinned wider. "I've had this sword for centuries, and will use it to skin you alive."

There was no time to think. Danton pulled out a spear, held it near the point with both hands and swung.

"You should let me eat her," Pin said, taking another bite out of the haunch.

Danton finished tying Missy to one of the chairs. The ropes were tight, and he was careful not to cut off the girl's circulation. "No, you have enough with the kill you did earlier. Where did you get it?"

Pin spat. "The stupid creature walked right up to the door. I surprised it when I opened it, then it came in thinking to kill me. Where were you all this time?"

Satisfied with the bindings, Danton walked to the hearth and sat down to finish cleaning the rabbits. The hunger that plagued this body almost made him bite into the raw flesh right there, but he knew the raw meat would not sit well in his stomach. He cut the carcass up and dropped it into the boiling water of the pot.

"I was hunting. The child, how soon after I left?"

"Not long. The sun was just starting to drop when it came up." Pin stood and walked out of the room. He returned with several small soft potatoes and yellow carrots. "I had just pulled these out of the ground out back before it came to the door. The pot was already over the fire for you."

Danton's stomach rumbled loudly. He watched the pot as Pin continued his monolog.

"It was quite a trick, getting your food ready while butchering the thing." Pin took another bite of the haunch. "Are you going to eat? That body of yours is making strange sounds."

You are evil.

"Pin."

"Yes, Danton?"

"The voice is growing louder in my head."

CLOUDS CHASED AWAY THE STARS, LEAVING THE HUT IN total darkness, save the embers glowing in the fire. Danton sat on the hearth, hugging his knees. Pin, balanced on his haunches, stared at Missy. Tears ran down her face and into the cloth that gagged her.

The night, quiet from Danton's admission, was only broken when he answered the voice that slowly drove him mad.

Why did you strike that little girl?

"She's a cannibal."

No, she doesn't eat people, she eats Hobs.

"But they are my people," Danton said. His voice, strained from hours of talking, cracked as he spoke.

You're an animal.

"No, I'm Danton, a Spear."

Would a Spear steal from someone? Would a Spear hurt an innocent?

"No, but I had to. There was–"

There was no choice? There is always a choice! You could have held her down. Better, you could have led her away from here.

"But that would have been suspicious. She could have told people, and they would have found Pin."

And he is a Hobs. So?

"It's... I've known him for years. He's saved my life many times."

Maybe it's time that he didn't.

"You want me to die?" Danton rocked back and forth.

Do you think you deserve to live?

"Everyone has a right to live!"

Even me?

"Yes, even you."

But you took that away from me by stealing my body.

Danton wiped the sweat from his forehead. He was trapped within the logic of the man-child. Now he knew it was time.

"But if I die, so do you."

That is something I can accept. My loyalty is to the Realm, unlike you. Animal.

"I am not an animal!"

What will you do if that Hobs of yours wants to eat the little girl, just like he ate the boy?

"I'll stop him." Yes, that is what he would do. He would stop Pin if he wanted to eat Missy. She was an innocent. Not only that, but a girl who was only trying to feed her family. And now she did not have food for her family, and they would be worrying about her. The family would know something was wrong and might try to find her. That would mean people searching, people moving about, and people discovering them.

If you are going to stop him, you better tie him up as well.

He almost rose to tie Pin up, but stopped as his stomach grumbled again. The pain of emptiness erupted through his body. He could hardly lift his arms and had forgotten to eat after his confession to Pin. No, he would not allow this to happen.

With a force of will that allowed him to go through the rituals of rejuvenation Pin put him through every few decades, he rose. Legs, wobbly from lack of food, trembled to hold his insignificant weight. A bowl, he needed a bowl. One was found and then filled with the stew. Soon, the hunger was sated.

Now he knew what was needed. Danton turned to Pin with a single-mindedness driving his actions.

"Pin, we will be letting Missy go before the sun comes up."

Turning to Danton, Pin snarled and extended a finger toward Missy. "This one will be dinner tomorrow."

"No." Danton stepped between the two. "She will be let loose and allowed to return to her family. This is what I have decided."

Pin jumped to his feet. "But I'll need food as well!"

"And you will not be eating Missy."

Pin made a fist and slammed it into his left hand. "I will not starve myself anymore."

"You have enough food from the child you slaughtered to last a week. There is no need to slaughter her as well." Danton grasped his sword hilt, but did not draw the blade. "I will not let you take her life."

Pin stared at Danton, then glanced quickly at the sword ready to be drawn. Tension built. It did not take long for Pin to look away and sit back on his haunches. He mumbled something and picked at his teeth.

Danton turned to Missy and removed the gag. She cried, but did not make a wailing sound like he thought she would. That relieved him, and with a tender hand, he brushed the hair out of her eyes and cupped her cheek.

"You'll be safe now. I'll see to it," Danton said.

"Why did you hit me?" Missy whimpered.

"I'm sorry. You were about to attack my friend there and I could not have that happen. There is something that you need to do." Danton dropped his hand.

"I want to go home." Missy's lower lip trembled and tears rushed down her face. "I want my mommy."

"Yes, I know." Danton pulled out her knife and saw the girl's eyes grow wide. "No, I will not hurt you." He reached around and put the weapon in her hand. "It will take you a while to cut through the bonds, and that will afford us some time to get away. Tell them about us if you must, or just say it was too dark to wander the forest. But at least give us time to leave."

Danton stood and started to walk away.

"They'll hunt for you."

He stopped but did not turn.

"I know."

TWENTY-TWO

Danton followed Pin through the doorway and out into the pre-dawn night. The chill of evening hung heavy in the air, and small puffs of mist escaped their mouths as they walked. There was no talking, and all he could do was stare at the back of his companion.

In two days, they would be at the outskirts of the Hobs' region of claim. Once there, another week would see them obtaining one of the many tunnel entrances to their underground city. He was close to home, and his wife, the Queen of the Hobs.

He missed her. The hope that she missed him as well still gave him strength. Who could tell? The Hobs, being very dissimilar to humans, reacted differently to situations. The first time Pin cast the rejuvenation spell on him, she had only smiled and ruffled his hair. That night was special, for three litters were born several months later.

After all this time, he could claim that most of the Hobs in their city were related to him. But why did they not look like him? Pin had explained it once, a few decades ago. It had to do with Hobs' seed. It was very strong and only a small amount of human made its way into the bloodline. And even though he couldn't see it in their faces, he knew their intelligence had increased beyond the normal Hobs. That did not help them when they attacked this land last year. The boiling of the

Hobs' blood caused the mind to lose the ability to reason, and that was the downfall of their attack.

He glanced skyward and marvelled at the splay of gold and orange that marked the dawn.

"Pin." The Hobs did not answer him. "You'll have to talk to me sooner or later." Danton lengthened his pace.

Pin turned his head and spat at the ground. It was a strange action for the Hobs and Danton wondered when his companion picked up such a human habit.

"I can tell you why," Danton said.

Pin stopped and then spun around to face him with smoldering eyes. "Why? You want to tell me why you released my meal?"

Danton took a deep breath. "You have enough food."

"Enough?" He swung down his backpack and pulled out a haunch of half eaten meat. "This is all there is left from that child."

"But there was a whole body there?"

Pin pulled out a dirk and cut into the meat. After several cuts, a trickle of white pus dripped out. "This is what I'm talking about. The child was diseased. If I keep eating its meat, I'd get sick, possibly die!"

Danton stared, mouth hanging open. He had seen Hobs eat rotten meat and not flinch. Something else must have infected the child, and he needed to find out about it. "What is that puss, and why can't you eat it? I've seen you eat all sorts of stuff before."

You are an idiot.

The declaration unnerved him. There was an honesty about the words, but it was not what worried him. The voice grew louder, and he did not know what to do about it.

It will not be long before you are ended, and I return.

"You will never return," Danton said.

Pin stared at him. "What are you saying?"

"It's the voice," Danton said. "The noise it makes is louder now. I... I don't know what is causing it."

Pin touched Danton's chest just over the heart, and the other hand guided him to kneel. Mumbling, he placed his other hand on Danton's forehead, closed his eyes and stamped a foot three times. After a minute, the Hobs dropped his hands and stepped back, eyes wide.

"Something is looking for the boy. Something is reaching forward to see you here." Pin reached into his bag and pulled out a little tied purse. He unwound it and emptied some bluish dust into his hand. "Keep your eyes open. This will sting." With that, he pushed the powder around in his hand and mumbled words of power. The powder glowed in his hand and smouldered. Once it smoked, Pin threw the powder into the air and blew it at Danton's face.

The powder hit and stung as promised. He kept his eyes opened. A scream erupted in his head. A young man's face looked at him, blood flowing from one nostril. His eyes went black and nothing could be seen. "Pin! You've blinded me!"

"No," Pin said. "This is temporary. You will see soon enough. Don't blink! Keep your eyes open. We are almost finished."

There was more chanting, then water ran over his head and washed away the powder from his eyes. The blackness started to lift from his vision. Pain receded. He could see the green of the grass in front of him and he wondered when he had fallen forward.

"You said the voice was loud," Pin said. "Why didn't you say it could tell what you were doing as well?"

"It didn't occur to me. Was that important?" Danton pushed off the ground and sat back on his heels.

"Important?" Pin snarled. "Very. The head can only hold so much before it breaks open. That voice was almost to that point. One of you would have been lost, and it was strong enough to cast you out." Pin grabbed Danton's hand and lifted it. "This ring only has so much power. And that sword of yours will only bind for a while. You have to fight to hold this body, or that child will take it back from you."

Danton nodded. He would fight to retain the body. This was his now, no matter how much the previous owner wanted it back. "What do I need to do, Pin?"

The Hobs stood there, one hand cradling the elbow of the other arm, and one hand stroking his chin. "If you were a Hobs, I would say nothing. But a human. Well, the good thing is everything matches. The body and the mind are the same thing, so it is just finding the right balance."

"Balance?"

"Yes, balance. It's what keeps you from falling apart. Food and water are a balance. Meat and bread are a balance. We need to figure out what will balance your mind in that body." Pin still stared at him.

"You're not mad anymore?"

Pin's hands dropped down to his sides. "We need to find a burial site."

Danton glared at the Hobs. "We're not digging up a body for you."

"No, not a body," Pin said. "We need mandrake root. It's part of the balance."

"I'm not digging up a body, Pin."

CRAGGILY TREES STUCK OUT OF THE BROWN GROUND, defying the death around it. Nothing about them said it was a graveyard except the small depressions in the ground with small stones set at their heads. The feeling of death had not escaped the area, and both Pin and Danton wanted to spend as little time in the area as possible.

"Here," Pin said. "This is the youngest grave."

Danton glanced at the grave. The depression was only an inch below ground level, and a stone marked the head. The thought of digging up a corpse shuddered through him. What was under that spot? After a few years, would the body under the dirt still be recognizable? It rattled through his mind; he imagined the person buried under there could be someone's daughter or mother. If they dug deep enough, could the person even be related to him?

Maybe years ago, a child was born to a woman who died. That child, found by a Wooder, was taken to Capital for training as a Spear. The child soon became a legend, and then the head of the Spears ten years after graduating. Maybe the name of the child was Danton. He remembered being told the story by the Wooder who said she found him. Something about the training made him understand something would give soon, and he did not want to be in the centre of it.

Pin dug with his hands, the same way all Hobs dug. The long nails at the ends of his fingers cut clear channels in the dirt. Soon, he was a foot under the earth and clearing a channel beside the mound. It went slow with just him going, and when Danton started to help the digging went faster. Something told him to go as fast as he could, and not rely on Pin to do all the work.

Soon the sun was overhead telling him it was noon. He understood things were going good, but when his stomach rumbled, it became obvious he would have to stop digging and eat.

You are lazy. How you became the leader of the Hobs army, I'll never know.

"You think that was an army?" Danton said. "How you were mistaken. That was a raiding party I commanded. The main army is still underground. Over five thousand at last count, and every year it grows by several hundred." Danton smiled at the thought.

You lie! There are not that many Hobs in the world. You only had a few hundred, and we decimated your army before you knew what happened.

"No, you are mistaken." Danton waved away Pin's questioning glance. "The force I brought to the surface was only a small group to raid. You and your friends found us before we could report back, and that is why there's not that many coming forth now. Why, that girl, Missy, could hardly find any of us."

Us? Who do you think you are? You're a human, not a Hobs. Is your skin green? Is your body stringy? No, you are a human, and now you are more human than any of us, using my body.

"There are things you know nothing about. A Hobs is more than just the physical body. A Hobs is a state of mind. A freedom that is not seen anywhere in the world except underground. And the love of the queen will free any Hobs who allows her close." Danton stopped walking away from the dig.

You are still going to die. Even if it means the end of me.

Danton believed it. That voice, the child whom owned this body before him, was strong willed. With the spell to dissipate the mind from his, this voice should not be heard, but still it was there. Pin was right. They needed to get back to the caverns and deal with this entity before it was too late.

"Danton!" Pin called out.

He glanced toward Pin and noticed the Hobs no longer dug into the ground. His hand was wrapped around a strange root with a large bulbous top and two large branches jutting out just below it. Under that was a long part of the tuber and under that it split into two parts. He did not recognize it at first until he noted between the two lower parts was a very small part.

"Pin, is that–"

Pin smiled. "A mandrake root."

"Is that what we need, Pin?" Danton heard of mandrake. A small amount could extend the act of love, and too much would cause pain and death.

"Mandrake," Pin said. "We will use it to drive the mind from you."

"I don't see how that will work, Pin."

"You don't see how anything will work. What is wrong with you? I am the one with magic, not you. Trust me."

Danton trusted Pin. For too many years the Hobs had kept him alive for some reason. Now was not the time to question him, so he left Pin to do the preparation.

The sun was lower in the sky now, almost hidden behind the hill to the West. A soft breeze rustled the brush, and he shivered. The night would be cold. He did not look forward to spending it in the open. These last few months saw him in the cold of the night too many times. He was tired of it.

He unslung his pack, then untied his tent. At least he would not be wet if it rained, and erecting it did not take long. He glanced over to Pin, who was still rooting around in the brush for something. There was no reason to hurry, but he wanted to get Pin's tent up as well, even though the Hobs rarely used one. It would make the morning easier, for if it rained the Hobs would not get rained on and be upset about getting too clean so close to his yearly bath.

A fire was the next job, and he found fallen branches scattered about. Soon he had a fire licking skyward.

Pin had stopped searching for whatever it was he wanted. He sat on the ground beside a rotted log and picked out grubs. Each one he examined carefully before whipping dirt off it and eating the wriggling insect in a gulp.

Danton pulled out the last of the rabbit from his pack and placed it on a round stone sitting inside the fire. He only wanted to heat the meat, for it was cooked the night before.

"We need to go as soon as there is light," Danton said, pushing the meat on the stone around with his dirk.

"Yes," Pin said, licking his fingers. "We are a couple of days out from the caverns, unless we run a little bit."

He thought of that. Running would tire them out faster, and this body burned through food so fast he was concerned about it. But run they must. So he nodded his agreement. Reaching back, he grabbed a water skin and drank heavily, then offered it to Pin.

"Yes," Pin said, taking the skin. He sloshed the water around and frowned. "We need more of this as well."

"We will need to find a stream or something." Danton cut a piece of rabbit off and ate it.

"There is one not that far away. Remember the march?"

Danton nodded. "Yes, I remember."

"There was a stream near here, about a few miles south. We could be there in the early morning at a run and not have to worry until we got underground." Pin found another grub and ate it.

"I wish you would cook them."

"Cook what?" Pin looked about him.

"The grubs." Danton waved at the one Pin had just pulled from the log.

There was a bark of laughter, and Pin almost spat out his food. "Cook a grub? You are mad. They splatter and lose all their moisture. Never cook a grub."

A light misting of rain came in, and Danton pulled his cloak tighter around him. "I'm not sitting in the rain. Good night, Pin." He got up and walked to his tent.

"Good night, Danton."

Yes, good night.

THE RUSTLE OF THE TENT FLAPS WOKE HIM FROM HIS slumber. Hands grabbed his legs and pulled him out into the cold, early dawn air. Twenty town folk stood around the camp, sombre and staring at him. Two of them held Pin just above the ground. A gag kept the Hobs' from screaming.

Missy smiled from behind a large, dark-haired man with no neck. His hands, balled into fists, hammered against each other with anticipation. A slight snarl touched the corner of his lips.

Pin pulled against the arms holding him. His eyes, wide as tea cups, stared at Danton with a plea for help. Small welts showed on the side of the Hobs face, possibly from a beating.

Why had he not heard anything? Then he noticed. The people were talking, but no noise made its way to him. Strong hands pushed him forward. Ten feet away from the tent, the voices of the crowd became audible. The shouts concussed against his ears with ferocity, and he stumbled. The men held him up against falling.

Missy stepped out from behind the big man, but he did not allow her to be more than an arm's length away. She approached Pin first, then slapped the Hobs. Daggers shot out from his eyes and he tried to snap at her hand. The girl just smiled, and held her hand in front of Pin, edging him to try again. Dark green flushed his cheeks.

Obviously tired of the game, Missy let her hand drop, and turned to Danton. She approached him, and with a smile on her face, said, "You left me tied up."

Danton shook the fog from his head. "Yes, but I did leave you a knife."

"Yes, you left me a knife," Missy said loudly. She spun about with arms spread. "You left me a knife in my hand. And each hand tied up against the other. What did you say to me before you left? Do you remember? Are you man enough to tell these people what you told me?"

"Yes," Danton said. He lifted his head, and before a word escaped his mouth, Missy stepped up and slapped him.

"Well?" Missy asked.

"I told you–"

She slapped him again, hard.

"Are you going to say it?" Missy shook her hand.

"You hurt your hand," Danton said.

She stepped forward, and this time, a small fist hit his jaw. Missy swore, shaking her hand.

"I know," Danton said.

"And I told you they'd hunt you."

Danton looked into her eyes. "I know."

TWENTY-THREE

Thomasyn glanced about the chamber, feeling uncomfortable with all the seers reclined around him watching the ceiling. Jerek nodded at him Dallia took his hand. He wanted to leave immediately, but Papion requested they stay for a few minutes and talk quietly while Bethany recited her story once again. Dallia kept asking her about the stars and the position of the moon in the sky.

Finally, after fifteen minutes, Thomasyn had enough. "Papion, we have to get to Jon and bring him back to Capital."

"There is no need to hurry." Papion glanced back to Bethany. "Are you sure the moon was full?"

"Yes," Bethany said. "It was full, I'm sure of it."

"A week," Papion said. "We have time. You have seen the future and now we know where he will be."

"How can you tell?" Thomasyn asked.

"The full moon is a week away. You are four days away at a fast march if you travel straight there."

Thomasyn thought about that. They had taken a week to get there last year, but that was travelling slowly, and taking their time to look at the country once they were past Salman. He thought about what Papion said, but wanting to get to his friend was overwhelming. There was the desire to save Jon, and find out what the mention of Danton meant to them. But bowing to their elders was instilled in them. He would have to obey their direction.

"Don't worry, Thomasyn. I'll make sure you get out in time to save your friend." Papion stood and looked at the others. "For now, I would like to check on the king."

Thomasyn wondered if the king had awakened from his slumber. He was told the man was tired and needed sleep, but it had been a long time and answers were needed.

A runner came into the chamber and looked around anxiously. He spied the group and approached as respectfully and quickly as possible. The grabbed Papion's arm and leaned into the man. They exchanged whispers and Papion swore under his breath. An air of anger surrounded the man, which started at the frown on his face.

Once the news was given, the runner left as quickly as he had come. The group stared at Papion, looking for an explanation. After a minute, Papion shook his head and addressed them all.

"There's a problem. The king awoke and confronted the Elven diplomat. He has the elf in the back chamber, a knife at his throat." Papion sighed. "We are lost if the king kills the elf. It will start a war we are not prepared to fight yet."

"We have an elf in the castle?" Bethany asked.

"There has been one here for many years," Jerek said. "We use diplomacy to keep them from attacking."

"What else is the Realm keeping from us?" Thomasyn asked. "It would be important we know everything."

"No." Jerek took a deep breath. "You only need to know what is needed. No more."

"I don't like it." Bethany stood a little wobbly on her feet. Papion reached out and steadied her.

"You need to allow your body to adjust from the dreaming," he said. "It will take time."

Bethany pulled her arm away from him. "I'm all right. We need to keep Darious from doing something he will regret in the future. Show us the way, Papion."

Thomasyn, Bethany, Sandra, Jerek, Papion, and Dallia rushed through the castle. The hallways bustled with excitement, and several of the militia ran toward the same destination.

They travelled deep into the castle. Past the area they had recovered to the back that faced toward the ocean. Never having been in this section of the castle, Thomasyn was mystified by all the tapestries and paintings hanging on the walls.

They walked in silence. And after several minutes, they came to an area unlike the rest. The tapestries changed from landscapes to pictorials of vast Elven armies marching in file. They carried bows and lances. Each brandished a large, curved sword. The images were foreboding to him.

Finally, after turning a corner, they came up against a pack of Elven guards. Their helmets, bronze and gleaming, sported nose pieces that ended in hooks. Thomasyn noticed the portrait of a dragon on each breast plate and every one of them in a different crouching or flying stance. Tanned leather short skirts embedded with iron rods hung from their waists, while only sandals adorned their feet. Each guard held a halberd level to the ground, and a bow slung across their back. Twenty militia held swords out as heated words exchanged between them.

Thomasyn pushed forward through the militia and stood before the Elven guards. He stared at them with a level glare, one hand on his sword hilt and his throwing bone in the other. He could not be mistaken for anything but a Spear. In a few seconds, the guards started to look away.

He took his hand off the sword and stepped forward. The elves stepped back and extended their weapons. He did not flinch, but drew his sword and kept the tip pointed downward. No one said anything. Then Bethany was by his side, her sword drawn as well.

"I will pass," Thomasyn said.

"No one will pass. We have orders…" The elf motioned with his head to the door where muffled yells came. "It would mean our heads."

Bethany spoke up, "It would mean your heads if you don't."

Thomasyn did not want to have a confrontation with the elves, but there was nothing he could do. She had already put forth the challenge to them.

The elf jerked his chin to motion behind him. "We know what he is like. It would be slow."

"And it will be fast with us," Thomasyn said. "Do you remember the past? How the Spears took down your invading army all those years ago?" He stepped forward again, his chest barely inches away from the tip of the halberd held by the speaker. "You don't want a fight here. We don't want a fight here. Step aside; you are not at the embassy, just a room in a castle that you have no right to block."

The elves looked at one another. They spoke in hushed tones. Most nodded and only two shook their heads. But once the speaker said a sharp no, they backed away from their position in acquiescence.

Thomasyn took the chance and rushed past. The door was locked. One of the guards humphed and a key ring jingled at his waist. Jerek grabbed it before the elf could react and handed it to Thomasyn. Soon, the door flew open. They all entered.

The sitting room was in shambles with chairs overturned or broken and pillow stuffing all over. A table on its side with a leg broken slowly rolled in the corner. Then he saw Darious. The king held the elf by the throat against a wall with one hand. His other brandished a saw tooth dirk against the elf's neck.

The elf tried to punch the clutching hand, but with his feet touching the floor on tiptoes, he could not muster much strength. Thomasyn wondered at how close the elf looked to Fletch and then thought of his friend in the hands of the elves.

"Darious, this will mean war between our two people," the elf gasped.

"Better war than a slave to you and your blood magic, Kalin. I will kill you for what you did. You made me a puppet and didn't even think of how it hurt my people." He pushed the blade higher, and the elf grabbed at his wrist.

"Our people have lived in peace for hundreds of years. Would you dare break such for open war?" The wind from his lungs rattled with exertion as he struggled to speak.

"Your people have invaded already. I have reports of elves posing as villagers. Gathering information. Causing chaos within my Realm." He thrust his body to the side, putting more pressure on the elf's neck. With a swift movement, he brought his knee up to connect with the elf's groin.

A whimper escaped the elf and his eyes crossed before squinting. Darious let go and allowed the elf to fall to the floor in pain.

"I should end you now, but no. I have a better idea. You will be cast out from the Realm. Sent back to your people in shame. Stripped of all wealth and power. Naked and branded a criminal." Darious took a deep breath. "They will disown you. If you are lucky, they will let you live in the sewers." He spat at the elf, whom crawled slowly away.

"My king," Thomasyn said, and knelt. He reversed the grip on his sword. Bethany copied him.

The Elven guards barged in after the Spears and surrounded their fallen comrade. The spokesman of the group turned to the king and asked, "Your majesty, what happened?"

Darious pointed to the elf. "Your countryman. He placed a control creature on me ten months ago. He tried to control me, and succeeded for a short time."

"A serious charge," one of the guards said.

Thomasyn stepped forward. "We burned the creature off him a day ago."

Darious took five steps to the Spears and motioned them to stand. "You will never kneel before me again. No more will you kneel to anyone, Spears. Both of you, I owe you my life."

Thomasyn inclined his head. "I live to serve."

"No, you serve beyond what is asked. And now the Realm owes you." He turned to the guards. "You have heard?"

The guards nodded.

"Then, you are to take this... diplomat back to your homeland. He is charged with breaking the international treaty, possibly for his own gain." He stared at the knife in his hand. "There has been too much violence over the last year. I want it to end."

Bethany bowed her head. "My king, there is something else."

"Bethany." His voice softened. "You disobeyed me, forced your way into the room, and helped save me. It is just a... a dream to me. Don't bow, you need not."

"My king." She glanced up into his eyes. "I only did what any would do."

"No, both of you go far beyond." He turned to Thomasyn. "What else is there?"

"There was a Spear who is under the influence of an elf. We don't know where–"

Darious cut him off. "Not here. My chambers. You and the group."

"Some of us are not here," Bethany said.

Raising a hand, Darious called in the militia's corporal. The man rushed in and knelt.

"There is a group that needs access to the castle. See that they are able to enter, and bring them to me." The man nodded and rose. "Ask my Spear friends here. They know what their names are, and corporal."

"Yes, my king."

"The elf and his guards are to be evicted from The Realm immediately. Out of the city, to the docks, and get them on a ship before the end of day. They are not to go to their embassy. Gather any of their staff that is Elven, and have them evicted as well."

"It will be done, my king."

<hr>

Darious sat before the court on the raised dais; the fingers of his left hand caressed the arm of the throne, while his right lay on his sword hilt. Twenty militiamen formed a guard beside the king, two rows of five on either side, on the steps just below the throne. Delegates from the Realm lined the gallery, and the counsel occupied the first two rows of chairs to the left. Each glanced about with wavering eyes.

To the king's left, in chains with his arms shackled to a crossbar on his back, knelt the elf ambassador. His hair, tangled and dirty, fell across his face. Directly behind, his guards stood stripped of weapons and armour. They held heads high to look defiant, but appeared docile. Tigers with teeth and claws removed.

Thomasyn watched the folly unroll before him. The king wanted to expel the elves, but the counsel disagreed. The concoctions of their words hammered against all who had witnessed it.

"This is an outrage," the representative wearing a long robe cowed out. "The Elvin delegate should be removed from shackles immediately."

"I concur," interjected a representative whose coat was covered in feathers. "I demand he be unshackled at once."

Con, standing just a foot behind and to the left of the king, leaned forward and whispered into his ear. The king nodded and waved a dismissive hand at the delegates.

"Are there any others who feel the same as these two council members?" He scanned the men, and three of the group took a step forward in support. "Any others?"

Thomasyn knew he would have to act fast. The militia with the king had sworn an oath of protection and promised to put their bodies in harm's way if need be. It was up to Bethany, Sandra, Master Chail, and himself to do the rest. For this purpose, they had dressed in full cloaks, melded into the wall with the power taught them when they were young. To the outside world, they did not exist. No one could see them. They were hidden.

"Step forward, you four. Make your claims, or hold your tongues."

The four stepped from behind the railing separating the king's dais and the floor. They walked with slow and sure steps. Their leader, the man in the long robe, nodded at the elf ambassador. Thomasyn would have missed it if he had not been attentive, the nod being so short. But it was there. Could this member be an elf as well? Or was he a conspirator looking to help out one of his own? It would not be easy to find out.

Two hours ago, Papion had probed the mind of the elf, only to find very little of interest. The creature was not complex, and his thoughts were easily read. All that came to the seer was flashes of four others whom he dealt with on the counsel. So when he reported this to the king, a fury came over him. His own people, the council, conspired against the Realm.

The Spears were told to stay hidden until called upon. The people would take their word for what happened, and justice could be served.

But the king needed open admission of their crime. This, he said, would make the rest of the Realm call for justice, and allow for the protection of the people against a possible invasion. Once that was taken care of, the dwarven people's new contract could be discussed without issue.

The four approached and stopped ten feet away from the dais. Each bowed, and the one wearing the long cloak took a step forward and began to speak.

"My King, our economy is in shambles. The Elven people are here to open trade with us as long as we keep their emissary safe. Now he is in chains, and due to return in shame along with his guards. How could this serve the Realm?"

"Council member Jarrab, I should have known you were involved in this farce. The Realm will survive and prosper with your house expelled from the land, along with your conspirators. Each will have–"

"You outreach yourself, king!" yelled the feathered man. "This is an outrage. My house has been a member of the council for centuries and we will–"

"Be expelled with him." The king exploded to his feet. All rose with him. "We have your statement. You have shown whose country you back by coming forward to protect the Elvin dignitary." He stared at the four men. "There are three ways we can deal with this. First, execute all of you for treason. Second, hand you over to the Spears to be used for training. Third, expel you from the country. Be thankful I'm being generous."

The four froze, mouths agape. The king made a motion with his hand. It was the signal. The four Spears rose slowly, revealing their presence in the assembly. It was the old trick. They knew how impressive it would appear, four figures standing with deliberation, appearing to walk through the wall. The people gasped.

"The Spears await your decision, which will it be?" The king sat once more, motioning the congregation to do so as well. The crowd settled down. "I suggest answering quickly, lest they sentence you before I can pass judgement."

To drive the king's statement home, and push the conspirators to disclose their own guilt, the Spears took a step forward. Each of the four councillors shied back and looked toward the king for assistance. The king stared back, showed no emotion.

With a flourish, the man in the long cloak spun and pulled a sword. He rushed forward, eyes wild. His vestige changed, morphed into an elf. His features lengthened, ears pointed, complexion lightened. The man lost over 40 pounds in a blink. He was not human.

Master Chail stepped forward, but Thomasyn rushed ahead, sword drawn.

The two weapons rang out as they clashed. The elf was well trained. His sword danced in front of Thomasyn. He countered every strike, be it high or low. With a side step, the elf tried to pass by Thomasyn's defence, but he pushed forward, causing the elf to step back.

With a flick, Thomasyn drove his sword tip down. It caught the elf by surprise. The tip touched the back of the hand. The cut was less than an inch. Blood flowed. Slow at first. But he knew it would be a torrent soon.

The Elven guards stomped their feet and started to sing a fighting song:

The fight of an elf
The tide of the world
We hammer away to succeed
An elf is one with nature's child
Forever fighting with glee

To see the world
To gain the right
To seek the poor
And take the fight

The fight of an elf

The tide of the world
We hammer away to succeed

Their song was interrupted when Thomasyn dove under a back handed slash and brought down his sword. The blade whistled in the air. The elf screamed. There was a clatter against the stone floor. The elf knelt, clutching at the stump of his right arm severed just below the elbow.

TWENTY-FOUR

Thomasyn watched as Darious paced the back of the King's Chamber. The king, muttering to himself, would not sit down. He could not stop watching the king and wondered when the man would wear out the rug covering the floor. The dwarven contract lay on a table in the middle of the room. With a flourish, Darious stopped, picked up a quill, and signed the contract.

Thomasyn cleared his throat.

"I didn't get that," Darious said.

"It was nothing, my king," Thomasyn said.

"Thomasyn, if I'm going to rely on your thoughts, I need you to speak frankly to me. Just call me Darious when we are alone." He looked at Master Chail, Bethany, and Sandra. "That will apply to the rest of you as well."

Bethany blushed, and the others nodded. Chail stepped forward.

"Darious, I have watched you grow into the role of king and was very surprised when the order came to sequester me away. It is to my relief that it was not truly you, but something the elves subjected you to." He stared at his feet.

"Chail, you have been indispensable to the Realm. Your training of the Spears has been a centrepiece to our world. You are needed at the training grounds in order to save what has been done."

"I don't think, my king, that Con did anything poorly."

"No, but Con is not you." Darious came up to Chail and put his hand on the Spear's shoulders. "The training is always done by a Master of Spears, and you, sir, are that master. My father was correct when he commissioned you as the head of training."

Chail bowed. "I am honoured to serve, King Darious."

Darious regarded to the three young Spears and stepped toward Bethany. He reached out and caressed her cheek. "Bethany. I loath to say this, but I must let you and the other two search for the one you lost." He dropped his arm. "I want you to come back, Bethany."

She blushed, then smiled.

"King Darious," Thomasyn said.

Darious turned to Thomasyn and inclined his head.

Thomasyn shifted in place. The king had a way of levelling his gaze that made a person uncomfortable. He could look into the soul, and that is what Thomasyn felt, his soul being bared before the others. He looked away first and glanced at his feet. "No disrespect, sire." He looked up. "We will find Jon, and Bethany will come back, but without her..."

"You misunderstand, Thomasyn. I am not holding her back from this." Darious glanced at Bethany. "Just that I will miss her while she is gone."

Chail stepped forward and put his arm across Bethany's shoulders. "She will return after finding our lost soul." He squeezed Bethany's shoulders. "Won't you, Bethany?"

She looked up at him. "Yes, I'll come back. Thomasyn and I will come back with Jon."

Darious took a deep breath. "Bethany, can I speak to you alone for a few minutes?" He glanced at the others and raised his eyebrows.

"Thomasyn," Chail said. "Let's give them a few minutes."

Thomasyn leaned against the wall outside the king's chamber. He wondered what they were talking about, but Chail refused to let him listen by the door. So he took up position opposite the door and examined the contents of his pack. After that, he pulled off three short spears and honed the edges with a stone.

With his last spear sharpened to a fine edge, he pushed away from the wall and took the five steps to stand beside Chail.

"Master Chail," Thomasyn said.

"What is it, Thomasyn?"

"We've only been gone for a year, but I…"

Chail waited, but after Thomasyn did not continue, he spoke out. "Thomasyn, you can speak to me about anything. But if you want my advice, you have to let me know what is on your mind."

Thomasyn glanced at the floor. "It's about Jon. And Bethany, Sandra, and me."

The silence reared up again. Chail waited patiently once more, but when Thomasyn did not elaborate, he prodded once again. "You have to be a little more specific than that."

"Sorry, Master Chail." He took a deep breath. "Meeting up with Sandra was a surprise. We talked a bit, and… well… I want to be with her," he confessed. But what else would he say? There was more that needed to come out, but he did not know what to do. And just as he saw Master Chail start to speak he blurted out, "I don't want to travel around anymore."

Chail closed his mouth. He stared at Thomasyn for a second. "Are you saying that you don't want to be a Spear?"

"No!" Thomasyn said. "Far from it. I just don't want to spend my life walking around the Realm. Sandra and I talked about it. The outpost she was assigned to, they need another Spear. We were thinking…"

"You want to know if you can settle down with Sandra," Chail said. "Maybe raise a family."

Thomasyn walked a few passes away. "Yes."

Chail waited, and Thomasyn started to fidget.

"There is no law that says you must travel throughout the Realm when you're a Spear. You were assigned to the Teeth, just like Bethany and Jon. It was supposed to last for several years, not a few weeks and travel back here." Chail held up his hand as Thomasyn started to interject. "I understand you were sent back by the Dwarven King. Maybe because you've been so far in the last year that you felt it would be your lot in life to walk the Realm from one end to another, but that is not true."

"It sure feels like it."

Chail laughed. "It would, wouldn't it? I never told you about my first wife, did I?"

"No, Master Chail."

"It was a year before I was asked to train the Spears in Flight. The outer reaches of the Sand Sea. Have you heard of it?"

"North East. Hot during the day and cold at night."

"We met there, in the City of Sand." Chail chuckled. "Aptly named. Sand was everywhere. You could not change clothes without it getting in some of the most annoying places.

"Her name was Kattie, and she was the most beautiful woman I had ever met."

"I thought you said Tess was the most beautiful woman you had ever met."

"She is, but I had not met Tess back then. I fell in love and married her in a whirlwind of excitement." He put his hand on the young Spear's shoulder. "She was pregnant within the first three months. Something went wrong. The child came out of her after six months, and the Wooder could not stop her from bleeding." He stared into the distance. "My son lived long enough for me to name him Eric, after my great grandfather. His skin actually turned blue. An hour after his birth, he died. Kattie died before him." He took another deep breath. "I'm glad she passed away first. Kattie would not have been able to take it if she outlived our son."

"Is that when you came to us?" Thomasyn asked.

"No. Master Shail sent for me first. He let me stay up there for a while before word came down that his wife wanted him to return home."

"I didn't know Master Shail was married."

"He was." Chail turned away from Thomasyn, and his voice became distant. "She was killed in an attack. Some gang of children, too old to be Spears when they were found, attacked her for the food she carried and the coins in her pouch. Shail had been visiting me here when it happened. His children were very upset, but he took care of them. He had requested the assignment to the Teeth after his children were old enough."

"Does he not love his children?" Thomasyn asked.

"Oh, on the contrary, he loves his children deeply, but they blame him for their mother's death. It was because of his love for them that he left. They need to find their way, and for that to happen, they need to miss him."

"I think that makes sense, but I still–"

The door opened and Bethany walked out. Her red eyes showed puffiness.

⸻

THOMASYN SHOOK HIS HEAD AS SANDRA STOOD WITH HER hands on her hips. She wore one of the light shirts packed so many weeks ago with a white shirt and leggings. He did not want her to strain her arm, but she argued the disc was implanted two days ago, and her arm was almost healed under the administrations of the Master Wooders. Bandages still bound her arm, though she assured Thomasyn that full range of motion would not be a problem.

"I still don't like it." Thomasyn did want to have Sandra stay. He was concerned about her getting hurt further. If she was injured again, he would not forgive himself. Especially if that injury kept her from continuing as a Spear.

"Thomasyn, I am as much a Spear as you and Bethany. You need me to help here. If I don't come, then who will be the third?" She glanced over at Bethany for support.

"I agree," Bethany said. "Sandra should come."

"See!" Sandra said. "Even Bethany agrees with me."

Bethany turned to Sandra. "Yes, we need a third, but if there was someone else, they would be the one standing there, not you. Your injury will hamper us for a while."

Thomasyn held up his hands in surrender. "I give. Sandra, you can come. Make the third, but I want you to stay safe until you are fully healed."

"Agreed." Her smile beamed brighter than the morning sun.

He touched his forehead in agreement, and they picked up their packs.

Bethany pointed at the door. "We have company."

Thomasyn glanced toward the door to see Master Chail enter, followed by Tess, Papion, Dallia, and Con. None of them looked happy.

"I see you're about to leave," Chail said.

"Yes, Master Chail." Thomasyn finished checking his pack and slung it on his back. Three short spears went into their holders along with the throwing bone. He shifted it on his back to balance the load.

Chail helped Sandra with her pack while Tess hugged Bethany.

Papion coughed and waited for them to turn their attention to him. Once they did, he focused his attention on Bethany. "You said in the dream that something was wrong with your friend Jon."

"Yes," Bethany said. "I saw him, then the face of someone else. Jon's name came to me and then Danton. I don't understand."

"Nor did I when you talked about it." Papion reached into his robe. "Then I took the time to read a few of the records on blood magic, and it is my belief that Danton's mind was transferred to Jon when he killed him."

Thomasyn gasped. A mind transfer? From Danton to Jon? It would explain a number of things. The issues on the road to the Teeth. The inconsistency in Jon's responses. How he seemed to be two different people.

"You must be protected from the magic that is being used." Papion took his hand out from his robe and dangled three pendants between slim fingers. "These may protect you."

Bethany took a pendant and held it before her. The light danced on the small twining of metal. Three distinct fingers of metal interlaced together and ended holding a red ruby. The stone shone with a fire from somewhere inside.

"Very pretty." She put the necklace over her head.

Dallia stepped forward. "My father is concerned that you may need to kill Jon in order to free him."

"Kill Jon?" Thomasyn asked. "No. We are bringing him home."

Chail frowned. "That may not be possible."

"Chail!" Tess said. "They can bring him back."

"Yes, they may be able to bring him back, but who will they really bring back to us? Jon, or Danton?"

Con folded his hands inside his sleeves. "That is the question. They could bring back either one, or both. I would rather see them just bring Jon back, but failing that, bringing them both back would be more desirable."

"Thomasyn will bring him back," Sandra said, taking his hand. She gleamed at him.

"We will bring him back," Thomasyn corrected, and squeezed her hand. "I could not do it alone, and without the support of two others, the task would not be successful."

"Spoken like a true leader," Chail said.

"Indeed," Con added. "You have grown much over the last year."

Tess hugged Thomasyn. "You have all been special to me." She looked at Sandra. "I'm happy that you two have found each other."

Sandra blushed.

"You have a journey in front of you," Papion said. "Only a week to meet up with our target."

"I will not do a forced march. Sandra still needs time to heal." Thomasyn took a deep breath. "As always, I wish you were coming with us." He levelled his eyes at Master Chail and wondered when they had become the same height.

"Then head out, Spears. And may your travel be light and quick."

They walked into the training yard toward the gates of the city.

***

Over the first day, they walked toward the Town of Lands. They passed traders and seekers of fortune whispering of open trade once again taking place. Pilgrims smiled at the Spears while travelling to secure land. And at one point, they saw a dwarf on a cart pulled by mules; the back stacked with armour and weapons.

As they approached the cart, the dwarf stopped and waved to them. The Spears halted by the dwarf to ask how they could help. The dwarf stood tall for one of his kind, just over four feet. His hands, dirty even beneath short nails, were strong when he shook Thomasyn's. Chain mail showed under a worn brown tunic and his leggings held steel bands sown into the leather. One finger pointed at the sword Bethany and Thomasyn wore and words in a craggy voice rumbled through lips hidden behind a long beard. All the Spears shrugged, not understanding what the dwarf said.

"I'm sorry, but what did you say?" Thomasyn asked.

"Graffnee." The dwarf pointed at Thomasyn's sword once again. "Sword Graffnee."

Thomasyn put his hand on the pommel of his sword. He thought of the day the weapon was given to him by Master Garion and Shail. They had said the swords were a gift to Bethany and him. The dwarves gifted them special to them, and the Masters of Spears did not mention anything different about them, but that they were dwarven forged.

"The swords are dwarven," Thomasyn said.

"Sword Graffnee. Made Graffnee." The dwarf reached into the cart and pulled out a sword in a sheath. He pointed to Sandra and held out the sword. "Sword Graffnee."

Sandra glanced at the sword, her eyes wide in wonder. The dwarf smiled and bobbed the sword toward her.

"You want me to look at the sword?" Sandra asked.

"Sword Graffnee," he said, then pointed at Thomasyn's and Bethany's swords, saying, "Sword Graffnee. Sword Graffnee."

She took the sword from the dwarf. "Thank you, but I don't have much money to pay for this."

"Beeka, beeka." The dwarf pointed at Sandra's sword. "Trade. Three points."

Sandra reached into her pouch but only produced one silver point and two copper butts. Her eyes dropped in disappointment. Thomasyn took out one silver point as well as five copper butts, and Bethany produced another silver point.

The dwarf looked at them, his brows knitted together and mouth scrunched to one side. "Neea, neea." He pointed to Sandra's sword.

Sandra unbuckled her sword and handed it to him. He smiled, turned, and put the sword into his cart. He faced Sandra again and smiled, lifting the corners of his beard.

The dwarf pointed at each sword and said, "Point, point, point." He then reached out and took the one silver point from Sandra. "Point." The coin disappeared into his pouch. "Three Spears, three points. Silver points."

"I don't understand," Sandra said.

Thomasyn peered at the dwarf, who simply smiled. Something was familiar about him, but he knew very few dwarves that... then it came to his mind. "Pon!"

The dwarf pointed his thumb at his chest. "Pon." He then pointed to Thomasyn and Bethany in turn and said, "Thomasyn, Bethany. Selling weapon for food. Coin buy food."

Thomasyn thought back, and did not remember Pon ever talking to them. It could be due to his speech, but why were his words so broken?

"Deep digger," Pon said, as if hearing his unspoken question. "No speak lots. Jon coming?"

Thomasyn frowned, and so did Bethany.

"We're looking for him. I'm Sandra." She reached out her hand.

Pon took hold of Sandra's elbow, thumb between forearm and bicep. "Meet good, Sandra. Jon lost?"

"More than you would ever know," Bethany muttered.

"Three dwarven sword. Silver point. Would give, but money exchange on weapon or only sorrow come from use."

Thomasyn remembered hearing something of the wives' tale. Never take a blade as a gift, always exchange something for it, so the blade never lacks ownership. Sometimes the old ways were the best. The dwarves must have used their captivity when they visited, as the price paid for the swords they had given Bethany and him. It was the only explanation.

"Did you come right from the Teeth?" Bethany asked.

"No, left before big feast. Sell, make money, buy food."

"The king is changing the contract, making it more favourable to the dwarven people." Bethany smiled. "Your king won. He was fair, and King Darious knows it. He signed the proclamation just before we left."

Pon smiled, then bade the three to lean close. "Problem coming," he said, putting a finger beside his nose. "Town of Lands? Elves? All problems."

"We're going to the Town of Lands. Is there a problem with the elves?" Sandra asked.

"Elves always problem. Town of Lands, you there first. Elves months away, but many ships come. Warn I do. Land they want."

Thomasyn perked up at the mention of the elves months away, and asked, "Are you saying there's going to be an invasion of the Realm?"

Pon shrugged. "Elves. 200 ships. Very angry."

"And how would you know this?" Bethany asked.

Turning back to his cart, Pon lifted the rest of the tarp and there, surrounded by weapons, the remnants of Fletch lay rotting.

TWENTY-FIVE

The firelight cast eerie shadows across the four. Thomasyn poked a stick at the fire before throwing another log on it. Sandra sat beside him, stealing all the heat she could from his body.

Pon belched, rubbed at his nose, and sneezed.

"May the Five," Bethany said.

"Kants," Pon said.

Thomasyn could almost understand him. The strange sounds of the Dwarven Language took time to figure out, but it was not that different from his own.

The dwarf pulled out a flask from his jacket, took off the cork stopper and drank deeply. He started to cough, replaced the stopper, then looked at Thomasyn. With a smile, he held out the flask.

"Denk," Pon said, tilting the flask to Thomasyn.

At first he hesitated, not knowing what the flask contained, but Sandra edged him on. Thomasyn took the flask from Pon, uncorked it, and sniffed. Peppermint greeted him. He took a drink. Fire erupted in his mouth as soon as the liquid touched his tongue. He gasped, taking the fumes into his lungs. Thomasyn started to cough uncontrollably.

Pon laughed, took the flask from him, and slapped Thomasyn on the back until he could breathe a little easier. He could feel the heat of his cheeks as he turned to the dwarf.

"How..." he gasped. "How do you drink that?"

Pon giggled, made a motion of drinking from the flask and swallowing. He then rubbed his stomach and licked smiling lips. "Gasy."

Bethany glanced over at Pon. "Easy for you to say."

Sandra rubbed Thomasyn's back. "You shouldn't have given that to him."

Pon shrugged. "Te Sanbed ta."

"I'm going to bed," Thomasyn said. He stood, bent over, and kissed Sandra. "We have an early start tomorrow."

"Then we should all turn in," Bethany said. She glanced at Pon, who smiled. "I'm not kissing you."

"Neper kown is ya listin." Pon stood and winked. "Dwarven bekast orow."

Everyone laughed except Sandra. "I don't get it."

"Means little or nothing," Thomasyn said. "Goodnight."

⁂

The crackling of a fire and a log thrown aside woke Thomasyn. A grunt of satisfaction reached him and then a dwarven swear word. The thought of Pon cooking worried him, so he dressed and exited his tent in a rush.

Pon clanked a few pans together and looked up. "Orn, Thomasyn. Bekast?"

"What are we having this morning?" Thomasyn asked.

"Id cak an oken." Pon held up some meat and a large bowl. "Dwarven bekast."

Thomasyn shook his head. The last breakfast he had from a dwarf contained an under cooked egg and burnt bread, this one did not. It seemed Pon was not the usual dwarf.

Two pans went on the fire, and the meat started to sizzle. Thomasyn sat on the log and pulled out his sword. He tested the edge and shook his head. The blade, sharp and honed, still did not need sharpening. He looked up to see Pon smiling at him.

"Ud dwarven leel. Ege eve arp."

"Yes, the edge is always sharp." Thomasyn sheathed the sword.

Bethany came out of her tent, followed by Sandra. The two walked over, sat beside the fire, and watched Pon turn the slices of meat. After a few minutes, he drained the grease onto the other pan and poured a batter into the hot grease. Another minute later, he used a knife to lift the edge of the batter, smiled, and jerked the pan upward. The batter came away from the pan, flipped in the air, and landed back in the pan.

"What is that?" Sandra asked.

"Smells good." Bethany leaned forward. "Is that pig?"

Pon nodded.

"And what is that?" Sandra pointed at the other pan.

"Pon Tate," Pon said. "Ned ony."

Bethany started to cry.

Sandra put her arm around Bethany and pulled her tight.

Thomasyn stood and walked to his tent. "Jon could find honey just about anywhere." He reached into his tent, fished around for a second, and then returned. He handed a small jar to Pon.

"Ony!" Pon held the small jar up.

Bethany sniffled. "We need to get to Jon."

"We need to eat first." Thomasyn watched Pon take the pan with the Pon Tate off the fire and set it down.

"At," Pon said, and cut a quarter of the Pon Tate. He used it to dip into the meat grease and drizzled honey over it.

The group copied his example.

Thomasyn was surprised by the flavours in the meat and Pon Tate. And once finished, he found his stomach filled with such a small meal.

Pon cleaned the pans and put everything away. His tent went onto the wagon and he motioned the others to do the same. "Asy ith ay."

Each one placed their packs on the wagon, and the camp was broken.

They travelled for the next three days. Pon cooked and kept the Spears enticed with his mastery of food. Each day grew warmer, and they made good time, even with the wagon slowing them down.

At the end of the fourth day, they reached the flats of the Town of Lands. People moved about in the town before them, and they all seemed to be heading to the centre square. A bonfire reached into the sky, lighting the town in a golden red glow. The town chanted in a frenzy.

Something felt off in the town, and the Spears convinced Pon to wait on the outskirts. At that point the reciting of the town could be understood, even with the unmetered pace, "Spear and Hobs, burn in fire."

It spurred Thomasyn. Bethany and Sandra ran beside him.

A large log, towering into the sky, proved to be the target of the crowd. Two figures stood there, tied to the towering monolith before them. A shock of blond hair adorned the one wrapped in the cloak of a Spear. Jon.

Thomasyn recognized his friend even from a distance. Fifty yards, and his legs pushed at the ground. Forty yards, and the scream of the Hobs beside Jon sliced through the air. Thirty yards, and they reached the outside of the townfolk. Twenty yards, and they pushed through the people. The crush of bodies slowed them, but nothing would stop their progress. Ten yards, and the town finally noticed them and moved aside as the Spears drew their swords.

A small girl with three large men taller than any the Spear had ever seen blocked their path. One carried a large torch, another, a bucket of black pitch. The third, the biggest of the three, stood strong, with Jon's sword in his hand. The sword the Spear had taken from Danton.

The Hobs screamed, spat and struggled against the bonds securing it to the log. Jon, his face lined with age beyond his years, leaned forward against his bonds. Anguish darkened the Spear's face. Then, without any word of warning, his face changed. The lines of age dissipated. Eyes went from squinted anger to wide terror. The change lasted only seconds, and then Jon slumped once again. Age transformed his once youthful visage to that of a man who had seen too much.

Thomasyn stopped before the three villagers. His breath steadied as he took in the scene. The sound of Bethany's sword clearing its sheath, and then Sandra's sword coming free, split the air around them. Missy smiled.

"Are you Spears here to take the side of the Hobs like this one?" she said, pointing to Jon. "Or do you desire to take the side of the Spear and demand we free them?"

"You cannot be judge and jury!" Bethany stepped forward. "The king decreed centuries ago that only a Spear may pass judgement."

"And when a Spear is evil?" Missy said. "He sheltered a Hobs! The same one who took my newborn brother last year. The one who killed my twin brother in the same hut that the Hobs used to destroy a whole clan last year!"

Jon's head came up, showing a young man once again. "Thomasyn!"

Bethany gasped. "You're going to burn them alive?"

"We have no Spears here to pass judgement," she said, adding a mocking slur to the name of the ancient protectors.

"We are Spears," Sandra said. "We will hear your claim and pass judgement."

The crowd laughed.

"The Spears have come to pass judgement," Missy said. "Oh, you Spears always show up when it is good for you, and not for us." The child spat on the ground.

Thomasyn stepped forward. "I will hear what he has to say."

"You claim the right?" It was the large one holding Jon's sword.

Bethany nodded and spoke before the others. "Yes. I claim the right."

A murmur passed through the crowd, and they shuffled on their feet.

"She claims the right!" The big man placed a hand on Missy's shoulder. "We must let her speak to the man."

Bethany rushed past them. She clambered across the stacked wood and stood in front of Jon. Thomasyn attempted to follow, but the large man stepped in front of him.

"The right is hers alone. She claimed it. She will be the only one. This we claim as our law. The Realm is no longer our home. We are the Land. We are our own."

The thought of a town removing itself from the Realm was inconceivable to Thomasyn. There was so much to gain by keeping the kingdom together. Why was this man denying the people their right to have Wooders heal here, and the Spears to enforce the law?

"And can I not claim the right as well?" Thomasyn asked.

"No," Missy said. "Only one may claim the right."

"But the Spears have the same rights as everyone else," Thomasyn said.

"The Spears left us after fighting the Hobs," said the large man. "They did not hunt down the creatures, and we were left with groups of them raiding our lands."

"You could have asked for help," Sandra said.

The man barked a laugh. "We asked for help. We sent men to Capital, and they were turned away after all their points were taken from them. Nothing came, save one note telling us we needed to pay for protection. We already paid for protection. Why would we have to pay more? No," he said, shaking his head. "We have no need for the Spears and the Realm."

Bethany came down from the captives. Her face, bleak with grief, and told Thomasyn there was a great problem beyond what they faced now. The crowd could be dispersed. The man, though large, did not stand like a worrier or leader. The other two did not have swords or weapons of any kind.

"It is Jon, but not Jon," Bethany said. "It is like another has his body for a time, and then he has it back. I... I fear we have lost him, Thomasyn." A tear fell from her eye and drew a line down her cheek.

"I demand a challenge!" Jon yelled. Everyone turned to him. The crowd grew silent. "Yes. I demand a challenge. By the Five if you think I am guilty, then death will follow me. But if I am innocent, no blade will harm me."

Missy shook her head. Anger filled her voice. "He cannot claim such!"

"But he has," the man said. "My daughter, it was our law. A claim of challenge must be met."

"No!" Missy cried.

"Yes," he said. "I will meet the challenge. I will be your champion, for your family was wronged by this... man."

Missy grew quiet. Her brows knitted together and she started to shake. Then, before her father could fully claim the right, she spoke. "No. You were also wronged. You cannot champion." She cast her eyes across the Spears. "I choose him to be my champion." Her finger pointed to Thomasyn.

The man dropped his head. "Do you accept, Spear?"

Sandra grabbed his hand. He looked over at her to see a slight shake of her head. Thomasyn lowered his eyes. There was nothing left to do. Their friend would either burn on a log in agony, or he could fight him and find out what happened. The choice, though easy, was something he did not want to make.

The years he had spent training with Jon, their time together in the barracks and on runs, all came together in one memory. They had a bond that went beyond friendship. It was a mutual respect for the fighting ability each claimed as their birthright as Spears. But to let the town destroy his friend out of malice, with no foresight, that was unacceptable.

With his mind made up, Thomasyn glanced back to Missy and said, "Yes, I accept."

"No!" Bethany cried.

"Thomasyn," Sandra said.

"Accepted," Missy said. She turned to her father. "Cut him down and bring him to us. He can use his own sword. This Spear will kill him."

"Kill?" Thomasyn said. "Nothing was said about killing." He did not want to kill Jon, but there was a chance that Jon may kill him.

The big man cut Jon free and cuffed Pin, knocking the Hobs unconscious. With a firm hand on the once tied Spear, he escorted him to the foot of the pyre. The crowd parted away, leaving a large circle opened for the duel between two fighters. Jon, looking old once again, motioned for the sword. The big man just dropped it two paces away.

Jon picked up the sword, and the lines of fatigue started to melt away.

Thomasyn entered the circle, with Sandra following him. She still held his hand.

"You didn't need to accept," Sandra said.

"Yes, I did." Thomasyn turned to her. "Don't worry, I know how Jon fights."

"So do I." Sandra rubbed her arm. "Remember, his body burns bright, and needs to eat all the time. That is his weakness."

"There are others." He squeezed her hand. "I love you."

"I love you too," she said.

Thomasyn leaned forward and kissed her.

"Be careful," Sandra said.

Bethany hugged him. "Mind patterns. He will find it, no matter how difficult you make it and use it against you."

"I will," he said.

"Are you ready, Spear?" Jon said.

The voice was different. The stance was different. The man before him was different. There was something, though, that was familiar about him. The little way a sneer crossed his face.

"You see it, don't you? The difference? I am not who you think I am." Jon held up his sword between them. "So, what do you do? Fight like you would usually or experiment and take the chance that something will not work the way you want it to. It is a hard decision, that of a Spear. Who is good, and who is evil."

There it was. The one thing that made him feel there was a difference. He did not face Jon. He did not face Danton. He faced someone else. A mix of the two, but who would be the prominent fighter? And could he overcome him to save his friend?

"You see it now, Spear. What was once your friend is no longer here. You face a fully recovered enemy, not the one he bested so long ago."

"Danton." Thomasyn lofted his sword. "But are you sure?"

"The Hobs." Danton pointed the sword at Pin. "He made it possible. I was dormant in the Spear's mind for a long time until this ring and sword came together in my hand. The balance is tipped. You will now die."

Danton pounced. The sword sliced wide through the air, hitting nothing.

Thomasyn ducked below the slice and thrust out his foot. He hit nothing. With a quick bound, he was back on guard. *I must keep from killing him.*

Swords clashed. Sparks ignited the air. Danton's left shoulder dropped slightly. Thomasyn twisted, and a fist hit his cloak. He grabbed Danton's sword arm and tugged.

Danton's body went over his back, tumbled, and rolled to face him.

"A good move. Very aggressive. You must have been trained well."

Steel flashed. Sparks. A block of a slash. The fight pressed.

Thomasyn marvelled at the quickness of Danton. He was faster than Jon ever was. His movements more subtle. Stance firmer. Danton pressed the attack. *A disabling blow. How can I not kill him?*

Two slices. A jab. Hammer strike. Hammer strike. Thomasyn defended, looked for an opening. He pushed forward the tip of his sword on a block. The hand was not there. Danton moved back.

"Good try," Danton said, waggling his finger.

Thomasyn dived forward, sword out.

Danton pulled back his hand, fingers splayed.

The tip of Thomasyn's sword touched Danton's hand. Not hard. Just enough to cut into the ring finger and draw blood. Danton slapped the blade away.

Thomasyn pivoted and slammed his sword against Danton's. The two handed strike sent reverberations through both swords.

Danton, shocked and disoriented, switched grip and shook his right hand.

"Lost feeling?" Thomasyn asked.

"AAAAAAAAAAYYYYEEEEE!" Danton charged. His sword, now held out, stuck forward.

Thomasyn dived forward into Danton, taking out his legs. In a second, Thomasyn was on his feet, ready to defend. Danton lay on the ground, heaving.

With slow movements, Thomasyn approached Danton. The man was attempting to push himself away from the ground. Red coloured his cloak.

Thomasyn reached out his foot and pushed Danton over to his side. The Spear's sword jutted from his side. With a hand, Thomasyn grabbed the hilt and pulled it out.

"Thomasyn!"

Danton's eyes changed. The face became young, and Thomasyn knew Jon was back. He knelt beside his friend.

"He is in me," Jon said. "I cannot control him–" His eyes squinted.

"Don't talk," Thomasyn said. "We can stop the blood, call a Wooder. Save you."

"No," Jon said. "He will always be here." He touched his head. A tear fell from his eye. "You must end it. He can never be allowed to come again."

"I can't," Thomasyn said, his voice catching in his throat.

"You must." Jon reached out. "You have always been my friend."

"No!" Tears fell from his eyes. He knew it had to happen. Papion knew what was needed, that is why they gave them all the charms. There was nothing left to do. "I'm sorry," he said, and drove his sword into Jon's heart.

THANK YOU

For reading the third book of the Spear series. Please take the time to either write a review or leave a star rating of the work.

Reviews and ratings are the life blood of the Independent Author and Small Press publishers. Each 5 or 2 star rating and written review tells other readers it is worth at least looking at the work. Please feel free to leave an honest review where you purchased this work.

About Douglas Owen

Douglas Owen is a writer of fantasy, urban fantasy, science fiction, horror, and crime fiction . His short stories have been published by Cedar Cave Books and Mash Stories.

Doug wrote an article series called A Written View for Self Publisher Magazine, Indyfest Magazine, and Indtale Magazine. He also spent two years as a circulation manager for Indyfest and Self Publisher Magazines.

He is an active member of The Writers' Community of York Region, and spent several years as their Special Events Coordinator, and once ran the communities special Book Shelf event, bringing authors and publishers to the forefront of the region.

Doug lives in Goodwood, Ontario with his wife and three cats who make sure he does not sleep past 5:00 on any given day.

Visit Doug on his website for updates- https://douglasowen.ca

Follow Doug on Facebook https://facebook.com/AuthorDouglasOwen